"What do we tell people?" Gabby asked.

What would they tell people? Everyone had a proposal story, and people loved to hear it. But their story wasn't exactly romantic, and that wasn't going to go over well, was it?

"Well, uh—" Seth swallowed. "Why don't we move you into my place first, and then we can take some time to hammer out the details."

"Something more palatable than we got married for health insurance?" she asked with a teasing smile. There she was—the old Gabby.

"Yeah, pretty much," he agreed, and they exchanged mildly amused smiles. "We always did get ourselves into messes, didn't we?"

And every single time, he'd been furious with her for dragging him along into trouble. A sparkle came into Gabby's eyes, and he was gratified to see it.

"So we just...keep the secret for a bit?" she clarified.

"You okay with that?" he asked. "I mean, people will ask questions once you've moved in, but by then, I'm sure we'll have something sorted out between us. United front, right?"

"United front."

Dear Reader,

This is the last story in my Home to Eagle's Rest miniseries, and I'll be sad to leave this mountain town behind. If you haven't read the other books in the series, I hope you'll pick them up.

If you'd like to connect with me, you can find me on Facebook, Twitter and my website, patriciajohnsromance.com. I love meeting my readers, and you'll find a few giveaways from time to time, too!

A very merry Christmas from my home to yours!

Patricia Johns

HEARTWARMING

Her Triplets' Mistletoe Dad

—

Patricia Johns

HARLEQUIN® HEARTWARMING™

Recycling programs
for this product may
not exist in your area.

ISBN-13: 978-1-335-51091-4

Her Triplets' Mistletoe Dad

Copyright © 2019 by Patricia Johns

Printed in U.S.A.

www.Harlequin.com

Patricia Johns writes from Alberta, Canada. She has her Hon. BA in English literature and currently writes for Harlequin's Heartwarming and Love Inspired lines. You can find her at patriciajohnsromance.com.

Books by Patricia Johns

Harlequin Heartwarming

Home to Eagle's Rest

Her Lawman Protector
Falling for the Cowboy Dad
The Lawman's Baby

A Baxter's Redemption
The Runaway Bride
A Boy's Christmas Wish

Love Inspired

Montana Twins

Her Cowboy's Twin Blessings
Her Twins' Cowboy Dad
A Rancher to Remember

Comfort Creek Lawmen

Deputy Daddy
The Lawman's Runaway Bride
The Deputy's Unexpected Family

His Unexpected Family
The Rancher's City Girl
A Firefighter's Promise
The Lawman's Surprise Family

Visit the Author Profile page
at Harlequin.com for more titles.

To my husband, my very own happily-ever-after.

CHAPTER ONE

GABBY ROGERS AND SETH STRAIGHT had driven out to Benton, Colorado, for the privacy— because if they'd done this in Eagle's Rest, their secret would be impossible to keep. Gabby pulled her honey-blond hair away from her face, then rubbed her hands over her arms. Her cream knit dress wasn't warm enough in the chill of the courthouse. She shivered. The old building was decorated for the holidays—Christmas was only two weeks off—but there were drafts coming from windows, and Gabby found herself wishing she'd left her thick winter coat on. Except that didn't seem quite appropriate for her wedding—even this wedding. In all her fantasies, her wedding day had never been like this—so sterile and logical. She'd been positive that when she did marry, it would be for love—what other reason made it worth it? But this was smart; they'd agreed on that much.

Times were tough right now. She was a

mother to triplet newborns, and that had changed her life in every possible way. The father wasn't in the picture. Just about the time she discovered she was pregnant, he'd revealed that he was already married. She'd been stunned, heartbroken. She'd been thinking he might be the one, only to find out he'd been lying from the start. So though she'd delivered her babies with his financial assistance, their relationship was over. Now she was on her own, back in her hometown of Eagle's Rest, Colorado, with a broken heart and trying to figure out where her ex's lies had started and ended. Recovering after childbirth and now realizing she had no way to afford her baby boys' expensive formula... This idea of marrying her best friend had made so much sense a few days ago, when she and Seth Straight were making their plans. They were getting married for mutual benefits, and love didn't have to factor into their arrangement. Love never steered her right, anyway, and Seth was the best man she knew. This was sensible... wasn't it?

"Are we crazy?" Gabby asked, looking over at Seth. She fiddled with the flowers and realized belatedly that she'd been slowly shredding a rose petal.

"Maybe." Seth shot her a wry smile. He had worn his Sunday best—a suit and cowboy boots, with his white cowboy hat tucked under one arm. The last five years had aged him, with some silver laced through his auburn hair, and eyes that were a whole lot sadder. He'd always been the guy who was so cautious and organized that she'd assumed heartbreak would skip him. But no one was immune, it seemed, so here they were, along with their mangled hearts.

Gabby missed her babies right now, and that lonesome feeling was squeezing out her other misgivings. This was the first time she'd been separated from her newborns since they'd been in the NICU at the hospital. Funny how the same feeling of panic seemed to rise even when they were healthy, growing, and safely being cared for by Aunt Bea for the afternoon. Gabby's mother was working a double shift, which was actually a good thing. This wedding was top secret and she had no idea how she'd explain it. One thing at a time.

Gabby glanced at the clock. They had five minutes until it was their turn in the judge's office. Then they'd be married. This would be very final, if she went through with it.

"Are you sure you want to do this?" Gabby

asked, stepping closer to Seth, searching his face. "Because we can still back out."

Was she hoping that he would change his mind? Maybe. It would be easier to step away from this solution if Seth pulled out first. And he was the rational one—the guy who was logical to the extreme. If anyone could find a good reason not to do this, it would be Seth.

"Do you have a choice?" he asked.

"There's always a choice."

"Yeah, but…" He shrugged. "Your mom is broke right now, and she'd be the one you could normally rely on, right? If you've thought up a better solution…"

"I'd considered contacting my father," she said quietly. "But he never paid my mother a penny of child support, so I doubt that he'd suddenly want to help with his grand-children. And Uncle Ted said he didn't have a job for me. I mean, he did give me some cash, but I need more than money—I need a way to support my kids."

"And you need my health insurance, right?" he asked, his dark eyes meeting hers.

"You know I do," she said.

Her newborn sons—Aiden, Beau and Andy—had been born prematurely and their digestive tracts hadn't been ready for regular milk. Their formula cost a small fortune, and her savings had been bled dry in the past couple weeks just trying to keep them fed. Uncle Ted, who was actually more of a family friend than actual kin, had given her a financial gift that had helped, but their need for formula wasn't going to end soon. Seth was the ranch manager at the Ross Ranch, and as management, he had decent health insurance. That was where this idea had come from.

Was it selfish of her to want to shield her sons from the gossip surrounding their conception, too? She wasn't proud of that, and in a place this size, people were going to talk.

"I don't see any other way you're going to get the help you need," Seth replied. "Unless you can suss up a job with benefits real quick. Besides, don't they always say you should marry your best friend?"

They'd been best friends for years, but kind of an odd couple in that respect. She was the fun-loving risk taker, and he was the overly cautious worrier. They were direct opposites in so many ways, but somehow their personalities clicked.

"Marrying your best friend... Yeah, I'm not sure they had *this* in mind," she said wryly. "I just need to know you aren't going to regret this. I'd hate myself for taking advantage of your health insurance if you're going to wish you hadn't. I mean, what if you fall in love with someone and—"

"I won't." He paused. "Look, we talked about this. This whole modern notion of marrying for love sets people up for disappointment. It used to be that parents chose their children's spouses by looking at the more practical things, like how well he could provide, how their personalities might click, how they could succeed if they worked together. And those marriages worked! We can't say there were thousands of years of marital misery, because there wasn't. I really think this is smart. We don't have sky-high emotional expectations from each other. But we do have a really solid friendship."

Look at him—logical to the extreme. But she did agree with him on this point. She'd already been burned by Craig, and it was her own stupid, romantic hopes that blinded her to reality. That wasn't her worry here.

"You might meet someone, Seth," she countered.

"I've already had the love of my life," he said softly. "You know that. There isn't going to be another love like Bonnie. Besides, you're my best friend, Gabs, and I want to help. But if you don't…"

The door to the judge's office opened and a woman in a black robe smiled and looked down at a notepad. She was short and middle-aged, with chin-length brown hair. She looked tired, Gabby thought, as the judge studied her tablet.

"Gabrielle Rogers and Seth Straight?" she said, looking up.

"That's us," Seth replied, then he looked down at Gabby and lowered his voice. "If you don't want to…"

Standing there in a knit dress that wasn't quite warm enough, a bouquet of white roses that Seth had splurged on in one hand and the ring box in the sweaty palm of the other, she found her options sweeping through her mind.

She could continue her search for a job— any job—that offered decent health insurance, and then put her sons into day care. She could do what other moms did and get used to this hollow, lonely feeling of being away from her babies. And in the meantime, she could see if the bank would give her another line of credit to cover the cost of formula until she could sort something out… *If* she could sort something out. She couldn't count on Uncle Ted to give more than he already had. She had three hungry newborns gobbling back bottle after bottle of specialty formula. God forbid they need more hospitalization or surgery… And Seth's offer had been so kind and generous. He didn't have cash to share, but he did have health insurance. Because of his offer, she'd felt genuinely cared for by a man for the first time in years. Besides, she wasn't about to follow her heart again, either. What she needed was a logical marriage—one that actually had a hope of lasting.

"Gabby?" Seth murmured. "What do you think? You want to do this?"

She nodded slowly. "Yes. It's a good plan."

"You sure?"

"Positive." She sounded more decisive than she felt. "Let's get married."

Another couple slid onto a bench behind them. The woman wore a lacy wedding gown over a bulging belly. The couple's fingers were entwined, and they leaned their heads together, whispering. They looked excited, those two. And young—*so* young. Good grief, were they even twenty? Her gaze lingered on the couple, and she sighed. By the looks of it, that bride was marrying the father of her baby. Gabby hadn't managed that—the father of her babies was already father to two preteens in Billings. Still, even though Gabby wasn't going to be an excited, dewy-eyed bride, she *would* be married. And life would be easier because of it.

"All right," the judge said with a smile. "Let's get started. Come inside, please."

Gabby went into the office first, followed by Seth. He'd always been the polite sort—ladies first and all that. She used to tease him about his old-fashioned ways. He'd have to loosen up if he wanted to catch a girl, she used to say…but then he'd married Bonnie, disproving that theory. And watching Seth using those antiquated manners on his wife, she'd wondered if she'd been the one to miss out.

Gabby felt Seth's warm hand linger on her back as the door to the spacious office shut behind them. Was he as nervous as she was? She glanced back and found his dark gaze drilling into the carpet in front of him. Whatever he was feeling, it was locked away.

A desk dominated one side of the room, but there was a nice open area by the window. There were two court-appointed witnesses sitting in visitors' chairs—an older woman in sensible slacks and a bored-looking young man whose hair didn't flatten all the way at the back. They each gave her a cordial nod. How many weddings had they seen today?

"Let's just take a look at your paperwork," the judge said, and Seth handed it over. They spent a couple minutes going over everything, and then the judge gestured for them to stand by the window.

"Let's get started, then," she said. "I normally do the vows over here by the window. It's a little nicer for pictures." She paused. "Do you have anyone to take a few photos?"

"Uh…" Gabby shook her head. "We didn't really think of it."

"Sorry," Seth murmured.

It hardly seemed appropriate to be taking joyful photos of this sort of wedding. They'd look like those stricken couples in old black-and-white photos—the ones where the bride and groom stood a foot apart in every shot.

"I'll take a few shots, if you like," the older woman said. "I've got my phone right here. I could email them to you."

Seth smiled. "Thanks. We appreciate that."

Did they *really* appreciate that? She'd have her own stricken pictures to pass down to her sons… She wasn't sure she wanted pictures. It was better to remember this day the way she wanted to—taking an intelligent step that would benefit them both—instead of seeing actual photos that might betray her memories somehow. But now wasn't the time to quibble. They stood where the judge indicated, and the older woman came and took a couple photos of them facing each other. Seth seemed more stable than she did—more resolute. Mind you, he'd been married before, so he knew how all this worked.

"Join hands," the judge instructed.

Seth held out his broad, calloused palms and he gave her a small smile. There he was—the best friend. It almost felt like a joke, an act they were putting on, two collaborators once more. Normally, she was the one who lured him into drama, and maybe that hadn't changed. His hand was warm, and he gave her fingers a reassuring squeeze.

"We're here together today to join you in marriage. Have you both come of your own free will?"

Gabby nodded.

"We need you to answer aloud with a yes or a no," the judge said.

"Yes," they said together.

"As expected," the judge said with a soft

chuckle. "So let's just get right into the vows then. Seth Straight, do you take this woman to be your wife from this day forth and for the rest of your life?"

Seth's dark gaze met Gabby's, but only briefly before he cleared his throat and looked toward the judge instead.

"I do."

"And Gabrielle Rogers, do you take this man to be your husband from this day forth and for the rest of your life?"

Gabby licked her lips. "I do."

"Rings?" the judge asked brightly.

Gabby picked up the ring box, which she'd set on the desk, and cracked it open. They'd bought very simple, cheap wedding rings. Gold, but barely, Gabby had joked earlier. But now, they seemed weightier, more important. She started to put the ring on Seth's finger, though he had to shimmy it the rest of the way past his knuckle. Then he slipped the matching slim band onto her hand.

"Repeat after me," the judge said. "With this ring, I thee wed."

"With this ring, I thee wed," they murmured together.

"Then by the power vested in me by the state of Colorado, I now pronounce you husband and wife." The judge smiled warmly.

"If you would like to share a kiss to commemorate your marriage, now would be an appropriate time for that."

And that was the moment that Gabby realized she'd never kissed Seth before. Not when they agreed to this wedding, not when they first saw each other all gussied up. Even when she'd broken up with boyfriends and Seth had been the one to let her cry on his shoulder... They'd never crossed that line because they'd never been attracted to each other.

She'd never kissed the man that she'd just married!

"Brace yourself," Seth murmured, as if reading her mind, then dipped his head down and caught her lips with his.

SETH DIDN'T KNOW what he'd expected kissing his best friend to feel like, but perhaps a little less wide-eyed shock on her part would have been nice. Her lips were tense at first, but after a moment, her eyes fluttered shut and they softened under his own.

Married. He hadn't thought ahead to the kiss after the ceremony, but with a judge and two witnesses expecting *something*, he felt he'd better oblige. He didn't want to embarrass Gabby on his very first day as her husband, after all.

He pulled back and Gabby's eyes opened again, and they exchanged a serious look.

"Congratulations!" the judge said with a smile. "This is a big day. We'll all just put down our signatures here—"

"I got that shot!" the older woman said with a brilliant smile, her phone held up in front of her. "Congratulations, Mr. and Mrs. Straight!"

A surge of guilt swept through him, and he attempted to push it back. He'd sworn he wouldn't take these vows again, but this was different, wasn't it? Bonnie had been his first love—his first kiss! He'd been a late bloomer in that respect. While the other guys were dating around, he'd been the serious one, focused on his career and not wanting to waste his time with the wrong girls. His parents had gotten divorced when he was twelve, and he'd never wanted to endure that kind of misery in his own romantic life. He'd always been cautious to a fault. And when Bonnie died in childbirth, the light of his life blinked out. He'd been prepared to keep their marriage healthy and strong for a lifetime, but he had no control over mortality. He'd lost a baby girl and wife all in one day, and he'd been in a fog of depression for two years.

Seeing Gabby again had flicked a light back on, scattered the fog and given him a bit more clarity at last, though he was determined to keep to his resolution to never fall for anyone again. But now, he'd just given his name to another woman for some very logical reasons, but it still felt like a betrayal to his wife's memory.

What exactly had he gotten himself into?

The paperwork was quickly dispatched, and the older lady had already emailed her snapshots to Gabby's account. They thanked her, thanked the judge, and headed out of the office, all without once looking at each other. The ring felt funny on his hand, and he fiddled with it with his thumb.

"Congratulations!" the young couple next in line said in unison. They got up from the bench and moved toward the office. "How does it feel?" the woman asked.

"Great." Gabby smiled and nodded. "Congrats to you, too."

Did she really feel great about this? He eyed her uncertainly. The judged called the next names, and the young, pregnant couple disappeared into the office.

Gabby shot Seth an annoyed look when she noticed his scrutiny. "What?"

"How does it really feel?" he asked, his voice low.

"Weird." She shrugged. "But a good weird. We'll be okay."

Seth sure hoped so. He'd done it for her, and for those three little babies. They were so small, and when they cried, his heart clenched in his chest like he was the one causing their distress. They'd reminded him of his own baby girl—Hazel Marie. She'd been too tiny to make it, but he'd had the opportunity to hold her, at least.

He pushed back the memory. He was doing this for those babies. They needed two things: food and their mother, and this time around, he was going to be able to protect a mother and her babies—make sure they had the long and healthy life that Bonnie and Hazel had deserved.

"I know I didn't speak up when she called us Mr. and Mrs. Straight back there," he said. Did he dare take that back? "It's no pressure. I was just… I don't know, acting the part for the audience, you know?"

"No, I get it." She put a hand on his arm. "I was, too. But I think I'll keep my own last name for now. It's simpler. My sons have Rogers as their last name, so—"

"No, no, that's perfectly fine." A wave of relief crashed over him. His last name was something he could hold back for himself… for Bonnie. He looked down at Gabby again, and she gave him a tight smile.

What was with them? They'd known each other for decades, and here they were dancing around each other like painfully polite strangers, discussing what last name she'd have now that he'd married her. Gabby had always been the irreverent type, and here she was meeting him toe-to-toe with manners. He went over to the coatrack and took down their jackets.

"What do we tell people?" she asked, as she pulled her puffy, cream-colored coat around her shoulders. A few people passed them in the tall main entrance of the building, and Seth caught the smiles cast in their direction.

What *would* they tell people? Everyone had a "how we met" or even a proposal story, and people loved to hear it. But their story wasn't exactly romantic, and that wasn't going to go over well, was it?

"Well, uh…" Seth swallowed. "Why don't we move you in to my place first, and then we can take some time to hammer out the details."

"Something more palatable than we did this for health insurance?" she asked with a teasing smile. There she was—the old Gabby.

"Yeah, pretty much," he agreed, and they exchanged a mildly amused smile. "We always did get ourselves into messes, didn't we?"

And every single time, he'd been furious with her for dragging him along into trouble. A sparkle came into Gabby's eyes, and he was gratified to see it.

"So we just…keep the secret for a bit?" she clarified.

"You okay with that?" he asked. "I mean, people will ask questions once you've moved in, but by then, I'm sure we'll have something sorted out between us. I don't want to look like I'm lying to my boss—I mean, our reasons for this marriage shouldn't matter so much to our friends, but my reputation at work matters. If they thought I was scamming the system, or whatever—"

"No, I understand," she said.

"United front, right?"

"United front." She gave him a nod. "You

sure you'll be okay with three babies in your house? And me?"

"I'll be fine." He'd been prepared for one baby a couple years ago. He could stretch for three.

"I do appreciate this," she said. "You have no idea, Seth. You're a really good friend."

Seth slid an arm around her shoulders, and for the first time today, some physical contact felt natural between them. He gave her a squeeze.

"Now that we have a marriage license, I'll get you on my insurance right away. I'm sure we can scrape up enough money for the formula between now and when it kicks in."

"I'm relieved." Gabby put a hand against her chest and her gaze misted. "I've been alone in this, and I don't think I even realized how worried I was until just now. I mean, to have the basics be almost out of reach... Milk! It shouldn't bankrupt a woman, you know?"

"You're *not* alone in this." He dropped his arm and caught her hand in his. "It's a burden shared, right? You've got me now."

She nodded, and he felt a flood of relief, too. They would be okay. Gabby was a good person, and she didn't deserve to be struggling on her own. Neither did those tiny boys. And for once, he was able to do something—fix something—and feel like he was making a bad situation better for someone he cared about.

They headed down the stairs to the main floor. As he held open the door for her, they were met by a rush of frigid air. It was snowing again—large flakes floating down in lazy pirouettes. Gabby pulled on a pair of gloves.

"How should we celebrate?" he asked.

"I wouldn't mind a piece of cake," Gabby said, glancing up at him. "To go, though. I miss my babies."

Cake. Yeah, that was oddly appropriate. Years ago, they would go out for cake together—normally when Gabby was mourning a breakup from some unworthy boyfriend.

"Yeah, you bet." Who was he to argue about what helped her feel better? As they turned down the street toward his truck, Seth spotted someone he knew ambling toward them. Heck, they both knew him, but what was he doing here on the *one day* Seth and Gabby needed a bit of privacy? He instinctively put a hand out to touch Gabby's arm. But she'd seen him, too.

Taylor Shirk was dressed in a pair of jeans

and a fleece-lined denim jacket. A cowboy hat was pushed back away from his face. They'd gone to high school with him, and they'd all known each other for years. He was staring at them with a look of shock on his face. Seth looked down at Gabby—she stood there with the bouquet in one gloved hand. She looked every inch a bride, even in a winter coat. They were in front of the courthouse, after all. He sighed.

"No way!" Taylor exclaimed as he approached. "Is this what it looks like?" Taylor glanced between them, then pointed at the bouquet. "Did you two just get married?"

So much for keeping a secret... Seth exchanged a helpless shrug with Gabby.

"We were hoping to keep it hush-hush for a little bit," Gabby said with a grimace. "You don't think you could keep a secret, do you?"

"Me? Yeah, of course!" Taylor laughed. "Wow. I mean, I had no idea you two were even an item. This is a total shock, I gotta tell you. How long were you hiding this relationship?"

"It's new," Seth said quickly. "We...uh— we just realized it was the right step, and we took it."

Not a lie. Maybe this wasn't going to be so hard, after all.

"Well, about time! Congratulations!" Taylor bent in and kissed Gabby's cheek. "You, too, man. Really, from the bottom of my heart."

Seth and Taylor shook hands, and Taylor belted out a laugh.

"But discretion, right?" Gabby pressed. "Taylor? I'm serious. Please."

"Yeah, yeah, of course." Taylor nodded enthusiastically. "You got it. I won't hold you up! Enjoy that honeymoon, you two!"

Seth caught Gabby's hand again and checked over his shoulder as Taylor went on his way. He was still laughing aloud, shaking his head as he wandered off down the street and then crossed to the other side, but he'd pulled his phone out of his back pocket and was typing into it. Seth tugged Gabby after him and they made their way to where his red pickup truck was parallel parked. Honeymoon. Yeah, technically, that was what this was, but it wouldn't be like anyone else's.

"He's not keeping that secret," Seth said, opening the passenger side door for her. Taylor Shirk was a good guy, but he was a talker, and he was probably texting the news now. The town of Eagle's Rest, Colorado, was about to be react.

"I know. I don't think we're getting the luxury of time here."

Seth waited until she'd hopped up into the cab, then slammed her door shut and angled around the truck and got in. The engine hadn't cooled off all the way, so the air that pumped into the cab as he started it was warm already. Seth looked over at Gabby. Her blond hair was tousled from the winter wind, and her cheeks were pink from the cold. On her left hand was the faint glimmer of that golden wedding band... His mouth went dry.

"What will people say?" Gabby asked after a moment.

"I guess we're about to find out." Seth tried to smile. "We're about to be the talk of the town, Gabs."

"I'd better tell Mom before she hears it from someone else," Gabby said, and her expression turned grim. "I just need some time to think up our story. Something that sounds less...pragmatic. We don't want to be charged with insurance fraud."

He definitely didn't want that! But this was a real marriage—maybe a convenient one, but they'd be living together, raising three kids together… How much more real did it get?

"Should we swing by today and tell your mother ourselves?" he asked.

"No. She's working a double shift at the restaurant, anyway. Tomorrow morning is soon enough."

"Right." Seth fiddled with the back of his ring once more with his thumb. It was time to get home and face their new reality.

CHAPTER TWO

THE DRIVE FROM Benton to Eagle's Rest was a quiet one. As Gabby stretched her legs out to feel the heat from the vents, Seth put on the radio to fill the silence. A few honky-tonk Christmas tunes about unrequited love were on various stations. She'd never been a fan of heartbreaking songs, but today they seemed more personal. She'd gotten married today, but she wasn't in love with her husband.

"Could you change the station?" she said.

"Sure." Seth flicked the station to an equally depressing song. He stuck it on a talk radio station and Gabby sighed. It was an improvement at least. Seth's broad hand rested on the top of the steering wheel, and he looked about as somber as she felt.

Gabby turned away from Seth, staring the window at the snow-laden farmland. She was thinking about her babies, and about this legally binding step she'd just taken. While a woman could do far worse than

Seth Straight, with his rugged good looks and his strong sense of personal ethics, she felt a wave of misgiving. She had terrible luck with men—and at the age of thirty, she could accept that her "luck" was rooted in her decision-making. She *chose* the wrong guys again and again. Whenever she followed her heart, it brought more pain. Her heart needed to stay out of this.

Seth had made better choices in his own life. His wife had been a saint. She really was perfect for him, even if she'd never trusted Gabby. Gabby, of all people, wasn't a threat to their marriage. She and Seth had never felt more than friendship for each other, but she could understand a woman protecting her turf. All the same, Seth had loved Bonnie deeply. It had been the kind of connection that people envied, including Gabby. If she could find a guy who looked at her like Seth had looked at Bonnie, she'd never complain again—as long as he was legitimately single. Sad that she now had to add that qualifier to her list. But Gabby had been taken advantage of one too many times, and while Seth wasn't the type to treat her shabbily, she had an even bigger reason to keep herself in control of her emotions. Her new husband was still in love with his late wife.

Gabby was willing to accept this arrangement for what it was—a convenience—but she wouldn't hope for anything more. This was a favor, nothing else.

Gabby looked down at her wedding ring. It was just a simple band, but it was already taking on meaning. It certainly would to everyone else. They'd all expect a passionate love story, and Gabby wasn't going to be able to deliver. How was she supposed to play this? Would their natural friendship look romantic enough to a casual observer? Would they have to amp up their physical contact in order to look the part? All things she should have thought through already, but she hadn't had the time. Her boys were her priority, and they needed their specialty formula. Plus who knew what other medical help might be necessary down the road with premature triplets.

They arrived in Eagle's Rest in the late afternoon and headed to the south side of town, where Gabby's aunt Bea lived. Bea was her mother's aunt, so unlike Ted, she was legitimate family. Small, boxy houses built in the sixties, with large yards and mature trees, ran up and down the street, and her aunt's house was second from the end. Most of the houses had Christmas decorations on their lawns—inflatable Santas, lights on the trees, wreaths on doors… The snow had stopped and watery winter sunlight filtered through the overhanging boughs of the trees. Gabby fiddled with the roses in her lap, then looked down at them.

"What do I do with my bouquet?" she asked.

"I don't know," Seth said. "Were you wanting to throw it or something?"

"No." Gabby sighed. "I just don't know what I'm supposed to do with it."

"Bring it back with us. Stick it in a vase."

He sounded so sure of himself that it actually sounded like a logical plan, as if that was what anyone would do with a bouquet after a secret wedding—stick it in the center of the kitchen table. But why not?

"Okay," she agreed. "I'll do that."

Throwing it away seemed wrong, and tossing it over her shoulder wasn't even a possibility.

"This doesn't have to be complicated," Seth said. "Keep it simple—isn't that what we said?"

Yes, that was exactly what they'd said, but that was before she'd said vows for the first time in her life…before she'd realized that this was her first marriage, and even if she annulled it right now, it would always be her first marriage. Her heart ached in a strange way. She wasn't sad, exactly, just overwhelmed by it all, and the only thing that would make her feel better was to pick up her babies and hold them close.

Bea Thibodaux's little white house had a towering oak tree out front that dwarfed the structure but gave some beautiful dappled shade for the summertime. Seth pulled into her driveway and turned off the engine.

"Are you coming in with me?" Gabby asked.

"Do you want me to?" He looked over at her uncertainly.

"You might as well," she said. "But mess up your hair, or something. You look too formal and wedding-ish."

Seth chuckled softly. "I'm not the one dressed in white."

Gabby shot him a smile. "It's cream."

"Same diff."

"Let's just try to get in and out without the neighbors asking too many questions."

"You give them too much credit," Seth shot back. "They won't ask us, they'll go ask your aunt once we're gone."

He had a point, and she shook her head. "I guess we can't help that. And we'll start telling people soon enough… Let's go in. I miss my boys."

She pushed open the door and hopped out of the truck. One of her aunt's neighbors came out the side door of her house with a snow shovel at the same time and shot Gabby a curious look.

"Hi," Gabby called casually, and headed toward her aunt's place as if she'd just gotten back from a coffee or something. The neighbor raised her hand in a wave, but didn't stop watching Gabby. Seth followed a moment later, and Gabby was relieved to see that he'd left the string tie behind and seemed to have dug out an older, more beaten up cowboy hat. Now he just looked like a really well-dressed cowboy. Hopefully, the neighbors would assume he was a date.

Aunt Bea pulled open the front door before Gabby even had a chance to knock, and the older woman looked immediately at Gabby's left hand, then over at Seth's.

"So you did it," Bea said, stepping back. "Come in, then."

Before they'd left that morning, Gabby had told her aunt the plan and sworn her to secrecy. Bea hadn't liked it, but she hadn't tried to stop them, either.

Gabby headed for the car seats where the

babies were all lined up and asleep. Andy was sleeping with his tongue sticking out, and Beau and Aiden were turned toward each other in the car seats, breathing in unison. Gabby squatted down in front of them and reached out to touch their tiny feet.

"Mommy's back," she whispered.

"I just put them down after diaper changes," Bea said. "So they should be dry. Except for Andy. He wets his diaper the minute I put a new one on... Lucky he doesn't seem to mind being wet, unlike Beau."

"Thanks, Auntie," Gabby said, reaching for Andy. "I appreciate it."

She put a hand under Andy's little rump and the other under his downy head and scooped him up. He settled with a sigh against her chest, and she felt the tension seeping out of her. This was what she needed—to hold her babies.

"So you're going ahead with the plan to move into Seth's house?" Bea asked.

"Yes," Gabby said.

"Well, I expect we can put Seth to work, then," Bea said, turning toward him. "Can you start carrying out some baby things? I've got it all ready to go by the side door."

"Sure." Seth looked relieved to have something to do. "I'll load everything up."

"Auntie, we're not telling people yet," Gabby added.

"Oh." Bea nodded. "Not even your mother?"

"I will tell her—tomorrow, though. I want a bit of time to think it out before I do."

"She's your mom," Bea replied. "I don't know why there's any explanation necessary besides the actual truth. She'll understand that you need to provide for your children. She knows what it means to be a single mother, after all."

"No, she'll feel like she let me down," Gabby said. "And I don't want her to think that."

Gabby's mother, Carol, had helped her get through college and earn her diploma to be a medical office assistant, and then Carol had lost a few jobs, one after another. None of it was her fault—just the fluctuating economy. She'd gotten into debt, and there was no way she could help Gabby pay for that expensive formula now. Gabby knew her mother would feel terrible if she found out that Gabby was marrying Seth only for health insurance.

"We just need some time to sort out our stuff," Gabby said. "But we were spotted in Benton by Taylor Shirk, so it probably won't stay a secret for long."

"I'll let you be the one to tell her," Bea said, and as Seth picked up a couple garbage bags filled with clothes and linens, the older woman added, "Welcome to the family, Seth."

Seth shot Gabby a half smile, then nodded to her aunt. "Thanks. Don't worry. I'll take care of these boys."

"And Gabby, too, I hope," Bea shot back.

"Most definitely."

The warmth in his eyes, the private smile he cast in Gabby's direction, and the way his muscles flexed as he hoisted the first bags—they were a combination that made it easy to pretend this marriage was something it wasn't.

The screen door banged shut as Seth disappeared outside, and Gabby looked at her aunt with eyebrows raised.

"You've got your privacy now," Gabby said. "What's on your mind?"

"What's on *yours*?" Bea quipped, and she reached for Gabby's hand, looking down at the wedding ring. "Why did you do this?"

"You know why." Gabby felt the tears rising up inside her. She was tired. She had missed her babies, and she really wasn't in the mood to argue about something that was already done.

"I thought you'd come to your senses before you actually went through with it," Bea said.

"Auntie, could you afford that formula for the long term?" Gabby demanded.

"No, but the church could have taken up a special offering—"

"No!" Then Gabby lowered her voice, because Beau and Aiden squirmed in their car seats. "Auntie, I'm not a charity. And I'm not going to be waiting on church collections to feed my children. Besides, I don't want them growing up with the stigma of how they came into this world."

"But you've married a man you don't love."

Gabby looked out the front window to where Seth was tossing the bags into the bed of the pickup. "Yes, I have. Look, he and I are good friends. We have been for years. We understand each other."

"How long will you stay married?" Bea asked. "Is this truly until death do you part?"

"I don't know. We'll see, I guess. There are no false expectations here."

"No?" Bea paced the living room, then turned back. "This is *marriage*. It isn't supposed to be the sort of thing you take a day at a time!"

"I know." Gabby rubbed a hand over her face. "Trust me, I'm aware. I'm not a child anymore, Bea. I'm thirty."

The door opened again and the women fell silent as Seth grabbed a folded playpen in one hand and a baby swing in the other. He met Gabby's gaze, then turned back to the door and disappeared outside once more. Bea pushed it shut behind him.

"There's no point in arguing about it," Bea said, adjusting her tone. She reached out and touched the back of her finger to Andy's cheek where he lay snuggled on Gabby's chest. "But I feel like I should at least warn you."

"Of what?" Gabby asked tiredly.

"You're playing with fire, dear. Those vows—they're no joke. When you vow to belong to a man as long as you live, whether you mean it or not, it joins you to him in a way you don't understand yet. It's not just business. It can't be."

"Well, it's too late now," Gabby said with a bitter laugh.

"You have to know that I wish you only happiness," her aunt replied earnestly. "All I can say is that you're in for the ride of your life."

Of that, Gabby was absolutely certain,

but whether it would be exhilarating or a wild regret, she wasn't sure. Still, her boys would be fed, and they'd have doctor's visits and medicine if they needed it. And that was what mattered. She'd deal with the fallout later.

"Thank you, Auntie," Gabby said quietly. "Cross your fingers for me, or say a prayer for me, but for crying out loud, don't tell your church my business, okay?"

Bea smiled wryly. "Wouldn't dream of it, dear. But the prayer chain is very discreet if you change your mind."

"Auntie!" Gabby caught the teasing glint in her aunt's eye. "I'm not going to tell anyone about the health insurance. You've got to keep my secret, okay? I don't want Seth getting charged for insurance fraud or something like that. We can't afford those legal fees. Besides, it'll only hurt Mom if she knew. So I'm asking for a huge favor—keep my secret."

Bea nodded. "I can do that. But just know, secrets have a way of coming out, anyway."

"I'll take that risk."

The side door opened again and Seth poked his head in.

"So how are we going to do this?" Seth asked.

"I've got the car seat bases in the back of my car," Gabby said. "And I think I'm ready." She gave her aunt an appreciative smile. "Thanks for everything, Auntie. I'll call you, okay?"

Bea nodded. "And if you need someone to mind the babies while your mom is working, I'm here."

Gabby leaned over and kissed her aunt's cheek. "I intend to take you up on that."

THE ROSS RANCH was about forty minutes outside of Eagle's Rest, out of the mountains and down in the snowy foothills. Seth was the ranch manager, and his little cottage was just up the road from the ranch hands' bunkhouse and canteen. As he drove past the main house and around the bend, he came to another cottage—what used to be an in-law arrangement, from what he understood. This was where Billy Austin lived—a ranch hand and a good friend.

Billy's wife, Grace, had just pulled up to the cottage. She was a teacher in town, and their daughter—now in kindergarten—hopped out of the car and turned to wave at Seth's truck as he came around the bend. He smiled and waved back. Poppy was a cute little girl, and he had a soft spot for the kid. But then Grace and Poppy both turned their attention to Gabby's car following his truck, and Grace brightened and waved. Here was hoping that in the car, with only a coat visible, Gabby didn't look too much like a bride…

It wasn't that he wanted to hide their arrangement, exactly, but he did want a few minutes with Gabby alone to adjust, at least. They didn't have their story straight yet, and Grace and Gabby were good friends. What they decided to tell people was going to matter, big-time.

The ranch manager's house was a small affair with two floors, and it was located on the other side of the bunkhouse and canteen. The last woman to share this house with him had been Bonnie. Pregnant Bonnie, always knocking water glasses and towels off the counter with her belly. It drove her crazy, and the memory brought back the sad ache. They'd set up a nursery together, all decorated in yellow and green because they'd wanted to be surprised about the baby's gender. When Bonnie and little Hazel Marie hadn't come home with him, he'd shut the door on that nursery and hadn't gone inside again.

Seth parked in his regular spot and waited

for Gabby to park next to him. The next few minutes were spent getting the babies out of her car and unloading a few necessities. They carried the car seats into the kitchen, and he glanced back at Gabby to see her appraising the place.

"Grace saw you coming here," Seth said. "How long until she drops by?"

"She texted me already." Gabby lifted her cell phone with a small smile. "I told her I'd give her a call later on, but I can't tell her until I've told my mom. You and Billy are pretty good friends. He'll require some explanations, too."

"Yeah." Seth shrugged. "This is just the start."

Gabby bent down to uncover the babies, and she smiled down at them. All three were sleeping. Right now, the least of his worries should be the explanations. He now had three infants in his home—and their mother.

"I've got two bedrooms upstairs," Seth said. "I thought you might be okay sharing with the babies."

He hadn't shown her the upstairs when he brought her here for dinner a week ago and they'd come up with this idea. That had still felt like private space.

"Sure, that works." Gabby nodded. "I need

to be close by for those feedings, after all. Every two hours. Did I mention that?"

"Yeah, I think you did." Energetic, fun-loving, free-spirited Gabby was a mom on bottle duty all night. Hadn't she sworn she didn't want kids once upon a time? *Kids are great, so long as they belong to someone else. You and Bonnie should have ten, Seth.* Now she was the mom, and his daughter was gone.

"Let me take that," he said, removing the bouquet from her shoulder bag. He retrieved a vase from the cupboard under the sink and filled it with water. He used to do this for Bonnie when he brought her flowers. Every two weeks. That was one of the things a book advised about keeping a marriage strong—regular flowers. And he'd always been particular about maintaining his marriage. Thing was, marriage was a whole lot more complicated than he'd anticipated, and flowers every two weeks weren't quite the magic answer he'd hoped for.

Seth put the bouquet into the vase and slid it onto the table. It felt right, having flowers in here again. And it also felt like a bit of a betrayal to Bonnie, too.

One of the babies opened his eyes and let out a whimper.

"It's about that time." Gabby reached for the diaper bag that sat next to the car seats. "Why don't we feed them first, then get settled?"

She was already adjusting to the space, and Gabby hoisted the bag to the counter next to the fridge and pushed aside a fruit bowl. It shouldn't irritate him—she lived here now, after all, but Seth liked things to stay the same, even if that was unrealistic. He and Bonnie had always had the fruit bowl just there because Seth would reach over from his spot at the kitchen table and grab a banana. His attachment to a fruit bowl's position had nothing to do with being picky. It was linked to his grief. And maybe his irrational guilt over arranging Gabby's flowers like that...

Gabby took out a can of formula powder, then went to the sink. In a few minutes she'd shaken up three bottles, then caught his gaze lingering on her. "What?"

He'd rather not start out with an argument. And he'd be wrong—it was only a fruit bowl.

"Nothing. Which baby do I feed?" he asked. This had been his idea, and he'd just have to get used to Gabby's touch about the place. Still... He moved the baby bag and slid the fruit bowl back into its rightful place. There. That felt better.

Gabby unbuckled the first baby and scooped him up. She planted a kiss on his forehead, and the infant's eyes opened and gazed up at her.

"This is Aiden," she said. "You'll know him because he's a little bit smaller."

She passed him to Seth, and he reached out awkwardly, his fingers splayed. It took a moment of careful adjustment to get the baby into his arms. The little guy barely weighed anything. His heart clenched, and he swallowed back a lump in his throat. He'd imagined doing this with his own daughter a thousand times before she was born, and he'd never gotten the chance.

"Hi, there…" Seth said, looking down into the squished little face. Aiden opened his eyes again and his mouth opened into a tiny O, nudging toward Seth's shirt, a baby's instinct for milk. It took him a few tries to get the bottle's nipple into Aiden's mouth, but once he did, the baby set to sucking.

"There," Seth said, and he felt a rush of unexpected satisfaction.

Gabby was cuddling another baby close as he slurped hungrily at a bottle. With a foot, she rocked the third car seat.

"This here is Andy," she said, looking down at the infant she was feeding. "Beau might hate a wet diaper, but he's a little more patient for his bottle."

Aiden stretched out a tiny arm—remarkably strong for such a little fellow. Their marriage might be a unique arrangement, but part of Seth's willingness to help her had been *because* of these babies, and he looked down at the infant in wonder.

"I've fed calves, and a couple of newborn goats, but I've never fed a baby before," he admitted.

"No?" Gabby wrinkled her nose. "Are you serious? I thought you used to babysit your cousins."

"They weren't babies," he said, casting her an incredulous look. "And Ian is only four years younger than me. His sister was like five at the time. So they all fed themselves pretty efficiently."

"Right. You just seem so much older than him."

"Thanks." He rolled his eyes.

"You know what I mean—you're more mature. He's always been a perpetual boy. I mean, he's fun, don't get me wrong, but…"

She was right about that. And Gabby would know—she'd dated Ian for a few months. In her defense, there weren't a lot of single guys to choose from in Eagle's Rest.

They were silent for a few beats, and Seth sobered, adjusting the baby in his arms.

"I was all set to figure out bottle feeding with my daughter," he said quietly. "I never got the chance."

When Seth looked over at her, he saw her eyes misting. She lifted her gaze to meet his, and her chin trembled ever so slightly. It was the mom in her reacting.

"I can't imagine losing a child, Seth," she said softly. "That's a heartbreak I don't think you'd ever recover from."

"Yeah, it's bad."

Understatement of the year. Losing his wife was one kind of grief, but losing his infant daughter was another. It was an aching emptiness—a loss of a hundred things he'd never gotten to try. A pregnancy was different from a baby for the father, and while he'd felt his child squirm in Bonnie's belly, he'd known that meeting the baby would make it all concrete. He'd be a dad in earnest then. When the doctors put her in his arms, she had suddenly become real...and so had the depth of his loss. All in that one moment. Because little Hazel Marie hadn't survived the delivery, and his hello and goodbye had to happen all at once. He realized then it wasn't the length of a life, but the depth of it, and his tiny daughter had sunk down into his soul.

He didn't know how to put all those feelings into words, and he'd never tried. He'd just covered the pain over as best he could with work and keeping busy. People had expressed sympathy, and Billy had spent quite a few evenings in this house, sharing beer and some companionable silence. It had helped more than Billy probably knew. A few aunts had brought casseroles, but mostly he just sank back down into a bachelor's life—meals for one and a whole lot of working. There was enough to do on a ranch that he could go day and night if he wanted to. And sometimes he did.

Aiden finished the bottle, and Seth put it on the counter.

"You'll need to burp him," Gabby said, putting her own bottle down and tipping Andy up to her shoulder. "Like this. Just pop him up there and pat his back a little bit. Aiden's a gassy one. He'll burp twice."

Just pop him up there… That was easier said than done. The baby was so small that Seth was scared of hurting him. He managed to get his hand under Aiden's head and when he tipped him up onto his shoulder, the tiny head tipped forward, too. Seth felt his gut drop. But then Aiden lifted his head and settled it down again in a more comfortable position, and there was a surge of relief.

"Okay, buddy," Seth said softly, and he gently tapped the tiny back the way Gabby was doing with his brother. Almost immediately, there was a resounding belch.

"Wow," Gabby chuckled. "Keep that up. He'll do it again."

Seth continued the soft tapping as he watched Gabby finish burping Andy. She put him back in his car seat and scooped up Beau.

"You've been so good, Beau," she crooned, tucking him into the crook of her arm. "Are you a hungry boy?"

Her voice was different when she talked to her children—softer, sweeter, more intimate somehow.

Aiden lifted his head again, and then he burped again, this time leaving a dribble of milk to soak into Seth's shirt.

"Sorry," Gabby said with a wince.

"No problem."

"You don't have to help with baby stuff, you know," she said. "Just having us here is enough."

"If you don't want me to—" he started, then breathed a sigh. "Thing is, Gabs, I kind of want to. If I'm going to be your husband, I guess that makes me a dad to them…sort of. Right?"

"Do you want to be?" Gabby eyed him, and he couldn't tell what she was feeling. But she was waiting for his answer, all of her body tensed. He'd learned a few things in his first marriage, like never to assume he knew what a woman was feeling. Honesty was probably the best call right now.

"Am I allowed to be a dad to them?" he asked cautiously.

"How long-term is this?" she asked.

"Uh…" He smiled hesitantly. "As long as we want it to be."

"That's not an answer, though."

"I'm assuming we're going to keep this going for as long as the boys need the insurance," he said. "That's on a purely practical level. As friends, though, we can stay married for the rest of our lives, if it suits us."

"If it suits us…" She sucked in a breath. "Kids needs stability."

"Yeah, I get it," he said with a quick nod. And emotional connection and passionate promises gave at least the impression of stability. But he and Gabby weren't there;

they weren't promising undying passion for a lifetime.

"I did grow up with a really great god-father," Gabby said. "You know how much Uncle Ted meant to me. I was thinking maybe you could be like him... That way, if we do decide to end this after a while, it won't be as traumatic for the boys, and you could stay in their lives in a meaning-ful way."

Uncle Ted. That had been a weird setup with Gabby's family—not that Seth had told her his real feelings there. Godparents mat-tered a lot in her family—more than in his, that was for sure.

"Okay, well...so I'll be a godfather kind of figure. And I can help out with the bot-tles and stuff."

When they got older he could teach them to ride a horse, and to fix a truck, and to use their manners. Maybe she was right, and being a godfather would be a longer-lasting relationship than a stepdad.

"Okay..." Gabby's voice softened, and she met his gaze with a gentle smile. "We'll just learn as we go."

That seemed to be parenting in a nutshell, really—learning as you went along. Billy's daughter had been dropped on his doorstep, and he came back to Eagle's Rest to raise her before Seth and Bonnie had started trying for a baby. Watching his old friend adjust to fatherhood had taught him a thing or two—namely, that a whole lot of love made up for whatever limitations a dad might have. If Seth had had the chance to raise his own daughter, he'd have bumbled along, he was sure, but the chance to bumble and mess up and fix stuff—that was more precious than most people realized.

When the babies were fed, Gabby changed diapers again. Seth stood back and let her do that one on her own. He was easing into this, and a bottle was enough to stretch his skill set right now.

"I guess I should show you your room," Seth said, when the babies were dressed once more.

"That would be great. They normally sleep after a bottle," Gabby replied. "I've got the collapsible playpen in your truck—"

"There's a crib," he said, and he swallowed against a lump in his throat.

"Oh…" Understanding registered in her eyes. "Hazel's?"

He nodded. "If that's okay."

"It's perfect," she said. "They're small enough we can lay them down sidelong and they can all sleep together. For now, at least. That's how they sleep in the playpen, anyway."

Hazel's crib… He hadn't looked at it in a long time, and his chest tightened at the thought of it being put to use after all this time. But these boys needed a home and a bed, and it was better to have that nursery used than to leave it empty of life and filled with grief.

Seth cleared his throat. "Should I carry one of the babies?"

"Please. Here's Beau."

She passed the infant into his arms, and Seth looked down at the tiny face of yet a different boy who needed him. Seth was a dad. Sort of. That was how he was seeing himself right now. He might not be biologically linked, but he was here…and he was married to their mother. He gave the baby a little pat on the rump.

"Hey, Beau," he murmured.

Beau was sleeping, pale eyelashes brushing his cheeks. Seth waited until Gabby had the remaining two babies in her arms, and then he led the way up the creaking stairs to the second floor.

"That's my bedroom," he said, nodding toward the closed door. "And this is…yours."

It was hard to say that Hazel's room belonged to Gabby and her sons now, but he opened the other door to reveal the nursery. It was spacious and bright, and there was a double bed pushed against the far wall. He'd come through the room and dusted all the surfaces, did some sweeping and generally tried to make it hospitable before he left to get married. Originally, this used to be the guest room, and he and Bonnie never did move that bed out. They'd figured it might be useful for feedings or something. But Gabby could use that bed, and the babies would share the crib until they could squeeze in another couple cribs.

Gabby stepped into the room ahead of him and looked around.

"It's beautiful," she said. "So bright. I love it."

He'd always liked that room, too, and he stepped forward to lower the side of the crib one-handed so she could put the babies into it. It took him a moment of fiddling—he wasn't used to actually using any of this stuff, but before Hazel was born he'd familiarized himself with it all. He was nothing if not prepared—his life motto, for all it had worked out.

Gabby laid the boys carefully on the

yellow-sheeted mattress. Andy stretched out tiny limbs and Aiden exhaled a comfortable sigh. Gabby took Beau from his arms and laid him next to his brothers. Beau and Aiden turned toward each other.

"They always do that," Gabby whispered.

"I wonder why," Seth said.

"They shared a womb." Gabby shrugged. "They all did. I'm sure their relationship— the three of them—will be one we'll never fully understand."

"Yeah."

We. That was the word she'd chosen, and it felt awkwardly endearing to be included like that. *We.*

Seth glanced around the nursery—at the owl decals on the walls, the rocking chair in the far corner holding a pile of knitted blankets he'd never actually put away—and he realized that it didn't feel quite so sad anymore. It wasn't that Hazel's memory was gone from this room exactly, but perhaps her memory had some company in the form of triplet boys.

CHAPTER THREE

GABBY CHANGED OUT of her wedding dress and into a pair of jeans and a sweater. That felt better—more like herself. She went downstairs and helped Seth unload the last of the baby supplies from the back of the pickup and brought them into the house. Next, Seth emptied a couple cupboards for her, and over the next hour, Gabby went up and down the stairs at least ten times carrying things to the nursery and taking a peek at the sleeping infants.

Seth was stomping around, not looking exactly welcoming. Three times now, Gabby had put something down and he'd moved it—a bag of baby clothes, containers of formula, her purse...and she was a little worried that he wouldn't be as able to adjust to her being around here as he claimed. It might be easier to have him out of the house for a while. When he came back, he could reel under the shock all at once.

"You have the week off, right?" Gabby asked as she sank down into a kitchen chair.

"Yep," he said. "I haven't taken my vacation time in a while, so Mr. Ross was glad to give it to me."

So much for having him out from underfoot. It felt different now—it *wasn't* the same as before.

"You're definitely uncomfortable," she said with a small smile. Might as well face this head-on.

Seth cleared his throat. "I'm used to facing marriage a little differently than this."

"I know…"

"I mean, my parents had that vicious divorce when I was twelve, so Bonnie and I—" He swallowed. "We really took our marriage seriously. It was top priority. We read marriage books and had our own plan that was supposed to keep us divorce-proof, and now…" He met her gaze. "I'm not sure how to do a marriage like ours. You know?"

"We said this was going to be pragmatic," she said.

"And it is," he agreed. "I honestly think this is smart, but I'm not sure how to do this now that we're…home. There aren't a lot of books on how to make a practical marriage work."

Right. Seth and his love of research.

"We should probably talk about money," she suggested. "You know, now—before there's any resentment."

"Probably," he agreed.

"Obviously, I've got to contribute," she said. "I could get my aunt to watch the boys while I work part-time somewhere. With them so young, it would be hard to do more than part-time, but—"

"No." His tone was closer to a growl, and she stopped, surprised.

"No, what?" she asked.

"No, you don't have to work. Three newborns are enough on your plate, and I didn't do this expecting you to pay me back."

"Yes, but I still need to contribute," she countered. "Realistically speaking—"

"How about…" he interrupted, and she saw the discomfort on his face. "With some cooking and stuff?"

"Are you asking me to be a housewife?" she asked, expecting to laugh when he did.

"Yes?" He smiled bashfully. "I know this marriage is a practical one, but it's been a hell of a long time since I've come home to a hot meal."

"A housewife…" She rolled that thought around in her mind, and found that it felt rather nice at the moment. She could spend her days raising her boys and taking care of this farmhouse…

"I'm not sure you'd actually like that," she countered. "I'd change things."

"Hmm." It sounded more like a grunt, and when she searched his face for a reaction, all she saw was granite. He was hiding his feelings from her—something she'd never cared too much about before, but it wouldn't make living together easy if she couldn't read him.

"I'd rearrange stuff," she pressed on. "I'd cook food that I like, and I'd probably want to paint some walls, or plant a garden, or—or…" She cast about, searching for the sorts of things that would occur to her, and she'd be halfway through before Seth even got to voice an opinion. "I might want to decorate for the holidays."

"Not yet," he said with a sigh. "No painting. No rearranging. I like things the way they are. Just for now. For a while."

So she *was* a houseguest, not a housewife. Good to know. He met her gaze with a hesitant smile. The sparkle in his eye made her breath catch ever so slightly, though, and she broke eye contact.

"Hey, we're making some ground rules here," he went on. "So if you've got something that's nonnegotiable, now's the time to put it out there."

"Okay," she said. "I'm not waiting on you hand and foot. That's something I won't budge on. I'm technically your wife, but I'm not your servant."

Seth grinned. "I never thought that was an option, Gabs."

"No slipper-fetching or reverence in your presence," she said, only halfway joking. "I'm not standing by with a plate of food warmed in the oven. So if that was in the back of your mind, you might want to encourage me to find a job to contribute financially."

"Gabby." He reached across the table and grabbed her hand. His dark gaze met hers and pinned her to the spot. She could make out the sandpaper of his stubble across his chin, and the few gray hairs that had worked their way into his beard. His hand moved slowly around her palm as if he didn't even realize how he was touching her—an absentminded kind of caress from a man who'd been married before. "You aren't that good of a cook."

That broke the moment, and she pulled her hand back with a laugh. "I'm better than nothing, you lout."

Seth seemed to realize how he'd touched her, and he closed his fingers into a fist, flattening his lips. "I'm just saying. We can make this work, but don't stress about me expecting you to be a servant. You *know* me."

Gabby did know him, but she'd never been married to him before. And when he was married, Bonnie had kept Gabby at a good distance. She hadn't seen too much of them. Maybe Gabby was worrying for nothing. He was offering a great deal here, and he'd already made it possible for her to feed her boys without worry. Now he was letting her raise them without worry, too. Maybe she felt a little guilty for all she was getting from this deal. She could do something in return, and maybe she wasn't entirely closed to the idea of keeping some food warm for him in the oven…

"I'll probably be cleaning up and stuff while you're working," she said. "Anything you don't want me to touch—like at all?"

"My bedroom."

There was a finality in his tone that sobered her, and she nodded quickly. He was giving her access to the house, but not to his private space. It was fair, but it also drew a solid line.

"Okay," she said quietly. "I leave your bedroom alone. And I won't change too much around here. I'm just warning you. I'm here. I'll…leave a mark, I guess."

"Yeah," he said, his gaze meeting hers again. "You're right. Look, I know you'll change a few things. I'm sure it'll be fine. I'll adjust."

It was good to talk this stuff out. They had a friendship worth protecting, and marriage was going to complicate that.

"We have about an hour before the babies wake," Gabby said. "Want to watch TV?"

Seth shrugged. "Sure. Why not."

It might help to get them back to where they used to be—buddies hanging out, appreciating each other's humor. Not husband and wife. Maybe in public they'd be the Straights and keep up some sort appearance of romance, but in private, they had to protect their careful balance. Because right now, that balance was the one thing that might help Gabby stay afloat.

"Be right back," she said. "I'll just check on the babies."

SETH PAUSED TO look up the stairs toward the nursery. Outside the kitchen window, the sun was sinking in the west, golden rays pooling on the kitchen floor. This was their first day married, and it was almost over. He felt a weird mix of happiness and guilt at the same time. It felt good to have company in the house again—maybe too good.

He glanced around the kitchen, and it seemed like some of those old memories had dimmed a little, just by having Gabby here, and that felt wrong. Like he was letting Bonnie down. Bonnie deserved to be remembered—vividly. But Gabby was even more vivid right now, the smell of her perfume already seeping into the other scents of the house. Gabby was *here*. He'd gotten so used to living with a memory that having a woman physically in his home made him uneasy.

And yet, Gabby *had* always been a good friend, and before Bonnie, when times got tough or one of them had a breakup, they'd always gravitated toward each other again. They built each other back up when life knocked them down. When he'd gotten married that became his wife's domain, but he'd missed Gabby in his life. Maybe too much; Bonnie hadn't ever been comfortable with their friendship.

Losing his family was the hardest knock he'd ever experienced. Gabby had been here for the funeral, but she'd had to go back to her life in Denver. So having Gabby here now felt like a bit of salve on a wound that had never healed. It wouldn't magically cure him, but it would ease the pain somewhat, even while the chaos she and the babies would cause grated on his orderly personality.

His gaze landed on her purse, sitting on the table next to those roses. There had to be somewhere to keep her purse out of sight. He glanced around but didn't have time to do anything about it, because Gabby's footsteps came creaking back down the stairs and she emerged into the kitchen again. Her hair tumbled down around her shoulders, and he noted how she carried the extra weight from her pregnancy. She was rounder, softer. The extra padding certainly didn't hurt.

"All right," she said, stifling a yawn. "They're still sleeping soundly."

Seth pulled his eyes away from her figure. Wife or not, her body wasn't his business. It never had been.

"So... TV?" Seth asked.

The TV was in the living room. It wasn't very big; he didn't tend to watch that much TV, truth be told. He hadn't spent much time in this house since Bonnie's death, preferring to be on horseback checking herds and cowboy teams. Horseback riding was something he and Bonnie had never done together, so riding alone was an escape from grief, too. He'd given himself permission to not think about all he'd lost when he was on horseback. He could be present in the moment and just ride.

"Yeah," she agreed. "I'm exhausted."

He led the way through to the living room, feeling mildly self-conscious. This was to be her home, too, but it didn't feel like it yet. This still felt like his turf.

"Still not up to a Christmas tree?" Gabby asked. She sank into the couch—the one spot where you could see the TV without a glare.

Seth sat down next to her, the warmth of her arm surprisingly comforting next to him. "I don't know. I didn't feel up to it this year."

Or last year. He'd obstinately avoided Christmas last year, and he'd refused to decorate at all. It wasn't like it would cheer him up to sit alone in this house with some tinsel and mistletoe, after all.

Gabby nodded. "Yeah, I get it."

She'd mentioned wanting to do some holiday decorating, and he eyed her for a moment. Last year, he'd been alone. This year, it wasn't just him rattling around in the house.

"Maybe a little bit of celebration would be okay. Did you want to put one up?" he asked hesitantly.

"It'll be the boys' first Christmas," she said. "It might be nice."

Of course—there was more to consider than his own grief this year, and a first Christmas was important. Maybe that was a good thing, because he was getting a little too accustomed to his bare, cold sadness.

"Okay," he said. "So we'll get one."

"I can take care of decorating things around here," she said. "You know, part of the housewife deal."

He smiled faintly. "Sure. Okay." He glanced over at her. "Have you been in contact with the babies' dad?"

"Nope."

"He hasn't reached out to ask about the boys? Nothing?"

Gabby shook her head. "He didn't come to the hospital, but he did pay the bill for my delivery. From what I understand, his wife found out about me before I found out about her, and she made a few demands—one of which was to cut ties with me completely."

"Huh." Seth sucked in a deep breath. "Maybe for the best. For his marriage, at least. Not for the kids."

"You think so?" she asked curtly, sitting up. "I had no idea he was married! It's not like I was trying to steal him or something. I think I deserved a few explanations, and if he'd wanted his wife in the room for that, all the better. But frankly, treating me like the bad guy was immature and cruel!"

"Yeah... Yeah..." He blinked at her. "I'm sorry. I didn't mean it like that. I guess I just figure you're better off without him. You know—like a Band-Aid. Just rip it off."

"I was with him for a full year, Seth."

"I know." He swallowed.

"I deserved some closure, at the very least!"

"He deserves to hurt just as much as you do," he said. "I'm not on his side. I think he's garbage. And now his wife has him back. If I were her, I wouldn't be feeling so lucky."

"Fine..." Gabby leaned back again.

"He owes you, you know," Seth added.

"I could sue him for child support, I suppose," she said. "But then I'd have to let him—and his pissed-off wife—into the boys' lives, and I'm not interested in that. Is that good for kids, to be around a stepmom who hates them? She's blaming the wrong person for his unfaithfulness. I wasn't the problem—he was. He was the one capable of lying to two women at once and getting away with it for a year, but she blames me. So I'm assuming she'd hate them, too, fair or not. And it's not that I begrudge her that, either..." Color tinged her cheeks, and she dropped her gaze.

"It's complicated," he concluded.

"It's complicated," she agreed.

"Will you tell the boys the truth about their dad?"

"I'll have to. Eventually. Right? I mean, I always knew about my dad, even if he wasn't in my life. It'll be the same for them."

Seth picked up the remote and flicked on the TV. There was a commercial with Santa Claus and spilled milk. For paper towels, maybe?

"I feel like an idiot," Gabby said with a sigh.

"For what?" he asked. "Trusting a guy who was supposed to love you to tell you the truth?"

"Something like that." She didn't take her eyes off the screen. "You know my track record with men. I feel dumb for thinking

Craig would be any different. I attract one kind."

"You aim too low," he said. She always had. She chose cowboys who partied hard and never fully grew up. She was always attracted to the bad boys.

"I had my reasons," she replied softly.

"Like what?" He adjusted to turn toward her a little bit.

"You have your bedroom, and I have my personal issues," she replied with a wry smile. "Privacy, Seth."

He chuckled and turned back toward the TV. He changed the channel a few times. "What do you want to watch?"

"Whatever. I'll fight for the remote another day."

Seth flicked the channel another couple times, then he glanced at Gabby.

"You said you don't want to find someone," Seth said. "And it might seem kind of late to ask, but why?"

"I always dated loser cowboys before," she said, glancing toward him. "No offense to your cousin."

"A fair assessment," he said.

"With Craig, I was actively trying to break the mold, to go for a better kind of man. And look what that got me. I'm not good at dating, or romance. But Craig... I really loved him. He was perfect—at least he seemed that way. He was sweet, attentive, adoring... I thought I might actually marry him."

"I'm sorry."

"Turns out he was husband material... just someone else's." She sighed. "But I have these boys now, and I seem to be good at being a mom."

"You're really good at being a mom," he confirmed.

"So I'm sticking to that," she replied. "I don't need a steady dose of romance and rejection. I just need some calm and a solid friendship."

Gabby tipped her head against his shoulder and he could feel the warmth of her body pressed against his arm. They used to sit like this when they were both single— a luxury they wouldn't allow themselves if one of them was romantically connected. So maybe it made sense that they could still sit like this. He reached over and smoothed her honey-gold hair down. Her head felt warm against his palm and she smelled sweet—a mixture of shampoo and that perfume she liked. Touching her head had been an automatic reaction, one rooted in a few years of marriage, he realized. He froze, then pulled his hand back. That was too familiar.

Gabby's breath slowed and deepened, and he glanced down at her again. Her eyes were shut, and she looked so incredibly tired. They'd had a big day, after all. Getting married, moving in. Who knew how much sleep she got with the triplets eating every two hours? He would let her rest. She obviously needed it, and he craved some quiet.

He flicked through another few channels, then chose an episode of a comedy show he'd recorded on the DVR. The tinny laugh track was just what he needed right now—someone to point out the humor he couldn't see.

Her head slipped from his shoulder and she jolted, then settled against his shoulder again. This wasn't the most comfortable position, after all, and he eased his arm free and put it around her so that her cheek rested against his chest instead. She shifted, still sleeping. Yeah, this was better.

But she was closer now, and with his arm around her, his hand rested comfortably on her hip. He pulled it back. That wasn't going to work, either...

What was with him? This wasn't the plan; marrying her was supposed to be safe, not tempting. He needed to get up, put some physical distance between them, but she was settled against him now, fast asleep.

It was ironic that their marriage was based on a mutual understanding that they'd keep things platonic. She was counting on him. Gabby had been through a lot, both romantically and physically. She'd been betrayed by her boyfriend and had been struggling to provide for her children. She'd married Seth for health insurance, not for anything he could offer otherwise. Besides, their arrangement was smarter than most other couples'. Even when he'd married Bonnie, he'd been in for a few jolts and surprises, all because of different expectations and hurt feelings when hearts were involved. His deal with Gabby made more sense. They weren't going to go over all those bumps and have all those stupid fights that newlyweds normally endured.

"Gabs," he murmured.

"Hmm…"

She wiped a little trail of drool from the side of her mouth. It was oddly endearing, and he chuckled.

"Shut up," she muttered. "I haven't slept a whole night in weeks. You'd drool, too."

"Yeah, I know," he said. "Rest here. You

deserve some sleep. I've got a few things I need to do."

He eased himself up out of the couch and she slipped down into a more comfortable position to nap. He looked at her for a moment, watching her face relax as she dropped back to sleep before his eyes.

Seth didn't actually have anything he needed to do, but he had to get out of her space, away from that sweet scent that enveloped her. He needed to get outside to cold air and a clear head.

This was day one of marriage, and so far he thought he'd done pretty well. They'd take some adjusting, but he and Gabby might actually make this plan work. They'd managed to move in together, take care of the babies together, and even talked through some pretty delicate issues like money and bedrooms. There was something to be said for pragmatism, but it lasted only as long as they followed their rules.

CHAPTER FOUR

GABBY COULD HEAR something sizzling in the kitchen as she blinked her eyes open. It took a moment to center herself and remember where she even was. Her back was kinked, and she pushed herself upright, stretching her spine and letting out a soft sigh. Then she looked around the room. Right. She was at Seth's place…their place now. How long had she slept? It felt like a year. She licked her dry lips and rose to her feet, listening. Other than the sizzle of cooking food, all she could make out was Seth's off-key humming. Stifling a yawn, Gabby headed toward the kitchen.

Seth stood at the stove frying sausages. He wore a blue-and-white-striped apron over his jeans and T-shirt, and the babies were in their bouncy chairs sitting in a line on the long kitchen table, one blanket covering all three of them up to their bare arms. None seemed to be dressed. Snow floated lazily down outside the kitchen window, and she looked over at the table again. It seemed longer. Had Seth put a leaf in it so all three babies' chairs would fit?

"Hey, you're awake," Seth said. "The babies woke up. I gave them bottles and changed diapers. Sorry—I didn't get them dressed again. I kind of ran out of patience with that, so I just brought them downstairs. Hope you don't mind. The kitchen stays nice and warm."

"No, no, that's great." She went over to the table and looked down at her infants. Aiden and Andy were awake, but Beau had gone back to sleep. She looked under the blanket and saw that the diapering was slightly crooked. So she adjusted a few tabs, then bent down to kiss Aiden's tiny toes. He cooed, and she brushed her lips over Andy's forehead, letting Beau keep sleeping undisturbed.

"Did I do all right there?" Seth asked.

"Yeah, it looks good. Thank you. I can't believe I slept like that. What time is it?"

"Six thirty."

She'd slept for almost two hours? She knew she was tired…but sleeping that deeply also felt mildly irresponsible. She was a mom now, and she'd slept through all three babies waking up.

"I'm making breakfast for dinner," Seth said. "I've got some hash browns, some boiled eggs and sausages." He glanced over his shoulder. "You used to like that, didn't you? Unless you've gotten more refined in your tastes in the last few years."

"Not really." She chuckled. "It smells great. But I feel like I'm a burden on you already."

"Nah." He flicked off the burner and tipped the browned sausages onto a plate, then added some potatoes and a boiled egg that rolled around. "You were wiped. You really needed that sleep."

Gabby moved the babies' bouncy chairs down to the floor so they could use one corner to eat, and pulled out a chair. Seth deposited a plate of food in front of her and handed her a fork and knife. It really did smell amazing, and her stomach rumbled in response.

"Thank you. This is really sweet of you," she said, and she took a bite of sausage. She'd been so hungry lately, since the babies were born. It was like her body needed extra sustenance to recover, and it never really tapered off.

Seth sank into the chair opposite her and nudged a ketchup bottle across the table in her direction. As a friend, Seth had always treated her a whole lot better than any of her boyfriends had ever treated her. And somehow, that had never been something she found attractive before. He'd been almost too nice. Too careful. Too polite. But then he'd turned all that niceness onto Bonnie, and Gabby had watched it as an outsider. Was that what a functional, happy relationship looked like?

She wished she knew firsthand, but her relationships tended to be quick, passionate and short-lived. Ironically, Craig was the exception to that, lasting a year. But marrying Seth had been the first logically thought-out move she'd made when it came to a relationship.

"We need to decide on our story," Gabby said. "I need to go tell my mother about the wedding tomorrow morning. I'd really hate for her to hear from someone else first. We need a story we can stick to so we don't look suspicious and get reported to the insurance company by some busybody."

"Yeah, I get that," he said, then took a bite. "And you're sure you don't want to just let her in on the truth? It would be easier, you know. And of anyone, I think we can trust your mother not to want to ruin your health insurance."

"It would break her heart." Gabby sighed. "Mom sacrificed a lot to get me through school and everything. And when she was out of work for six months, she got into a lot of debt. She doesn't have a penny to spare right now, but she'll feel like she's let me down, anyway. Just trust me on this."

"Okay. So what do you want to say?"

Gabby looked down at the wedding ring on her finger. She liked it, actually. She liked how it looked—settled, comfortable. But it reminded her of her dreams of finding Mr. Right, too, and that stung a little bit. She'd officially given up on that. Even if she and Seth decided to end this marriage eventually, she wouldn't be looking for love again.

"We're kind of lucky," Gabby said. "We get to choose our story. Most people just have to make do with however they met. Remember how Colleen and Mike met at the hospital when that restaurant poisoned everyone with bad clams?"

"Yeah. But that was a good story," Seth replied.

"No, it wasn't! It was awful. I mean, interesting, but not exactly beautiful. It involved a lot of vomiting."

Seth chuckled. "But life isn't always beautifully arranged. At least they met."

Gabby shrugged. "I want something a little more picturesque, if you don't mind."

"So…" He took another bite and chewed thoughtfully. "What kind of story do you want?"

"Something I can tell with my head held high," she said.

"What was your story with Craig?"

Gabby sighed. "I met him at a work holiday party. He was an X-ray technician at the medical center where I worked."

"That's not a terrible how-you-met story."

"It was okay, I guess," she said. "I just… I want a better story. This is the one I'll be telling for a very long time, presumably."

Would she be telling it for the rest of her life? She wasn't sure about that. Eventually, they might decide to stop their charade, but for the foreseeable future, people would be asking how they got together after all these years of just being pals.

"It has to be believable," she went on. "And up until a week ago, I was in Denver and you were here. So… Do we tell people we were in contact before I came back?"

"Sure. I mean, we've been friends for

years. And we *were* in contact, weren't we? We were texting and stuff."

"What made you propose?" she said. "What flicked the switch between friends and more than friends? Grace is going to ask."

"Okay, so… I swept you off your feet in the city."

"Except you've been here the whole time, and no one knows that better than Grace and Billy. Besides, I was almost eight months pregnant with triplets. You weren't going to be able to sweep anything. And after I had them, they were in the hospital for three weeks, and my mom was traveling back and forth to help me out with them whenever she had a few days off. She knows you weren't in the picture."

Seth smiled ruefully. "All right. So let's stay as close to the truth as possible. We'll say you came back home to Eagle's Rest, heartbroken over your loser boyfriend, and when we saw each other again, everything was just…" his voice softened "…different."

His gaze warmed, too, and he watched her for a moment. Was that how falling in love worked for him—all in a moment? It normally took Gabby a little longer. Then he dropped his gaze again and speared another piece of sausage.

"That's it, then?" she said. "We saw each other, and...*whammo*?"

He was silent for a moment. "I asked you out for dinner. We talked for hours. When it was time to go our separate ways again, I had this crazy idea that maybe we should never say goodbye again. And...you didn't think it was so crazy."

Gabby blinked. They really had had dinner together—right here at his place, as a matter of fact. They had talked for hours... Except she'd been telling him her story about Craig and how heartbroken she was, and about how she needed a job. In fact, she'd suggested she might be able to work at the ranch. There weren't any openings, though, and he'd had another idea...

"It's close to the truth," she said hesitantly.

"It'll make it easier to remember," he said.

"So how come we snuck off and got married in secret?" she asked.

"It's eloping."

"I always wanted a big wedding. Mom knows that."

Seth shrugged, then gave her a slow smile. "We didn't want to wait. Simple as that."

He did make it all sound rather simple

and believable. Just two people who realized they loved each other and got married.

"So, we're wildly in love, then," she said.

"Only explanation for our quickie wedding," he replied. "Besides the truth."

"Can you keep up that kind of image in
public?" she asked. "I mean, we have to be
realistic here. You know how small Eagle's
Rest is. They all know us."

"You mean, can I act madly in love?" His
expression grew faraway and it seemed like
he was imagining how that would work, too.
Telling the story was one thing, but acting
all lovey-dovey…that was something else
entirely. "What do you want that to look
like? Hand-holding? I open doors for you?
We share a few private jokes?"

"That might be enough," she agreed. They
didn't have to go overboard, did they?

"Except for the hand-holding, that was our
friendship for years, Gabs," he said. "Until
I got married, at least."

She smiled at that. "Seth, you were my
best friend for a long time. And I don't want
to undermine what we have. This is just…
for appearances. At home, we can go back
to being our regular selves."

"Are you going to eat?" he asked, nodding
toward her plate.

Gabby looked down at her full plate and took a bite. It was delicious. So for the next couple minutes, she dedicated herself to eating most of the food on her plate.

"Do you think it's enough to look like best friends in public and let people assume it's… more interesting…in private?" she asked.

He chuckled. "I'll do my best, okay?"

"Do your best at what?" she asked.

"At making this all look believable. It matters to me, too. I mean, I've got friends and family who I'd rather not explain the details to, as well. So…"

Gabby smiled. "Thanks."

Seth would do his best. What was that going to look like with her? She'd seen him in love before, gazing adoringly at his first wife. She knew what Seth looked like when his heart was in it…

Was she going to get a chance to be on the receiving end of that kind of attention? It didn't matter, because it wouldn't be real. Seth wasn't in love with her. And she'd be wise to keep that in mind, or in the emotionally vulnerable state she was in, she might end up falling for it, too.

LATER THAT NIGHT, Seth stood in the living room, looking out the window at the full moon. The house was quiet now, except for the mournful howl of winter wind sweeping around the building. Gabby had gone up to bed already, and overhead, he suddenly heard the hiccuping cry of one of the babies. They were up again, it seemed, ready for more milk.

Normally on evenings he couldn't sleep, he'd take it as some sign from the universe that he should check things out on the ranch, see what was going on. The work was a constant in his life that let him cover up his emotions when he was tired of feeling them.

But tonight, it wouldn't be so simple. He was supposed to be on vacation, for one. The ranch was organized to survive without him for a few days, and he really should respect that. Second, this was his wedding night, and no amount of work was going to erase that fact from his head…

This wasn't exactly the kind of wedding night a man looked forward to. But it was more than the fact that this marriage was an emotional sham. He felt guilty. He looked down at the simple gold band on his finger. The one from his first marriage was platinum, with a tiny engraving of a leaf. He and Bonnie had chosen their rings together, much like he and Gabby had. Except with Gabby they were looking for rings that were as cheap as possible, and with Bonnie they'd been thinking more romantically and the price hadn't mattered as much. It was a bit of a relief to have a wedding ring on his hand again. He'd been happy in his marriage—proud, confident. Marrying Bonnie had been the best choice of his life. So looking down to see a ring on his hand felt oddly right, which only made him feel worse. He'd sworn he wouldn't get married again. Bonnie had been his one and only, and if he'd been a better husband, if he'd stuck around after their fight instead of taking off...

He'd gone out of the cell phone service area, and he'd noticed only when he checked his phone and saw no bars, and then he'd started back. She hadn't called for an ambulance—she'd been too certain that she'd reach him any minute, and halfway convinced it was false labor. But if he'd been home that night like he should have been, facing their problems, he might have gotten her to the hospital sooner. She might have survived that delivery. Their daughter might have, too.

Everything had taken longer, from getting her to the hospital to the arrival of a specialist. And now, two years after he'd laid her to rest in the local cemetery, he was married again, and his new wife was upstairs.

"It's not the real thing, Bonnie," he murmured.

He'd taken to talking to his late wife over the last two years. It helped make the house feel less lonely, helped him sort out his thoughts. And it helped keep Bonnie closer, too. He sighed and rubbed his hands over his face.

The moon shone bright and silvery, the light spilling over the snowy front yard, the gravel road and the bunkhouse beyond. He'd always found this scene soothing, but tonight it wasn't helping.

"What did I do?"

A few days ago, this had made sense. This marriage hadn't been for himself, it had been for the tiny boys. Gabby needed health insurance for her children. She needed as much formula as these boys could drink. She needed doctor's appointments and reassurance that if anything went wrong, there would be medical help. He could provide all that for his friend.

He pulled out his laptop and sank into the La-Z-Boy chair. He had a copy of the marriage license and of Gabby's ID, so tonight he figured he'd start filling out forms to have her added to his health insurance. This was the goal, wasn't it?

He looked at the license—the names, the dates, the number—and his heart nearly thudded to a stop.

Married! He'd stood before a judge that very morning and taken vows with Gabby Rogers. It was ironic that it was seeming crazy only now. It didn't matter what reason he had for marrying Gabby, they were legally wed, and the woman upstairs feeding babies was no longer just his old friend. She was his *wife*.

Overhead, the babies were quiet again, and he heard the soft creak of floorboards as Gabby moved down the stairs. He looked up as she came into the living room.

"Hey…" She wore a bathrobe wrapped all the way up to her chin. She looked bleary and tired.

"You should go get some more rest," he said.

"Yeah. I should." She smiled hesitantly. "I just wanted to say thank you, Seth. This is…huge. It's the biggest gift anyone has ever given me. And I'm not taking this for granted. I'm not taking *you* for granted."

"What are friends for?" he said with a small shrug.

"Not normally for gestures this big, and I know that full well." She fiddled with the golden band on her finger just as he'd been doing a few moments before, and he couldn't help but look at it. Her slim fingers looked pretty with the simple wedding band, and he couldn't help but admire it. No, it wasn't expensive, but it would do the job—it would tell the world she was married. To him. That flutter of uncertainty rose up inside him, and he attempted to bat it away. She needed him to be the strong one right now, to make all this seem normal.

"You're welcome," he said, then nodded toward the computer on his knee. "I'm starting the forms—as much as I can fill out right now, at least. We'll see if we're missing anything."

"That's for the medical insurance?" She came over and perched on the arm of his chair. She smelled good—like soap and something sweet—and sitting there so close to him, her warmth emanated against his shoulder. She felt good there, comforting almost.

"Yeah." He swallowed. "I thought I'd get started on it."

"Can I help?"

"Sure." He nodded. "It might go faster that way."

Gabby leaned closer, scanning the form he'd started on. "Here, let me put in my last address, and my doctor's name in the city. I can look up his phone number."

She took the laptop from where it balanced on his leg and typed for a few moments. He watched her, the screen's light glowing on her skin, the way her blue eyes shone, her wavy hair mussed from sleep.

"There." She handed it back.

"Thanks." He scanned the next couple pages. "Here, I need to put our marriage license number in. And the date of our wedding."

He typed them in, then paused, looking at the date. The date of their marriage—this really was official.

"We have an anniversary…" Gabby's voice was soft, and she looked over at him with a small smile turning up her lips.

"Looks like." He chuckled. "I guess I'd better make sure I remember it, huh?"

"You'd better."

He smiled, but he hadn't been entirely joking. He'd have to commit today's date to memory. Even if their marriage was for their own reasons, their friendship mattered, and he wouldn't be forgetting the day they took this big step together. He checked the appropriate numbers on the paperwork, pressed Save and continued on to the next screen.

"Here it says we'll need to mail them a copy of the marriage license and a copy of your ID to finalize you on my insurance, but this is surprisingly straightforward." He looked up at her. "I kind of expected more hoops to jump through."

"Me, too." She shrugged. "Small blessings, right?"

Seth met her gaze. This was like old times, sitting in front of a computer, writing a résumé for a job… In fact, it had been a job at this very ranch that he'd been applying for. And he remembered how she'd sat with him, helping find the best way to express himself. She'd been better with words than he was. If he remembered right, he'd been dating Bonnie at the time. It was after their wedding that Bonnie had put her foot down about Gabby in his life.

But it wasn't the same. Even if she didn't love him romantically. Even if he didn't love her romantically, either. They were joined.

"We're really married," he said quietly.

"Yeah. It's our wedding night." Her cheeks

tinged pink as she echoed his thoughts from earlier.

But he wouldn't be taking her upstairs. She wouldn't be sharing his bedroom or his bed.

"Not like other wedding nights, though," he countered.

"No," she replied. "But the marriage feels more monumental tonight than it did earlier today. Does that even make sense?"

"It's had time to sink in, I guess," he said.

He felt it, too. The shift. The closing of the circle. When he'd married Bonnie he'd felt his heart close around her, and marrying Gabby had sparked a protective instinct inside him. Not romantic love, exactly...but pride, maybe. A desire to make sure she stayed safe.

"Our friendship isn't the same anymore, is it?" she asked.

"It would have changed, anyway," he said. "We've both been through a lot. I've lost my wife. You became a mother. We're not the same people we were before, so even if we hadn't taken this step, our friendship would still feel different. I don't think we could avoid that."

"You're probably right." She stood and tightened the tie on her bathrobe.

"Let's just remember why we're doing this. It's for your boys," he said. "They need some stability and I can provide that. They're the priority, right?"

She nodded. "They sure are."

"Okay, then." He was trying to sort out his own emotions tonight, too, but he'd do that alone.

Gabby turned toward the living room doorway. "I'd better get to bed. The boys will be up for another bottle in two hours. I can't wait until they start sleeping longer between feedings."

"Good night," he said.

He wouldn't be going upstairs until she was already asleep—it would be more comfortable that way. He wasn't sure he could walk down that hallway knowing she was lying in her bed listening to his footfalls. Later, maybe. But not on their wedding night. He wanted to stay down here in the darkened living room, looking at the light of the moon on the snow.

The stairs squeaked as Gabby headed on up. He wasn't alone in this house anymore, and he was glad for the company in a way. He needed someone to pull him out of his natural inclination to just continue mourning. But…

"I'm sorry, Bonnie," Seth murmured. And he was sorry for how disrespectful of her memory all this seemed. Bonnie had been his one true love, and Gabby...she was a pal. Bonnie had been worried that they'd had deeper feelings for each other than they admitted. Mostly, she'd worried that Gabby's feelings ran deeper than she claimed. And here they were, married to each other.

It was almost like Bonnie was being proved right. Except it wasn't like that. Tell that to his guilty conscience.

CHAPTER FIVE

THE NEXT MORNING, Gabby looked over her shoulder at the triplets' car seats in the back of her car. The babies were all asleep; a car ride would have taken care of that, anyway. They'd loaded up the trunk with all the baby things they'd need for the morning, and Gabby felt a wave of anxiety. This was it—the beginning of their charade for the rest of the town.

Seth sat next to her. He was a big man, and he filled up the entire passenger seat, his hat balanced on his knee. He smelled good. She liked his aftershave.

"You ready to go make this mom-official?" Seth asked.

"As ready as I'll ever be." She shot him a smile. "Mom's going to be suspicious, though. I just know it."

"Maybe not. Mine wasn't," he said.

His mom? She shot him a look of surprise. "What?"

"I called her last night. I was printing off

those forms for the insurance agency, and I saw she was posting stuff on Facebook, so I knew she was awake."

"Did you tell her the truth?" Gabby sucked in a shaky breath. She had in-laws now, too, she suddenly realized. She'd have to explain to more than just her mother. She'd have to deceive more than just her mother...and in-laws might not be so quick to forgive that kind of thing. It was a risky start to a family relationship.

"No. I told her what we'll tell your mother. Fair is fair, I guess."

"Thanks." It did make it a bit less complicated, but the stakes felt just a bit higher now.

"Before I met Bonnie, Mom used to tell me to date you," he said with a smile. "She's feeling really vindicated now. Mama's always right—or something like that."

"Oh...well, I can see her enjoying that a bit," Gabby said. "So they're happy...for you? For us?"

His mother was remarried and lived in Nebraska.

"Seem to be," Seth said. "She and my stepdad want us to come see them in Nebraska for Easter, so..."

Easter... It seemed a little soon to be

planning family trips, and her stomach did a little flip. But it also sounded so blessedly ordinary. In-laws, and Easter bunnies, and traveling together... Maybe by then, they'd feel more comfortable in their new roles.

"Do they know about my sons?" she asked.

"Yeah. I told them that first," Seth replied. "I just said that the father of the boys had left you. I didn't elaborate. But they're happy—really happy. Mom thought she'd never have grandkids after... Hazel."

She swallowed. "She's probably still grieving, too."

"Yeah, she is, but she's also really looking forward to spoiling the boys rotten," he said. He caught her eye. "They're happy for us. I promise."

And that was something—because with her own misgivings rising up inside her, Gabby could use a little optimism from the people around them. And they were getting that—grandparents getting ready to love her boys. That was a good thing. She'd wanted all of this—a husband, kids, more family. They'd just gone about it a little more directly than most.

Gabby started the car and backed out of her parking spot, then headed down the drive toward the main road. She followed the road toward town, and the farther they wound into the mountains, the higher the trees grew—towering pines that lined the highway. She could see an eagle resting on a snowcapped tree limb that looked too frail for its massive weight, and then the eagle flapped, the bough bending and the snow dusting down, and it soared off into the sky and out of sight. She never did get tired of seeing the eagles. They were awe-inspiring. And when she'd been living in Denver— dating Craig, working her medical office job—she'd missed the eagles more than she'd thought she would.

The Welcome to Eagle's Rest sign came into view around another corner, followed by signs announcing the ski lodge, the downtown core and some hiking trails at the next exit.

Her mother lived in a little apartment building off the old end of Main Street. It was from the seventies, with wooden siding and tall evergreens blocking out the light for the apartments in the front of the build- ing. It looked "woodsy," but dated. Gabby drove into the visitor parking area, and then turned to Seth.

"So...happy newlyweds, right?"

"It'll be fine." A smile curled at the corners of his lips. "Come on. Let's get it over with."

They got the baby bag, and Gabby carried one car seat while Seth carried the other two. She had to admit that having Seth here to help her with carrying car seats made things easier. When they got into the front doors, Gabby punched her mother's code and waited to be buzzed in.

"That you, Gabby?" her mother asked. "Let me come down and help you with the babies—"

"No, it's okay, Mom," Gabby said into the speaker. "I've got Seth here. Just let us in."

Carol was on the third floor with a side view that wasn't blocked by those massive trees, and by the time they got to her floor, she was waiting with her apartment door open and a smile on her face.

"There you are!" Carol said. "Oh, my little peanuts!"

Carol took one of the car seats from Seth and cast him a smile. "This is nice of you to help Gabby out today, Seth." Her gaze paused at the wedding ring on his hand, then she led the way into her one-bedroom apartment.

What was her mother thinking, seeing

that shiny new ring? Seeing as she didn't say anything, she probably assumed he still wore his wedding ring from Bonnie—although that one had been platinum, not gold. It might be a detail she'd missed. Everyone knew how hard Seth had been grieving. Gabby and Seth exchanged a look.

Gabby followed her mother into the apartment, and Seth took up the rear. For the next few minutes, Carol got her grandsons out of their car seats and gave each of them a kiss. She held Andy first and cuddled him close. Beau started to squirm, and Gabby handed him over to Seth, then scooped up Aiden. It felt like a normal visit, and watching her mother holding Andy, Gabby wasn't quite sure how to bring up her news.

"I'm so glad I had a day off," Carol said. "I haven't seen my grandsons in forever."

"In three days," Gabby said with a low laugh.

"Like I said, forever," Carol said, and she looked up at Gabby with a smile. It was then that her gaze landed on Gabby's left hand, and Carol froze. Gabby licked her lips.

"Gabrielle?" Carol said quietly. "Do you have something you want to tell me?"

"Actually, yes," Gabby said, and she gave her mom a hesitant smile. "I'm… I mean,

Seth and I... We, um—" Gabby looked down at Aiden in her arms, then over at Seth.

"Got married," Seth finished for her.

"We got married," she confirmed with a breathy laugh.

"You got..." Carol's voice faded. "Oh, my goodness! Gabby, are you serious? When?"

"Yesterday," Gabby said with a nod. "It was a big secret. But, yeah. We're married!"

Carol adjusted the baby in her arms, then moved closer to Gabby and lowered her voice.

"Married?" Carol met Gabby's gaze questioningly. "Legally?"

"Yes, legally. How else does a person get married?"

Carol sighed, and Gabby looked over at Seth. This might be a sham marriage, but she did care about his feelings. Seth met her gaze for a moment, then walked discreetly across the small living room. He adjusted Beau up onto his shoulder and fixed his attention out the front window.

"Mom, just be happy for me," she pleaded.

"Sweetheart, I don't mean to rain on your parade here, but three days ago, you were crying over Craig, and today you're married to Seth? I mean, we all love Seth, but—"

"I know, it was quick," Gabby interrupted.

"He's a good man," her mother whispered. "But this is rather fast."

"We had dinner together, and we just realized it was right! I can't ask you to understand. I know you and Dad dated for a whole lot longer, but I know Seth inside and out. And I realized that I'd had this great guy in my life all this time, and when he asked me to marry him, I said yes. And here we are."

And not really a lie, either. As it turned out, the truth, minus a few pertinent details, was a rather nice story of how they got together.

"Here we are, indeed." Her mother was silent for a few beats. "You didn't think to tell me you were getting married? You didn't think I'd want to be there?"

Gabby felt tears gather in her eyes. "I'm sorry, Mom. It was…spontaneous. I guess I didn't want you to talk me out of it."

"I would have wanted to see my only child get married!" Carol fixed Gabby with a wounded stare.

"I'm sorry, Mom." What else could she say? "Please be happy for me…"

"Do you have pictures?"

"I do, actually." Gabby pulled out her cell phone and found the email. She hadn't stopped to look at those photos, and she was mildly afraid that the truth would be glaringly obvious in those images. But as she showed her mom the first shot, she stared down at a lovely picture of two people looking nervously down at their joined hands. Her dress was nice, a simple cream knit that showed off her new, maternal figure. And Seth looked serious and handsome, the light setting off his dark eyes just right.

"Oh…" Her mother sighed, and Gabby saw tears well in her eyes.

The next few photos were variations on the first, and then there was the picture she'd actually forgotten about—Gabby with her eyes shut, her face upturned, and Seth's lips pressed gently against hers in the very first kiss they'd ever shared.

"I wish I could have been there," her mother said. "If you'd told me—"

"I was a nervous wreck," Gabby said. "If you were there, I might not have made it to the vows. It was better this way—just the two of us."

Carol looked across the living room to where Seth stood with his back to them, legs akimbo, backlit by the window. Gabby looked at him, too. Seth always had been a good-looking guy, and now he was her husband. She wasn't used to thinking that.

"What about Seth's parents?" Carol asked.

"Seth told his mother last night. I wanted to tell you in person, or I would have called you, too."

Carol nodded. "And they're happy for you?"

"Yeah." Gabby smiled hesitantly. "I was scared they wouldn't be, but they really are."

"Welcome to the family, Seth!" Carol called. "You can come back now."

Seth turned, and he adjusted the baby in his arms. "Is it safe?"

"Perfectly." Carol crossed the room and held out one arm, her other occupied with Andy, who was sleeping in his grandmother's embrace. "Let's have a hug, now."

Seth bent down and Carol gave him a pat. Looking at her mother hugging her husband, both of them holding a baby boy, Gabby felt a stab of guilt at her lie.

Was her mother really going to be happier believing that Gabby had up and married Seth in a romantic whirlwind? Was the truth maybe better, after all?

Except the truth came with the hidden burden that Gabby and her mother couldn't afford to provide for these children on their own. At least romance took the burden off her mother's shoulders and made it a spontaneous leap instead of a calculated step.

The truth would have to be Gabby's burden to bear alone.

SETH BENT DOWN and accepted the side hug from Carol. He felt awkward, like he didn't really belong in the room for this conversation. Beau was snoozing peacefully up on Seth's shoulder, and he kept a protective hand on the baby's diaper. These babies had changed everything. If he and Gabby were still just friends, he wouldn't be here. She'd take care of her own family stuff. Except he was now a husband, a stepdad, and a part of this family.

That made him feel a bit nervous. The Rogers women were a passionate duo, and then there was Gabby's aunt Bea, who was known to be a pretty strong personality around town. And her uncle Ted...not really an uncle, but definitely part of the family. Seth had been happy to listen to her stories about various family dramas without ever having to dip his toe in those waters.

Yet here he was.

"You'll be good to her, right?" Carol said,

meeting his gaze earnestly. "You won't break her heart?"

That was an easy one to answer.

"I'm not going to hurt her," he said.

Besides, her heart wasn't invested in this marriage—at least not on a romantic level. But he'd most certainly take care of her. That was why he suggested their marriage of convenience to begin with. Gabby was special to him. She'd been there for him through thick and thin for years, and this marriage wasn't for him, at all. It was all for her.

"And you're ready to take on three boys?" Carol asked.

"Yeah. I mean, not really, but I'm sure I'll figure it out. I don't know anyone who's actually ready for triplets."

Carol smiled at that. "You have a point. But marriage isn't easy. Take it from me. It takes two people who want to make it work, not just one."

"Yeah, I know." He'd been married, after all. He knew what it took to keep a relationship going, but what he had with Gabby was different. This relied on a well-established friendship, not something so fickle as romantic love. He couldn't tell her mother that, though. "Gabby and I aren't kids. We know what we're getting into."

"We always think that, don't we?" Carol raised an eyebrow. "Well, Seth, of all the men Gabby could have chosen, I trust you. You're a good person."

She was trusting him to tell her the truth, too, to be open and honest. That stung a little.

"I try to be," he said, and he glanced over Carol's head to find Gabby watching him with a small smile on her face. Was he doing okay with this first introduction as the husband, then?

"You know that Uncle Ted hasn't seen the babies yet," Carol said, turning toward Gabby.

Gabby popped a soother into Aiden's mouth, and glanced at her mother with a tired look.

"I've been a little busy, Mom."

"I know—and I completely understand now that I know what you've been up to. But Ted has been asking about you, and you know how he worries."

Seth knew Ted Charleston from his years of friendship with Gabby. He'd always been pretty close with both Gabby and her mom. It seemed strange that a man with a family of his own would care this much about seeing Gabby's infants himself. Whatever…

Seth pushed the thought aside as Beau's diaper started to rumble.

"I've got a live one here," Seth said, and he looked down at the baby uncertainly. Beau's face was crunched up, and he wriggled again, producing another rumble.

"All right. You finished, Beau?"

There were no more rumbles, so Seth grabbed the diaper bag from the back of a chair where Gabby had left it, and looked around.

"I'll get you a towel," Carol said. "You can just use the couch. That old piece of junk has seen worse, I can assure you."

Carol came back with a towel, and Seth set to work. It wasn't quite so bad as he'd feared, except the tub of wipes was next to impossible to open.

"Here..." Gabby leaned over and pressed a button. The lid popped up.

"Oh." He smiled ruefully. He'd get better at this with a more practice.

"Ted bought you some baby stuff," Carol said, turning to her daughter. "I told him you'd be here today, so he might come by. It depends if he can get the time."

Seth wiped Beau's little bottom, and slid a new diaper underneath him.

"Cream..."

Gabby passed him a tube.

"How thick?" Seth asked.

"Like well-buttered toast," Gabby said.

He chuckled. "You and your buttered toast."

She was a bit of a stickler over how her toast was buttered. Anytime they got breakfast together, he'd watched her butter her toast from edge to edge with the attention to detail that a drywaller would use.

Still, he used her imagery and slathered some cream onto Beau's bottom, then secured the diaper. He cleaned his fingers off on another wipe, and then picked Beau up again. He grabbed the balled-up diaper.

"Where's the garbage, Mrs. Rogers?" he asked.

"Under the sink—" Carol began, then she held out her hand. "Maybe I'll just take that. And you might as well call me Carol. We're family now."

"Mom, I was thinking…" Gabby eased Aiden back into his car seat and looked up at her mother from her crouched position. "I want to contact Dad."

Carol came back into the room, but her face had paled. "Why would you do that?"

"He's a grandfather now," she said. "I figured he might want to know."

"I doubt he'd care," Carol retorted. "He left when I was pregnant with you, and he never came back. What makes you think he cares about your babies more than he cared about you?"

"Craig left me, too," Gabby snapped. "Is that the same thing? He's not going to care about his children because he was married to someone else?"

"Maybe not!" Carol said. "He's not exactly a man to be trusted, is he? And he didn't bother coming to see them when they were born. I'm sorry if you don't like to hear this, but I doubt he's going to put much effort into ever meeting them. These beautiful babies are an inconvenience to him!"

"People can change!" Gabby turned to face her mother. "Craig's priorities might change over the years. Dad's might have, too, for that matter! Besides, how much of Dad staying away was because you hated him for leaving you?"

Carol's face paled and she clenched her jaw. "Are you blaming me now for what he did?"

"I'm saying it's a bit more complicated than you make it sound. He's not the devil. He's my father."

"Sweetheart, take it from me. Just enjoy

your babies and your husband, and leave your father alone."

Gabby rose to her feet, and Seth could see that she was trying to calm herself, but she was angry. "If he ignores me, I'm fine with that. In fact, I kind of expect it. But I just want to try. I'm a mom now, and… I feel like he deserves another chance to be in my life if he wants to take it."

"Your father isn't worthy of your heart-break."

"I'm not heartbroken," Gabby snapped.

"Not yet," her mother retorted. "Trust me to know him better than you do. Okay?"

Seth looked down at the baby in his arms, his heart beating just a bit faster than usual. Gabby's argument with her mom didn't involve him, but the tension in the room felt almost palpable.

There was a buzzing sound, and Carol went over to a panel on the wall. She pushed a button and leaned closer to the speaker.

"Yeah?"

"It's me."

"Come on up, Ted…" Carol pushed a different button and turned back to them. "Seth, you might not understand all the dynamics here, but Gabby's dad is only going to cause pain. It's a fact. So I might seem a bit extreme, but I know what I'm talking about. If you're the one who's pushing her to do this—"

"No one makes up Gabby's mind for her," Seth said. "I promise you that."

"It isn't Seth," Gabby sighed. "It's me."

Carol fell silent, and Seth looked over at Gabby, watching the conflicted emotions flicker through those clear blue eyes.

"I just thought..." Gabby said after a beat of silence. "It was tough growing up without a father."

"You had me," Carol said, and she sounded wounded.

"I know. And I'm not complaining. I had a great childhood, Mom. Never mind. I'll leave him alone."

"Thank you." Carol gave a curt nod. "Just appreciate the people you have in your life, Gabrielle. That's the way to be happy."

There was a knock, and Carol went to answer it. Ted Charleston stood in the doorway holding a couple gift bags. He looked down at the baby in Carol's arms and smiled wistfully.

"Hey," he said quietly. "Wow. Here's one of the main guys, huh?"

"This is Andy," Carol said. "Come on in, Ted."

Ted nodded a hello to Seth, then smiled in Gabby's direction. He was a tall, slim man with silver hair and a good-natured smile. He had the natural look of a politician, although he'd skipped that profession.

"How are you, Gabby?" Ted asked. "You look like you're doing okay."

"I am. I'm feeling pretty good," she said. "Hi, Uncle Ted. This here is Aiden, and Seth has Beau."

"Wow…our Gabby is a mom, huh?" Ted said. "I'm proud of you, kiddo. Do you think I could hold Aiden?"

"Of course." Gabby seemed to grow a little younger as she smiled at Ted, then she eased the baby into his arms. Ted's expression softened as he looked down at the infant, and his eyes even teared a little. Seth knew that Ted had been a big part of Gabby's childhood, but seeing them together like this, it hammered home just how important her godfather had been to her. He'd been…like a dad. This was the role Seth was taking for the time being, wasn't it? Godfather, but doing all the stuff a dad would do.

Gabby was right; these boys did need more stability than that. Maybe he did, too.

"We have more news, actually…" Gabby

looked toward Seth and sucked in a breath. "Seth and I got married yesterday."

Ted's eyebrows shot up. "What?" He adjusted Aiden in one arm and reached for her left hand, as if that were the only way to make sure this was a fact, then looked toward Seth.

"We're married," Seth confirmed with a smile and a nod.

"They're…" Ted turned to Carol and they exchanged an unfathomable look.

"I just went through all of that," Carol said. "They're married, and they're happy."

There was a silence, and Ted nodded a few times as if silently making his peace with all this. Then he said, "I brought baby stuff, but no one told me I needed to bring champagne."

Gabby laughed. "Oh, Uncle Ted. Baby stuff is perfect. Trust me. We need everything we can get."

Ted looked down at Aiden again. "I'm happy for you, Gabby," he said. "And if he gives you any trouble, just let me know."

"Probably not necessary, but she should keep that in mind," Seth joked, holding out his hand.

Ted squeezed Seth's hand a bit harder than necessary, and Seth felt both the challenge and the warning in the older man's grip. Funny, how when Seth suggested this plan to begin with he hadn't thought of the in-laws he'd get as a result. He'd been lonelier than he'd ever imagined possible for the last two years. A family—even Gabby's rather intense one—was terrifying and...nice.

CHAPTER SIX

WHEN THEY GOT back into the car, Gabby leaned against the headrest and shut her eyes for a moment. She'd been worried about announcing her marriage to her mother—mostly because no one knew her quite so well as Mom did, and if anyone was going to see through this sham marriage, it would be her.

From the back seat, she could hear the babies fussing. She opened her eyes and sighed. Aiden especially seemed annoyed at being strapped into his car seat, and Andy joined the chorus back there. It made her feel helpless, like she wanted to scoop them all up just to make them stop crying, but they'd never get home that way, would they? She pushed her arms out straight, white-knuckling the steering wheel. It was hard to focus when her entire nervous system was taut with the desire to hold her babies.

"Let me drive," Seth said.

Gabby blinked her eyes open and looked over at Seth. He didn't wait for a reply. He pushed open his door and came around to the driver's side and opened it.

"Come on," he said. "I'll drive and you can… I don't know… Not drive us into a wall out of frustration."

Gabby smiled wanly and got out. While he pushed the seat back a bit and settled in, she opened the back door and checked the babies once more. They only cried harder when she tried to comfort them, and spat out the soothers she put in their mouths.

"You'll be okay, boys," she said softly. "Come on, now. Car seats are just one of those things you've got to put up with…"

"Gabby, get in," Seth said, as he readjusted the mirrors. "Once we start driving, they'll calm down."

They would; she knew he was right. She got into the front seat and did up her seat belt. As Seth backed up, the babies' cries grew less insistent. A car ride—that was what they needed—and having Seth drive was actually a bit of a relief. He pulled out of the parking spot and headed toward the main street, the babies' cries filling the car.

Streets in Eagle's Rest were narrow, since the town itself was tucked into a small valley, mountain peaks towering up all around them.

"Let's take the scenic route," Seth said.

"We can drive past the lake and then head back."

That would be an extra twenty minutes of driving time. "I don't want to waste the fuel, actually," Gabby admitted. "I need to make this tank last as long as I can."

Seth looked over at her for a moment, then licked his lips. "We're married. You aren't on your own."

"But my gas tank might be," she said with a low laugh.

"Your gas tank isn't on its own, either," he said. "I'll fill your tank. Okay?"

"Our arrangement is about medical insurance," she protested. "I know you wanted me to be a housewife of sorts, but—"

"I told your mom that I'd take care of you, and I was serious," he said, signaling the turn and pulling out into traffic. "These boys need a drive—and so do you, I suspect. Forget about the fuel."

"I'm not used to this," she said. "I have a bit in the bank that Ted gave me. I'll have to pay you back."

"No, you won't. It'll balance out," he said.

Gabby hadn't really thought through the financial ramifications of their plan. She didn't want to take advantage of Seth. Sure, if they were legitimately married for love, she'd feel better about melding their finances, but as it was, he was doing enough for her without a wife spending his money out from under him.

She'd need to get a job, maybe after a few months when the boys were older, so that she wasn't taking advantage of Seth's giving nature. It was only fair.

Gabby watched as the familiar streets and shops of Eagle's Rest swept past her window. Christmas lights and festive window displays were in bright contrast to the newly fallen snow. Some shop owners were outside shoveling their stretch of sidewalk. In the back seat, the babies were quiet now, and when she twisted around to check on them, she could see Beau's face, still wet from tears, but his eyes were shut, and he was making sucking movements with his little pouted lips.

"So how long have you been considering getting in touch with your dad?" Seth asked.

"Oh…" Gabby leaned her head back and let out a long breath. "Ever since I got pregnant, actually. I had to wonder about him—if this would change things for him."

"And your mom isn't keen on that, I take it."

"Regardless of how their marriage ended,

he's still my father. If it were you, wouldn't you want to know that you had grandchildren?"

"If it were me?" Seth's glance flickered toward her as he pulled to a stop at an intersection. "Yeah, of course. But I wouldn't have just walked out on my pregnant wife, either."

"There is that…" The stories of her father weren't flattering. He was a self-centered man who'd cared more about his own comfort than he had for anyone else. He hadn't even cared to come back and see his daughter. But that man was half of her DNA.

"You've told me a little bit about your father over the years," Seth said. "But what happened with them? Like, why did they split up?"

Gabby sifted back in her mind through the information she'd gleaned about her father. "He was one of those macho men who figured he was the boss, and Mom hated that. They used to fight a lot. Mom said he drank. One day, after a particularly bad fight, Dad packed his bags and left. They'd been married for about three years."

"Yeah, I knew it was about three years," he said. "About as long as Bonnie and I were married."

"Yeah…" Had she just offended him? She wasn't sure.

"I guess having been married before, I wonder about different stuff now." Seth paused. "He worked in marketing, right?"

"He was the one who did the first ad campaign for the ski lodge and really put them on the map. So he wasn't all bad. He was also pretty smart, I suppose." Gabby sighed. "But he wasn't any good at being a family man. And that was the part that mattered to us."

Seth, on the other hand, would make a good father and partner. If she were like every other woman and went for a man just like her dad, she'd be doomed to heartbreak. But she'd logically chosen someone who was her father's polar opposite.

"That was something me and Bonnie really worked on," Seth said. "Well, you know about my parents' divorce, so we tried to make sure we wouldn't end up the same way."

"Yours were always fighting about money, weren't they?" she asked.

He'd told her stories about his parents' epic fights before.

"Mom was a spender, and Dad was really thrifty. They didn't agree on much of anything. Still don't. I think it's easier to slide into that than people think. That's why I think our plan is so smart. There are no crazy emotions to get in our way. We talk about stuff—logically, realistically."

"Is our way the secret to having a happy, drama-free marriage?" she asked with a chuckle.

"Imagine giving our single friends advice," he said with a grin. "Find your best friend, have a clear and logical discussion about your expectations for the future, and then elope."

"No one is taking that advice," she said.

"Maybe not, but I do think we're onto something."

Gabby smiled. This was turning out to be a whole lot simpler than she'd ever experienced before. No fights. No misunderstandings. No aching disappointment. Maybe they *were* onto something.

"I think planning is key," Seth went on. "Bonnie and I both read a bunch of books on relationships and marriage. For all that worked…"

"But you two were happy," Gabby countered. "Honestly, you had the kind of marriage that everyone else envied."

"Yeah. Still, like your mom said, marriage

is tough." His tone was wooden, and for a moment, there was silence between them. Had his marriage been less idyllic than everyone thought?

"So, who was Uncle Ted to your mother?" Seth asked after a beat of silence. "Was he in love with her?"

"What makes you ask that?" she asked with a short laugh.

"I don't know. I've always wondered that. He hung around for a real long time for a buddy."

"You and I are married, and we're buddies," she said. "There were extenuating circumstances. Mom had me."

"Okay, I can see that." He smiled faintly. "Babies do inspire some guys to step up."

"But no, there was no romantic connection," Gabby said. "He was already married to Ramona."

"That doesn't always stop people," Seth said.

"Well, it would stop my mother! And Ted, too, for that matter."

"I know, I know… Sorry, I didn't mean for it to sound like that. I know that Ted was your father's best friend, and when your dad left, Ted helped her get back on her feet."

"He always hated the way my dad treated my mother," she confirmed.

"Ramona was okay with that?" he asked.

"Yeah."

"She's not *Aunt* Ramona, though."

"It's…a unique situation," Gabby said, and she felt a twinge of annoyance. Sure, their family dynamic was strange, but she felt oddly irritated at being questioned about it. Uncle Ted had been there for them—and not just in those first few months. He'd taken being named godfather very seriously, and he'd given her birthday gifts every year, paid for her to go to camp for a few years running… He'd been the strong male figure in her life. Her mother had told her that she might not have a father, but she had a godfather to make up the difference. And Ted had tried to do just that.

"Is Ted still in contact with your father?" Seth asked.

"No," Gabby replied. "I asked him about Dad recently, and there is no change there. He lost contact with him."

"Huh." Seth fell silent. But there'd been something in his tone…

"You don't think it's true?" she asked, turning toward him.

"I didn't say that," Seth replied. "Why... don't you?"

Gabby shot him an annoyed look. "It might be an unconventional setup, but it's ours."

"Okay. Sorry," Seth said. "The point is, you want to find your dad."

"I do and I don't," Gabby replied. "My mom sacrificed everything for me. She worked two and three jobs at a time, put away every extra penny to pay for me to get through college... I mean, she's the one I have to thank for raising me. I never knew my dad. He's never even seen me."

"So the part of you that doesn't want to find him...is that because he doesn't deserve to be in your life, or because of your loyalty to your mom?" Seth asked.

"Does it matter?" she asked testily.

"Not really," he replied. "I was just curious."

"Maybe a bit of both," Gabby said, adjusting her tone. "Sorry. You hit a nerve, I guess."

As they exited the town and headed down the old, cracked highway toward the lake, Gabby looked out the window at the towering pines. There had been a time when she would have given anything to meet her father. She used to make up stories about him as a girl, giving him excellent excuses for having stayed away. She used to imagine him coming back to town to find her, full of apologies and reassurances that he'd been thinking of her every single day since he'd left.

It hadn't happened. So, what was she expecting to happen if she tracked him down?

"I have to tell Bonnie's family about the wedding," Seth said, breaking into her thoughts. "Now that we've told our parents."

"Oh…" She looked over hesitantly. "They're in Denver, aren't they?"

"Yep."

"Have you seen them recently?" she asked.

"I drove down for a family memorial thing for Bonnie last year. It was nice to see everyone, share some memories."

"Are you afraid they'll think less of you for having moved on?" she asked.

"I haven't moved on," he said, his voice low.

His words stung, but she wasn't the only one with some emotional complications.

"They know I loved her," Seth went on. "But Bonnie wasn't really keen on you and me staying friends. She was a bit jealous."

"But you explained to her that we had no romantic feelings for each other," she countered. "Right?"

"Yeah…"

"What does that mean?" she demanded.

"Well, obviously, she wasn't really comfortable with our friendship. And my explanation didn't change that."

Gabby sighed. She knew that. Bonnie had been jealous—but it had been unfounded. Gabby's feelings for Seth had never gone beyond buddy, and neither had his. Bonnie had had Seth's heart with zero competition there.

"Wait…" Gabby turned toward Seth, her stomach dropping. "Does her family know she felt that way about me?"

"Yeah."

"How do you know?"

"She talked to her mom three times a week. I'm willing to bet her mom knew!"

Yeah, Gabby was willing to bet the same thing.

"Do you regret marrying me?" she asked quietly.

"I just need to sort this out," he replied. It wasn't quite an answer.

"When will you tell them?"

"Soon. I'd hate for them to hear from someone else first," he said.

He didn't say anything else, and she exhaled a shaky breath. Seth had given up his right to continue grieving publicly when he married Gabby. He'd have to maintain some appearances of a happy marriage now, and she hadn't fully appreciated the emotional toll that would have for him. Seth would have to tell Bonnie's family that he'd married *her*, the woman Bonnie had been so uncomfortable with. And he'd have to say that it was for love. That was going to be an insult, and Gabby couldn't see any way around it. Telling Bonnie's parents about their wedding was going to break his heart.

Gabby wouldn't blame him if he had some regrets. Because while babies might inspire some men to step up and help, Seth had given more than anyone could have expected.

And she had a few half-truths to tell, too. Gabby had to call Grace and give her the news that she was married.

THAT NIGHT, Seth sat on the edge of his bed, the door shut. The pinprick stars outside his open curtains seemed more distant in the wash of moonlight. The wind whistled past the house, fingers of ice creeping up the windowpane from the inside. He pulled the curtains shut. It was cold out there, but warm inside, since he'd turned up the thermostat for the benefit of the babies.

He peeled off his T-shirt and tossed it toward the hamper in the corner. He missed, and it landed close by. Bonnie used to hate his "laundry corner," as she called it. And for a while after her death, he'd made sure every stray sock wound up in the hamper, as if he could apologize to her that way. It was silly—he knew that—but for a while it had comforted him. But now he was back to his old habits. This was who he was, apparently, and laundry near the hamper was good enough until he picked it all up later.

Besides, there hadn't been a woman in the house to be annoyed by that sort of thing… until now. And his bedroom was his own domain. This was where he could relax, and miss the hamper if he wanted to. At least in this room, he could be himself and forget about appearances.

He heard the murmur of Gabby's voice through the wall. She sounded like she was talking on the phone, because it wasn't the softened voice she used with the babies. He strained to make out what she was saying. This was her regular voice—a break of laughter, a pause, and then her muffled words: *"I know. It's fast. But we had dinner together, and we just...knew it was right, I guess. And here we are..."*

Her voice faded as she moved away from the wall. What was it about having her here that made him smile when he didn't even realize he was doing it?

A month ago, this distraction from his own routines would have driven him crazy. But he realized he liked the sound of Gabby's voice in his house. She wasn't just another woman, she was his best friend, and her presence in the next room was oddly comforting. He could hear her moving around, the sound of babies crying every few hours, the tender tone of her voice as she soothed them back to sleep...as if that voice could soothe away his pain, too.

He'd been noticing how beautiful she was, how curvy, how good it felt to joke around with her... And having married her added in a whole new confusing dynamic. He couldn't just be pals with his wife. Even if they kept romance off the table, there was a certain amount of obligation, protectiveness, a sense of "us." They were more than friends, no matter which way he looked at it.

His cell phone rang, and he saw that it was his aunt. Maybe it was better to pull himself out of this funk tonight and follow Gabby's lead—get some of these personal wedding announcements out of the way. So he picked up the call.

"Hi, Aunt Selena," he said.

"I heard something from my friend Theresa," Selena said. "Something about you getting married again? I told her she was crazy, but…"

For the next few minutes, Seth filled his aunt in on all the pertinent details—the wedding, the triplets, all this happening so close to Christmas… He'd added that into his story of how he'd proposed, how the magic of the season had tugged him along. And that wasn't entirely wrong. Christmas made even the craziest wishes feel possible. It was nice to chat with his aunt about something happy for a change. But one thing was driven home as he said goodbye: his aunt had heard from someone he didn't even know. The news was out there, and in a town this size, it traveled fast. Denver wasn't that far away, and he'd need to call Bonnie's parents soon before someone else did.

There was a knock on his bedroom door, and he realized he couldn't hear Gabby chatting in the other room anymore. His heart sped up just a little bit as he headed over and opened the door.

Gabby stood in the hallway wearing that bathrobe cinched up at the neck. Her hair hung loose around her shoulders, but her face was clean of makeup, making her look different than he was used to seeing her—more vulnerable maybe. Her eyes looked softer this way—ocean blue next to her creamy skin. So beautiful…which ironically was something he wasn't supposed to be noticing about his wife.

Gabby had a tablet in her hands.

"So who did you tell?" he asked with a wry smile.

"Grace. She's thrilled. She says congratulations and she can't wait to do all sorts of couple things with us."

Her gaze flickered down to his chest and some pink bloomed in her cheeks, then she looked back up to his face. Right. He was standing here bare-chested in front of her, because he'd forgotten to grab his shirt.

He stepped back. The hallway was dark, and she came into his room a few feet. Seth snatched up his shirt from the floor and put it back on. He was glad she'd knocked. Funnily enough, he'd started to miss her since they'd said good-night and retired to their own rooms.

"My aunt Selena is pretty excited about us, too," he said, pulling the shirt down over his abs. "She's going to spread the word."

"So it begins," Gabby said with a soft laugh. "Are you okay with that?"

"Yeah, it'll make it easier. I won't have to call every last person this way."

"I was afraid you might be regretting this," she said hesitantly.

Had he made her feel that way?

"No, I don't regret it." He winced. "I'm sorry if I made it seem like it. I'm just... It's complicated, Gabs. You know that. But I don't regret this."

"Okay." She held her tablet across her chest, and he nodded down to it.

"What are you doing?"

"Oh..." She licked her lips. "It's actually why I knocked. You know I've been looking online for my father. I mean, not constantly, but from time to time. This is the first time I've found someone who looks like it could be him."

Gabby held out the tablet, and Seth looked down at an open web page. It was an employee profile for a marketing company, from the looks of it. When he took it from her hands for a closer scrutiny, his fingers slipped over hers. Her skin was soft, and having her standing this close to him… She smelled nice, too. He sucked in a breath, refocusing.

Hank A. Rogers, Marketing Director.

There was an email address and a phone number. Seth looked up at Gabby.

"Do you know where your dad lives?" he asked.

"Mom said he moved to California, and this is a California-based company. He was working in advertising back then." Gabby took the tablet back and looked down at the screen, chewing the inside of her cheek.

"Rogers is a pretty common last name," Seth said. "But I mean, how many Hank A. Rogers can there be in one state?"

"Eight." Gabby smiled wanly. "That I could find. But this one is the most realistic match that I can see."

"So you really do want to find him," Seth said.

Gabby shrugged, then sighed. "I don't want to hurt Mom or make her feel like all she did for me isn't enough, but he's my dad, Seth. Even if he's a jerk, I want to meet him. I want him to see his grandchildren."

"Do you want to find him badly enough

to hire a private investigator?" Seth asked. "Then it wouldn't just be you Googling him. It could be someone searching who has access to more information."

Gabby shrugged. "I don't know yet. But I'm considering emailing this Hank and telling him who I am. If he's my dad, he'll recognize my last name, at least."

"Even if he does recognize your name, he might not answer you," Seth pointed out. "This might not give you any more answers or comfort than you had before."

Gabby pressed the tablet against her chest, then nodded. "I know. He's stayed away this long. It's not like I'm expecting one email to change him into a new man. Maybe I'm courting disappointment here."

Gabby turned back toward the hallway. Seth remembered how she used to talk about her father when they were teenagers. She'd solidly hated him back then. *If my dad came back now, I'd have nothing to do with him. He didn't love me enough to even send a card all these years, did he?* There hadn't been any hint of her father coming back, but she'd been prepared for it, all the same. Deep down, she'd been hoping, even if her plan was to reject him.

"You asked if I thought this could be

him," Seth said, and Gabby stopped at her door and turned back. Her blue eyes glittered in the low light. "And it could be. It looks like a likely match to me, too."

She nodded, a smile toying at her lips. "Yeah, I thought so, too."

"Are you going to email him?"

Gabby hesitated, then nodded. "I am. I have no idea if I'll ever hear back, but I'm going to try and see." She smiled. "Sorry to bug you."

"No, it's okay. I was just..." He glanced back into his room, which suddenly looked a whole lot less cozy than it had a few minutes ago. "Thinking, I guess. You can bug me anytime. You know that, right?"

"I'll try to keep it to a minimum. Good night, Seth."

She closed her door first, and Seth stood there for a moment looking at the soft light that shone underneath it. Then he closed his door.

Funny how being an adult of thirty didn't actually make anyone feel any stronger or more pulled together. Rejection still hurt on the deepest of levels—for Gabby, for him—but Gabby was willing to face the hard stuff, anyway. At least, she was now. It was probably time he did the same.

Seth picked up his phone and pulled up the address book. He'd call Bonnie's parents tonight and tell them the news.

They deserved to know. And maybe he deserved a bit of discomfort.

He dialed the number and waited while it rang. On the third ring, Bonnie's father, Bill, picked up.

"Is that you, Seth?"

"Yeah, it's me. Hi, sir. How are you?"

"Not so bad, I guess. Merry Christmas."

"Merry Christmas." The salutation sounded wooden in his mouth. "How is everyone?"

"We're doing okay. Janet's pregnant, so that's exciting."

Janet was Bonnie's younger sister and Seth nodded a couple times. "That's great. Congrats to her and Tim."

"I'll let them know…"

"Look, I have some news of my own," Seth said. "And I'm not looking forward to telling you."

"Did you find someone?" Bill asked.

"I did, sir."

"Who's the lucky lady?"

"Gabby Rogers." There was a pause, and Seth listened to Bill breathe for a moment. "You remember her, I take it?"

"Your friend," Bill said. "The one Bonnie hated."

"*Hate* is a strong word," Seth countered.

"I know. The one Bonnie wasn't crazy about."

"Yeah…her." Seth grimaced. "There was nothing between us until very recently. It's important to me that you know that. When I was with Bonnie I was faithful—emotionally, physically, in every single way."

"I know that, Seth," Bill said. "You loved my daughter well."

He'd tried. Maybe he hadn't done as well as her parents believed.

"I, uh, got married again, sir," Seth said.

"You did?" Bill sounded genuinely surprised. "I thought you said this started up recently?"

"It did. This was fast. Gabby's got triplet newborns, and…it was fast." Seth cleared his throat.

"Triplets!" Bill said.

"Yeah…"

"Is that tough for you, after Hazel?"

"It is, actually." It was a relief to admit to it. "They're adorable. I'm definitely attached, but they remind me of all the stuff I didn't get to do with my own daughter, you know?"

"Yeah, I do," Bill said quietly. "But those babies need a dad, too. Are they boys? Girls?"

"Boys."

"They definitely need a dad, Seth. And you'll be a good one."

The compliment made a lump rise in his throat.

"I just wanted to let you know," Seth said awkwardly.

"And see if I'd be upset?" Bill asked.

"Maybe," Seth admitted.

"You don't need absolution from me, Seth," Bill said. "You can't mourn forever. You loved her deeply, you mourned for her, and you have to keep living."

Seth felt tears prick his eyes. He hadn't been doing much of that—the living part.

"I still feel a bit guilty about that," he admitted, his voice tight with emotion.

"Hey, you're young. We knew you'd love again. I'm happy for you. Really."

Except Seth hadn't fallen in love again—and he couldn't explain that. Somehow, he didn't think it would make things any easier for Bonnie's parents, either, to know the truth of their arrangement.

"Thank you, sir," Seth said. "I'd better get going."

"You have a great Christmas, Seth," Bill said earnestly.

"You, too, sir. Goodbye."

As he hung up, he let out a shaky sigh. Have a great Christmas… Easier said than done. Even if Bonnie's father could be happy for him, Seth was having trouble being happy for himself.

CHAPTER SEVEN

GABBY COULDN'T FALL ASLEEP. Maybe it was her nap that afternoon, or maybe it was her sudden misgivings from pressing Send on that email to the man she suspected was her father, but as she lay in the center of the bed, listening to the soft breathing of her babies, she just couldn't drift off.

The email had been simple enough:

Dear Mr. Rogers,
I'm writing to introduce myself, because I believe you are my father. My name is Gabrielle Rogers and my mother is Carol Rogers from Eagle's Rest, Colorado. If I have found the right man, you left when Carol was still pregnant with me. I want to meet my father. I have no requests for money or demands for a relationship if that is a worry for your present life. But I would like to meet you.

I hope to hear from you, even if you aren't the right man. Knowing one way or the other would help my search.
Gabrielle Rogers

Her father… She hadn't heard many good things about him. He'd abandoned them, he didn't care about her existence, but he was half of her. Did he ever think about that?

The fact that she'd managed to fall for a man like Craig was sobering to her—another man who could turn his back on his children without a second thought. How many men had this predilection to walking away? And why did she attract them?

Gabby rubbed her hands over her face. It wasn't only the email keeping her awake. She was hungry. Perhaps it was because some of her more immediate worries had lifted off her shoulders, but she was eating more now. She'd been constantly worried about her children, every time she measured out those three bottles of formula… every time their appetites seemed to grow and she realized she'd go through that tin of formula faster than anticipated. She'd been worried about diapers, about new sleepers, about what people must think when they saw her out in public with her boys in car seats with faded, secondhand covers. She'd started eating a little bit less every meal, thinking that if she could control her grocery budget, she'd have more for the baby things.

But with those marriage vows, her worries had lifted, and she could take better care of herself again.

She swung her legs over the side of the bed and the book she'd been reading before she'd turned off the light fell to the floor with a thunk. She bent down to pick it up and listened. All was quiet. The leftover sausage and potatoes from supper were calling to her. Her stomach rumbling, she tossed the book back onto her pillow and swiped up her bathrobe.

She paused at the bedroom doorway and looked toward Seth's closed door. It was nice here, not being alone. It was comforting to have a bedrock of friendship she could rely on. But living together like this was so much more intimate than she'd anticipated, and the memory of Seth standing shirtless in the doorway came back to mind. It wasn't just about sleeping arrangements; there were all the other details of a private life. Like listening to the sound of the shower running, or the smell of his aftershave that lingered there when she got her turn. Seth was just so…masculine. It might seem silly to be realizing that only now, but the buddy she'd hung out with was different than the husband she shared a house with.

Gabby crept down the stairs as quietly as possible, the baby monitor in one pocket of her bathrobe. A couple of the stairs squeaked, and she hoped that Seth wouldn't hear her. She'd have to learn which steps to skip if she was going to keep from disturbing him.

Gabby left the light off and headed quietly to the fridge. She pulled the door open and found the leftovers she'd been craving. As she waited for them to heat in the microwave, she tugged her bathrobe a little closer around herself against the cold of the kitchen. The space was bathed in the soft moonlight. This house needed something cozier…cookies in a jar on the counter, a Christmas tree in the living room, some holiday cheer. It was almost Christmas, after all, but looking at this house, she'd never know it.

The microwave beeped, and she pulled out her meal. As she turned toward the table, she saw a large, dark figure standing by the stairs and she startled, nearly dropping her plate.

"Hey," Seth said.

"Oh, my goodness, Seth!" she said, letting out a breath of relief. "You scared me."

Apparently, he knew which stairs not to step on.

"Sorry." He shot her a grin, then headed toward the fridge. "Got hungry, did you?"

"Yeah. I guess the stress is down and I'm catching up a bit."

He pulled open the fridge, looked inside for a moment, then shut it again.

"I can share," she said.

"Nah. I'm not actually hungry." Seth met her gaze in the dim kitchen, his eyes glistening in the moonlight. "I called Bonnie's parents."

"Oh…" she breathed. "What did they say?"

"Her mom was asleep. Her father was up. He said he didn't expect me to mourn forever," Seth said quietly. "He said I deserved to keep living."

"You do," she said.

Seth sighed, then shrugged. "People keep saying that as if I'm not living doing things my own way. The people we love are still a part of us. They don't just melt away. Bonnie's still here." He thumped his chest.

"She always will be." Gabby licked her lips. "This isn't easy for you, having to tell people about me. Having to explain yourself. I know where we stand, but other people don't. I'm sorry about that."

"It's not like it was easy for me before you came back to town," he replied with a sigh. "It was just me and my memories in this house, and now…"

She waited for him to continue, but he didn't.

"Are you saying you like having me here?" she asked, and a teasing smile turned up her lips.

"Yeah, I like having you here." He met her gaze, and something in his dark eyes softened. "But I'm not exactly easy to live with, I know."

"You aren't so bad," she said. "So far, you cook for me and help with the babies. You're pretty close to miraculous."

He met her gaze and a smile tickled the corners of his mouth. "What about you? Did you send that email?"

"Yep." She smiled faintly. "I'll have to see what happens, but I'm glad I sent it."

"Are you going to tell your mom?" he asked.

She shook her head. "I'm keeping it to myself for now. So… I'll have to trust you to keep that secret, too."

"I'm your husband," he said. "I have your back."

And she knew he did. She'd have trusted him with her secrets as her buddy, too. She was safer with him than she'd been with anyone.

"People are talking now," he said after a moment of silence. "Word is spreading about our wedding."

"It's not so bad for me," she said. "I get to say I married a cute cowboy."

Was that a blush she saw on his cheeks? He looked down. "It's different being married, isn't it?"

Here in this chilly kitchen, he was so close… His broad shoulders, that warm gaze. But it wasn't just being so close to him, living in the same house. Those vows had shifted things between them.

"Yeah, it is," she agreed. "I didn't know it would change things like this."

"I never knew how to be married," he said, his voice low. "I know you think I was this perfect husband to Bonnie, but I wasn't. I was a pain to live with. We butted heads over stuff, and I wasn't always very good at seeing things from her perspective. The thing is, I tried to make up for it with flowers and reading books about making women happy. I did everything I knew how to get better at being married, but I wasn't as good at it as we pretended in public."

"Marriage was harder than you thought," she said.

"Marriage is probably harder than you think, too," he countered.

"Seth, you were the kind of husband women wished for. Trust me."

"Not you," he said. "I think you saw through it."

"Why do you say that?" she asked.

"Didn't you? Every time Bonnie and I fought and we bumped into you, you'd ask me how I was, and…it seemed like you knew."

"I actually didn't," she whispered. "That was just me trying to catch up with you, pretending I didn't miss you as much as I did."

For the few seconds Bonnie would allow it.

"I guess everyone keeps up some appearances," she added.

"I might not be the catch you think I am," he said, and she heard the earnestness in his voice. Was he warning her? Or did he really fear he wasn't going to be good at being married this time around?

"We're doing this the smart way, remember?" she said. "We're going into this with our eyes open, and we don't have wild expectations. This is rational. And I know you, Seth. You're a good guy."

"A good guy and a good husband are two different things."

"You're better than my dad was," she said, breaking eye contact.

"I'll definitely be able to surpass him," he said with a smile in his voice.

"You think you're not the hero everyone thinks you are," she said, "but I've often wondered how much I'm like my father, too. I've hated him for years, but... I might be more like him, or like his side of the family, than I want to admit. So you might want to keep your eyes open for that."

Seth chuckled. "Do you suspect you take after a great-grandmother with terrible taste in men?"

"It's possible," she said, but she laughed. "Maybe I'm the spitting image of some woman in a photo somewhere who married a drunk, had thirteen kids and was grateful to be widowed by fifty."

"That's very specific."

"I've had a good many years to wonder about Dad's side of the family," she said. "My dad might be a piece of work, but there's a whole family behind him that I don't know about. There has to be a reason for…this fun mix of genes that produced me."

"Give yourself a bit of credit for the woman you've become," Seth said, and the laughter left his voice. "You're tough. You're smart. You're determined. I know other women who would have been knocked down by now, but not you. You just keep getting up. That's not DNA. That's character. You're really something. I wouldn't have married you if I thought otherwise."

She was silent for a moment, and the moment seemed to deepen around them.

"If I take the credit for sticking with it when times are hard," she said quietly, "then I have to take the blame, too. There are a lot of things I deeply regret. I joke around, Seth. But I'm embarrassed. My life hasn't turned out the way I'd hoped."

"You've had bad luck," he said, and he reached out and caught her hand in his. "That's it."

"It's more than bad luck." She smiled faintly. "I have…patterns. I wanted to break them. That's why I was willing to marry you. You're a good guy—the kind I normally steer clear of. You're the one smart choice I've made so far."

"I am pretty spectacular," he joked, then laughed softly. "I mean, look around you. By marrying me, you've got a small, drafty house, an emotional wreck of a cowboy, and leftovers from the fridge."

"Don't forget the health insurance," she said with a slow smile.

"Yeah, yeah…" He hadn't dropped her hand, and as he looked down at her, the laughter melted away. In its place, she saw sadness, loneliness, longing.

"Thank you for marrying me," she whispered.

Seth ran a finger down her cheek, and he stepped closer. "I am glad we did this…"

"Are you really?" she asked softly.

There was something about that moonlight spilling in over the kitchen sink, something about the chilly air winding around her bare legs… Seth's gaze moved down to her lips, and for a moment, she stood there with his hand against her cheek. He was close—so close that she could feel the warmth of his chest emanating against her, and if he just dipped his head down a couple inches…

But a kiss wasn't a part of their plan.

They had to keep their friendship solid, and she swallowed, moving her gaze away. He dropped his hand and stepped back, cold air flooding between them.

"I'm going to head up to bed," Seth said softly.

That was probably a good idea, and she nodded. Her logical mind needed to kick back in, because being this close was shutting all her reservations down. Seth paused and leaned in once more, and she tipped her head back, looking up at him in mild surprise. His face was so close that she could feel his breath against her lips. Then he reached behind her, and she heard a drawer scrape open. He smiled, slightly teasing, then bit his bottom lip and stepped back. That cold air whisked between them once more. He held a fork in front of him.

"You'll want that," he said.

"Oh…" she whispered.

"Good night."

Gabby listened to Seth's footsteps heading up the staircase, and she let out a shaky breath. If they got their hearts entangled in this arrangement, they'd lose the one element of their relationship that had been their strength: their friendship.

Her eyes moved around the darkened

kitchen again, so bare of any Christmas cheer.

If anyone needed a little Christmas just about now, it was them. They were both sad, both dealing with their own griefs and burdens, and perhaps both a little susceptible to their own loneliness. With some Christmas cheer to distract them, maybe they could keep their heads so they didn't start looking for comfort in each other's arms. Her boys were going to have their first Christmas, but so were she and Seth. This would be their first Christmas together in their unique partnership, and even if it was nontraditional, their family deserved to be celebrated.

She was going to decorate—get a tree, a wreath, some candles, some holly…but the one thing she wouldn't get would be mistletoe.

WHEN GABBY GOT up the next morning, the house was quiet. She dressed while the babies slept. Seth's bedroom door was partway open, and she peeked inside. The bed was made and everything looked neat. He'd left early.

Heat hit her cheeks when she remembered last night. The memory was almost surreal.

She and Seth had never been like that together before—the attraction, the way his eyes had smoldered when he looked down into her face…

She needed to get a handle on things again. Whatever had happened last night couldn't happen again. And maybe it would help if they had something else to focus on besides each other—like a little bit of Christmas cheer.

The boys woke up then, and Gabby fed them, changed them, got them dressed in some new clothes—none of them matching. She couldn't afford that right now. By the time she'd finished boiling a pot of oatmeal, the back door opened and Seth came inside, shaking snow off his coat.

"Good morning," she said.

"Hey. I, uh, was just checking on a few things at the barn."

Avoiding her. She understood, but it stung a little. She'd wondered how Seth would react in the light of day. But he was back now, and he met her gaze easily enough.

"You hungry?" She held up a bowl. "I made oatmeal. It's not fancy, but it's good."

"Yeah, that would be great. Thanks."

He took off his coat and hat, and came into the kitchen. She dished them both up some oatmeal and brought the bowls to the table. The babies were in their bouncy chairs on the floor, all three of them awake.

"Hey, buddies," Seth said, crouching down in front of them. He tweaked each baby on the foot. "You're up and at 'em, are you?"

"They slept in a little bit this morning," Gabby said. "I guess I did, too."

"Don't worry about it," he said. "They say you're supposed to sleep when they sleep, right?"

"For what that advice is worth," she said.

Seth rose to his feet and cast her an uncomfortable look. "I'm sorry about last night."

"It's fine." She shook her head.

"No, seriously." He cleared his throat. "I...guess I was just falling into some old habits. I mean, I'm used to being married, and that's normally a bit more physical, you know?"

Her breath caught at that. Yes, she was getting a sense of what she was missing out on here... But she couldn't take Bonnie's place in his heart, or in his arms.

"Normally, marriages are a little more... intimate," she agreed.

"I'm just getting used to things," he said. "It'll get easier."

"It might help us feel more normal if we could do something fun together. Do you have an artificial Christmas tree?" she asked, taking a dribbling bite.

"No, we—I—used to chop one down."

"Do you have Christmas decorations?" she asked.

"A few." He eyed her.

"I want to decorate." She smiled, waiting for his reaction.

"Oh…"

He hated it. She could tell by the look on his face. They needed to develop a few friendship routines again, and there were lines she dared not cross with him.

"I told you I'd be touching things and moving them," she said. "Seth, some Christmas will be good for both of us."

He sucked in a breath. "I know. All right. Fine. Let's do it."

"Good." She grinned. "I was thinking of picking up a few decorations today. I have some money in savings, and—"

"I can pay for it," he interrupted.

"No, this matters to me," she said. "I'm the one who wants to decorate. And it won't cost much. I can do this on a dime."

His expression turning melancholy again. "If we hadn't gotten married, and I was back in town, we'd do something, you and I," she went on. "Granted, it might have been dinner at the Chinese food place, or I'd have invaded your kitchen with all the ingredients for Christmas cookies, but we would have made the holiday ours, somehow. Just because we have a home together and this feels a whole lot more domestic than either of us is used to yet doesn't mean we shouldn't make this Christmas ours."

"Ours." His voice was low.

"In our own way," she qualified. "For the boys, if nothing else. I want them to have pictures of their first Christmas to look back on—happy pictures."

How much would she explain? Would she and Seth be married at that point? Even with a marriage, there were too many uncertainties still.

"Fine, but let's keep it small," he said.

"We'll keep it small." She met his gaze. "It'll give us something…to do."

"You're probably right," he said. "I didn't decorate last Christmas." He looked away and cleared his throat.

"I know," she said softly.

"I spent the day with Bonnie's parents. They didn't decorate, either."

It would have been a terrible time for

Seth, and Gabby felt her throat tighten in sympathy.

"This Christmas will be different," she promised him. "We'll do it together—learn how to be happy again."

"If it were left to me, I wouldn't bother," Seth said.

"But it isn't left to you," she said. "I'm your wife now. A housewife, no less." She smiled hesitantly. "I'll take this on as part of my job around here."

Seth was silent, then he sighed. "It's the babies' first Christmas, and I'm their stepdad now. So they'll have a proper Christmas. Should we go to the store this morning? It might be good to get out of the house."

"That would be nice." She took another bite of oatmeal, and as she looked at him, she could see how much he needed her—as a friend, as a support. Seth had been alone for too long already.

Gabby was feeling more cheerful. Christmas wasn't always an easy time of year when a person was alone, but they were together now. And of all times to start this new marital home together, maybe Christmas was the best—a fresh chance to add

trembled a little, and she wouldn't meet his gaze. "I hadn't realized how protected I'd feel being Mrs. Straight. But I could get used to this."

Was that how she felt being married to him? Safe? Maybe he could stand between Gabby and the unkind parts of this community. He felt a little taller, a little stronger as those thoughts settled into his heart.

"What about those?" Seth asked, nodding to some Baby's First Christmas ornaments.

"They're a little pricey," Gabby said. "Clothing matters more than tree ornaments, don't you think?"

"I'm paying, Gabs," he said, his voice low.

"No, I'd said—"

"Come on," he said. "Get three of those for the boys. I'm paying for this. We're starting out right. Okay?"

"Then I'll pay for the rest," she said. "You can get the special ornaments."

Gabby and the boys were his—on paper, and in a deeper way, too. This was his new family, and they were going to have Christmas. He might have been reluctant before, but not anymore.

"Maybe I'll make some cookies, then," she said with a small smile. "You know, to keep with our deal."

He chuckled. "I wouldn't turn them down."

"You're getting your own slippers, though," she joked.

He laughed. "Even after I go chop down a tree?"

They headed to the cashier, and Seth put down their items on the counter. He pulled out a credit card as the cashier rung up their order. From the stroller, one of the babies started to whimper, and Gabby bent over the car seat.

"Hey, sweetie…" she crooned. "Waking up?"

He was a dad out with his family shopping for Christmas decorations. Funny how this kind of thing could sneak up on a guy. Seth looked over at the chocolate bars, then grabbed a couple and added them to the rest of his purchases.

"Merry Christmas," the cashier said with a smile as Seth paid.

And as simple as that, he'd stepped back into the busy, bustling, cheerful world around him. His mouth felt dry, and for a moment, the canned Christmas music overhead felt louder than it was before. He'd been holding back after losing his wife and daughter, refusing to rejoin the world, unsure if it was even possible. But here he was…

"Merry Christmas," he said, and he grabbed the bag of decorations, then put his other hand on Gabby's back as they headed for the door.

He was officially a dad with a family.

THAT AFTERNOON, Gabby stood in the living room, holding those three red stockings. There wasn't a fireplace here to hang them over, but she could turn it into a cozy room with a little work. It seemed a bit barren with only a TV, a love seat, a recliner and that beautiful hardwood floor. There was a throw blanket tossed over the arm of the love seat, which was the only bit of warmth in the room.

"You're very tidy, Seth," Gabby said, raising her voice to be heard.

"What?" he called back.

"You're very—" she started to repeat, when Seth came up beside her and handed her something that crinkled. She looked down to see a caramel chocolate bar. "Tidy."

Seth stood next to her, the bulk of him filling up the room in a comforting way. She plucked the proffered treat from his hand.

"Chocolate. You're already doing just fine as my husband, I'll tell you that."

Gabby shot him a grin and he smiled bashfully. "I saw this dad with his kids, and the girl wanted a chocolate bar, but he told her she had to have a proper meal. And I figured we're adults, and we can ruin our proper meals all we want."

"Amen to that." She tore open the wrapper and took a bite. The caramel treat was exactly what she needed right now, and as she chewed, she looked around the room.

"So what's wrong with being clean?" Seth asked, opening his own and taking a bite.

"It's just..." she started, but when she met his frank gaze, her teasing evaporated. She could see exactly why this room was so tidy and bare. It matched the careful look in his eyes. This tidiness made Seth feel more in control, somehow. "Nothing. I'm probably going to mess it up. That's all."

"What are you looking for?" he asked.

"Where to hang the stockings," she replied.

"Maybe on the windowsill," he said. "I can hammer in three nails."

"You don't mind?" she asked. "They have these weighted stocking hooks so you don't have to use nails. I should have thought of them."

"Marketing genius," he said. "Two dollar stockings hung on twenty dollar stocking hooks. I saw them, but nails are cheaper."

She shrugged. "True, but they're also more permanent."

Seth was silent for a moment, then he cast her a cautious look.

"Is this...permanent?" he asked quietly. "Between us, I mean. We've never quite nailed that down."

"As permanent as marriages are these days," she said with a hesitant smile. What did he want from her? She wasn't entirely sure. He was the one whose heart was breaking at being married again after losing his one true love. If anyone was going to back out of this arrangement, she figured it would be him.

"I'm serious," Seth said. "I know I'm helping you out with the health insurance, but I want this to be more than that. I was serious about planning for the long term here. Like—having nails in that windowsill that we use year after year."

"You think you'll want to keep us around?" she asked, but the joking had slipped out of her tone, because she realized that she really wanted to know. Now that he'd experienced the reality of a marriage to her, had anything changed for him?

"Yeah, I think so," he said, and he forced a short laugh. "I mean, I want to be more than a godfather figure in their lives. I don't want to be the guy who was married to their mom for a couple of years and who just tries to be there for them. They need a dad they can rely on. Besides, I like having you around like this. I like having a life together. And I'm not going to fall in love again. That's over for me."

"I'm not going to risk this on falling in love again, either," she said. "I'm not good at romance. I've said it before. So…yeah. I think we could both bank on using those nails in the windowsill for a long time to come."

Seth smiled, relaxing. "I think we're pretty good as a team, Gabs. I know this might sound selfish, but this is my chance at family, and…a real family takes commitment."

Commitment… She nodded, feeling a smile tug at her lips.

"You just keep bringing me chocolate," she said.

Seth chuckled. "So, we're going to do this

for the long haul, then. We're going to grow old together."

"If you still want me around when I'm old," she said. Had he really thought this through? He'd agreed to help her in her time of need, but did he want the old lady version of his best friend?

Seth sobered. "That's what I mean. I want to stick to our vows, be able to count on each other. We were doing this the smart way, right? And that meant choosing someone we respected and deciding on the kind of marriage we wanted. Well... I don't know about you, but I want to commit to this, be a family. I don't think we'll get the family we want without actual commitment."

For as long as they both should live. He thought he wanted this, but would his optimism last?

"If you change your mind—"

"I'm not changing my mind, Gabs." He caught her hand.

"And you want to be the boys' dad—the one they grow up with all their lives," she clarified. "You want to stick together as we get older and take care of each other. You want to be grandparents together."

"Yes. You can call me Pops, and I'll call you Gram-Gram."

"You're joking…"

"I'm not, actually," he said, the smile slipping. "I'm serious. If you want to, that is."

"I do want that."

He grinned. "Good. I was going to go out and find a tree today. I figured you could take care of the rest of the decorating, and I'll do my manly duty and chop down something appropriate."

He sounded more cheerful already.

"Okay," she said. "Just show me where the hammer and nails are."

Seth turned back toward the kitchen and Gabby followed. He opened a cupboard and pulled out a toolbox, then put it on the counter.

"Everything you could possibly need," he said.

Outside, Gabby heard the growl of an engine coming into the drive, and Seth went to the window.

"It's my aunt Selena," he said.

Seth opened the door and a moment later an older woman came inside carrying a gift bag with some tissue paper pushing out the top. She was plump, with a rosy smile and curly gray hair. She looked around and when her gaze landed on Gabby, her smile broadened.

"Hello, Seth," she said, giving him a hug. "I hope you don't mind me just dropping by like this. I actually expected you to be working."

So Seth's aunt had come to check on her. His aunt was going to be hers now, too…sort of. Wasn't that how this worked?

"I took a few days off," Seth said.

"Your honeymoon." Selena's smile turned strained. "Oh, I'm sorry…"

"No, no, Auntie, come on in," Seth said. "I was about to head out, and the babies are sleeping, so you'll get Gabby to yourself for a bit, after all."

"Am I chasing him out?" Selena asked Gabby. "Because I can come another time."

They last thing Gabby and Seth needed was "honeymoon" time.

"Not at all," Gabby replied. "He's going to chop us down a Christmas tree. Your timing is perfect. Can I get you some tea, or something?"

Seth shot Gabby a smile. "See you in a few hours."

Seth headed out, leaving the women in silence for a moment.

"I brought you a wedding gift," Selena said, holding out the gift bag.

"Thank you." Gabby accepted it.

"I didn't know what you'd need. I mean, gone are the days when a young couple needed everything from a toaster to sheets, right?"

"Right," Gabby agreed, and she pulled the paper out of the bag to reveal a crystal picture frame. "Thank you. This is beautiful."

"For a wedding picture," Selena said.

Gabby put the frame on the counter, and for the first time, she started to think about putting out a wedding picture. Would that be too much? In their home, they were supposed to be friends. But they were married friends, after all.

She filled a kettle and plugged it in, then went back to the table, where Selena had gotten herself settled.

"I'll have to put a picture in there as soon as we get some printed," Gabby said.

"I was hoping to see the babies," Selena said. "Triplets. I can't imagine how busy the two of you must be."

"They'll wake up pretty soon," Gabby said. "If you stay a few minutes, I wouldn't turn down some help in feeding them."

Selena beamed. "I'd love to. And before I forget, we're having a family Christmas party on the weekend. I know everyone would love to meet you and the babies."

"This weekend?" Gabby paused.

"Saturday evening, at seven. My husband and I are hosting it. Seth knows the way."

"That sounds really nice," Gabby said. "I'll talk to Seth."

"You know, I'm so glad that you and my nephew are married," Selena said earnestly. "The last couple of years have been such agony for him. I'm sure you know how much he loved poor Bonnie—and I'm sorry to talk about her—"

"No, it's fine," Gabby said. "He's still grieving in a lot of ways."

"You were friends, the three of you, weren't you?" Selena asked, softening her voice.

Gabby paused. "Well, when he got married, it changed things. Bonnie wasn't really excited about Seth and my friendship, so…"

"Oh, I see." Selena pressed her lips together.

"But she was good for him," Gabby qualified.

"She was," Selena agreed. "And I was worried he wouldn't pull out of his mourning. When you lose someone, you always grieve on some level. It doesn't just go away, but Seth didn't seem like he was willing to be happy again, so I'm relieved to see that you've pulled him out of that. I mean, he blamed himself. But you know all about that, I'm sure."

Had she pulled him out of his grief? Maybe not as much as it appeared. But she and Seth were going to have a Christmas together, and that was a step forward. Seth's family would have a different insight into what he was going through, she realized. She'd been a good friend, but family got an inside view. Did she dare ask Selena for a little more information?

The kettle started to boil, and Gabby went to get a pot of tea started. She got out the tea bags, but up until this point, she'd had no reason to use anything larger than a mug.

"What are you looking for?" Selena asked.

"A teapot." She felt her cheeks heat. "I'm still a little lost in Seth's kitchen."

"Over the stove," Selena said. "And it's your kitchen now, too."

Gabby opened the cupboard over the stove and spotted the teapot. She managed to get it down on her tiptoes, and went about making the tea. Selena fetched some cups, and within a couple minutes they were both settled at the table once more.

"You said that Seth blamed himself,"

Gabby said, stirring a teaspoon of sugar into her mug of tea.

"Because it took him so long to get back to the house that night," Selena said. "It wasn't his fault, of course. He just got caught up with work, and he missed her call."

Gabby's chest tightened. "He missed her call?"

Two years of talking, two years of confiding...and he hadn't told her that. Had they been as close as she'd thought?

"The thing is," Selena went on, not seeming to notice any change in atmosphere, "Bonnie didn't like living out here. She wanted a house in town—something with a cute little yard and neighbors on both sides. Of course, Seth never breathed a word of this to me, being as private as he is."

"Of course," Gabby agreed. "So, Bonnie told you?"

"She needed to vent sometimes. We women do, right? But she'd been asking him to move to town, and he could drive to work here at the ranch. She wanted a part-time job when the baby got older. Anyway, when I saw how hard Seth grieved, I just thought..." Selena paused.

"You thought he blamed himself for not

moving with Bonnie to town," Gabby concluded.

Selena shrugged. "I could be wrong."

"They seemed like the perfect couple," Gabby admitted softly.

"Oh, sweetie," Selena said, reaching out and putting a hand on Gabby's. "It's just appearances. Every couple has to sort things out. Just like you will for the next forty or fifty years. That's the nature of marriage."

"You're right, of course," Gabby said. It wasn't jealousy or newlywed nerves that had tweaked her, even though she knew that was what it must look like. It was a new sense of understanding Seth's deep grief, his guilt over being happy again, and his refusal to even entertain the thought of falling in love again.

Was this guilt over Bonnie's death the reason he'd been willing to marry her to begin with? Was this what was holding him back from finding the real thing again?

"He doesn't open up easily," Gabby said quietly. And she should know. He could have told her that. She'd been telling him pretty much everything for years.

"Dear, none of them do." Selena shot her a smile, and Gabby felt her nerves relax. "You're good for him in a whole different way. I can tell. Just keep doing whatever it is you're doing."

Was this what it was like to have in-laws—people who cared for a man as much as his wife did?

From upstairs, Gabby heard one of the babies start to cry. Then another joined in, their wails filtering down toward them and making Gabby's heart yearn in their direction.

"Care to help out with feeding?" Gabby asked hopefully.

"I'd love to." Selena stood up. "Lead the way."

She cared about Seth, probably even more than was wise for her to do in this marriage of convenience. But she realized that helping him to get over his grief with Bonnie would very likely unsettle their arrangement.

Because when Seth's heart healed, he wouldn't want a family based on a loveless arrangement. He'd find himself falling in love again eventually…and it wouldn't be with her. It never had been Gabby who filled his heart. But she knew that she would help him heal, even if it ruined this careful balance.

Seth didn't think he'd get the family he longed for without commitment, but once his heart healed, he'd be able to see more clearly. And he'd want to love again. He *deserved* to love again, and to share his house and his heart with a real wife, not just a convenient match that allowed him to avoid his feelings. Even though Seth wanted to be her boys' father, in the end, he'd likely be the loving godfather. And a godfather was a good addition to any child's life. She knew that from personal experience.

So why did the thought bring a lump to her throat?

CHAPTER NINE

SETH PULLED THE blue spruce tree through the back door, the boughs giving some resistance but ultimately bending as he hauled it through. It hadn't seemed that big out in that wooded stretch of land beyond the west pasture, but as it erupted into his kitchen, boughs springing outward again, he realized it was bigger than he'd thought.

His aunt's car was gone, and the kitchen was empty as he laid the tree on the floor. The house smelled good—like chicken and potatoes. And there was the spicy scent of gingersnap cookies mingled in there, too.

Gabby had cooked—and he felt a wave of gratitude for that. He always had felt loved when there was a meal waiting for him. Bonnie used to have supper waiting. His mom had, too. And while he knew that his relationship with Gabby was different, the meal made for him certainly meant that she cared. Friendship was a kind of love that he didn't take for granted, either.

Overhead, he heard Gabby's voice and the irritated cry of one of the babies. She was busy, obviously. He took off his boots and ambled into the living room. It looked different in there—messier, mainly. A laundry basket full of unfolded clothes sat on the recliner, a few piles of folded baby clothes on the couch. Three red stockings hung on the windowsill. It was already different in this house. Gabby was spreading out. And it only made sense, seeing as they were making a life together, but it might take a little longer to get used to. He headed back into the kitchen, toward the smell of food and the tree in the middle of the kitchen floor.

He'd need Gabby's help; putting up that tree was not a one-man job. In the meantime, he opened the oven and found a casserole dish covered in foil. When he peeked inside, he saw some baked chicken legs, some potatoes. She'd set it aside for him, it seemed, and it was pretty obviously leftovers. There were some pots and a used plate in the sink.

Seth turned off the oven. He found a pot of steamed broccoli on the stove top and set about dishing himself up a plate of food. Overhead, Gabby sang "I'm a Little Teapot" about three times through, and that seemed to quiet the babies down. It was definitely different coming into a house full of life. He wondered why this wasn't a more painful reminder of the family he'd lost. But Gabby was so different than Bonnie, and she wasn't a wife in every sense...

The cries stopped as Seth finished his last drumstick, and he heard Gabby's footsteps on the stairs. He looked up to see her come down into the kitchen with one of the babies in a bouncy chair—Aiden, he would guess, since he was still the smallest—and she looked over at Seth in surprise.

"I didn't hear you come in," she said, and her gaze moved over to the tree in the center of the kitchen. "Wow—now that's a tree."

"Think it'll do?" he asked.

"Oh, definitely!" She sounded properly impressed.

"The food is great, by the way," he said. "Thanks for cooking."

"No problem." She disappeared into the living room, then came back without the baby. "I'm just bringing them so they can watch us decorate the tree."

"Sure..."

Was that safe, exactly? If they put the tree in the corner and set up the babies on the far side of the room... He was already thinking ahead.

In a matter of days, Gabby had filled up his home, and it was entirely different than this house had ever felt. *She* was different— funny, sweet, no-nonsense. She was different in the intimacy of a shared home, and living with her had revealed a softer side to her than he'd seen before. She felt less like his buddy now than he was entirely comfortable with. She'd quickly become a part of things around here—her and the triplets—in a way he hadn't expected to enjoy. He was feeling protective, more so than he'd ever been with her before. And added to that, the babies seemed to give a new purpose to making a living—and to dragging a blue spruce all the way from the edge of the south pasture up to his little house.

He finished the last of his meal and took his plate to the garbage. He scraped the chicken bones into it, then poked his head into the living room again. Aiden's eyes were open and he was looking around in that near-sighted baby kind of way.

"Hey, buddy," he said.

Gabby came up behind him holding the other two infants, and without asking, she tipped the first baby into his arms, waited until he'd gotten him adjusted and then handed over the second one.

"Okay…" he said uncertainly.

"I'll be back with their bouncy chairs," she said, and then disappeared behind him once more.

Seth looked down at the babies. They were both awake, too, and when Beau, the biggest of the three, started to whimper, he bounced the boy gently.

"Mommy's coming back in a minute," he said. "I got you a Christmas tree, you know."

He felt a wave of pride being able to say that. They were too little to care, but one of these years, that announcement would be met with excitement. And a year or two after that, he'd have three helpers to tramp out there with him and chop it down. There were worse things than having a stepdad who did right by a kid.

Gabby came back into the living room with two more bouncy chairs, and she set the boys up on the far side of the room.

"Gabby, did the guy—your dad—did he ever respond?" he asked.

Gabby froze, then straightened. "Nope."

"Oh…" He'd been afraid of that. "Look—"

"It's not a big deal," she said with forced brightness.

That was the old Gabby—the buddy. She'd pretend things were better than they were, and it used to be comforting. Maybe it let him worry less, be more certain that she'd come out of whatever was troubling her. But he'd seen a gentler side to her, a more hopeful and vulnerable side. This reaction was false, and he was now close enough to see it.

"I think it is a big deal," he countered quietly.

"He hasn't been in my life this long. I don't know what I was expecting."

"I think you were expecting common courtesy," he said.

Gabby's cheeriness faded, and she shrugged. "Like I said, I haven't gotten anything from him up to this point, so I don't know why that would even surprise me that he doesn't want contact. Mom was right, after all. I need to focus on the family I've got."

"Right." Seth cleared his throat. "That makes sense."

He was now close enough to see when she was faking her optimism for his benefit, but it didn't make him any good at helping her feel better.

"Speaking of which, your aunt said that they're having a family Christmas party this Saturday," Gabby went on. "We're invited."

"Oh…" He paused. A family party… It

was one thing informing his extended family of his marriage, and quite another to introduce his new wife to everyone at the same time. The thought was mildly intimidating, and he swallowed.

"I thought it might be nice," Gabby said hesitantly.

"Do we want to do this so soon?" he asked. "I mean, it's a whole evening with my side of the family, and if we go, it'll be mostly focused on us."

"And Christmas," she said with a small smile. "You know, doing this, getting married at Christmas, was actually a good idea. People have their own holiday hopes, which will serve as an excellent distraction. Besides, it might be better to just bite the bullet. I'd rather do that than entertain them individually."

"Hmm." He sighed.

"We either go to them, or they'll come to us," she said. "Besides, I could use a bit of extra family right about now. I have a few Christmas hopes of my own."

"Yeah?" he asked. "Like what?"

"Oh, I don't know... Forgetting about our problems and just enjoying the holiday."

And if her dad was ignoring her, maybe a big family gathering would be soothing.

At least he could provide a houseful of extended family. He was good for that much.

"First things first," he said. "Let's get this tree up."

Seth went back to the kitchen for the tree and carried it through to the living room. The babies were way across the room, but he still kept a pretty close eye on where they were and where these branches stopped. For the next few minutes, he and Gabby got the tree straight and centered, and when Seth had fully tightened the last of the screws in the tree stand, he brushed off his hands and pushed himself to his feet.

It smelled good—all fresh and piney. The top of the tree just brushed the ceiling, and he tried to feel festive, happy. But it wasn't in him. He wasn't ready for this. He wanted to be. He wished he could just plow ahead into a festive mood, but he wasn't.

"I've got sap on my hands," he said, his throat feeling tight. He left the room and went to wash his hands. It was Christmastime again, and he was doing the same thing Gabby had been trying to do—pretend everything was okay when it wasn't.

He might not be ready to move on, but when he'd married Gabby, and later when he said he wanted to stay married, that was exactly what he'd committed to. But still, he couldn't just pretend that Bonnie and Hazel hadn't existed, hadn't been the center of his Christmases in the past. He looked toward the living room, listening to Gabby's soft humming, as an idea formed.

This Christmas, he wasn't going to be able to just wait it out numbly. There were a few other ornaments upstairs—the personal ones—and if he was having a Christmas tree, they belonged there, too. Christmas was about family...including the one he'd lost.

Gabby looked up as he came into the room, the cardboard box balanced in one hand. She'd finished winding the lights around and had just plugged them into the wall socket behind the tree. The lights blinked to life and Gabby stood up.

"I, um—" Seth licked his lips. "There were some ornaments that mattered to me..."

Gabby came around the tree, her gaze locked on him, but she didn't say anything.

"I got an ornament for Hazel's first Christmas when she was still in utero," Seth went on. "I don't know—it wasn't technically her first Christmas, because she hadn't been born yet, but she was still with us, you know?"

Gabby nodded. "Yeah. They're just as much a part of things, even when they're still on the inside."

Seth smiled wanly. He used to sit next to Bonnie, his hand on her belly, feeling the kicks and jabs. He hadn't known if they would have a boy or a girl, but he'd known that he already loved this baby.

"Bonnie and I got a few ornaments, too, over the years and—" He stopped. "I don't know if that's stepping over the line to bring them out, or..."

Would he offend her? He wanted to be a good husband, as far as that went between them. And he'd heard a few horror stories about widowers keeping their late wife's ashes in the house, stuff like that. He'd always sworn he'd be a little more considerate than that, but then he'd never experienced that depth of loss when he'd made those gallant decisions about his future grief, either. In fact, he'd sworn he wouldn't marry again, at all.

"This is your tree, too," Gabby said quietly. "They belong here. Do you really think I'd try and erase your past? I'm your friend. I'm not jealous."

Seth nodded, feeling a wave of relief. "Okay. I just wanted to check."

Gabby pulled out the boxed ornaments they'd bought for the boys' first Christmas. She took a moment to unpack them—three blue teddy bears holding signs declaring both the year and the fact that this was a little boy's first Christmas—and hung them a few inches apart, right in the front of the tree.

Seth opened the cardboard box and pulled out a few ornaments and put them on the tree—the generic variety of reindeer, a sled, a snowman. Then he got to the one he'd been looking for. Hazel's ornament was a pink ball with a sleeping baby painted on the side. It read Baby's First Christmas, and the date was in the calendar year before her birth. He'd always known there'd be some explaining to do with that ornament, but now he was glad he'd bought it. She deserved to be remembered, to be celebrated. Her time on this earth had mattered, despite how short it was. He paused, unsure where to put Hazel's ornament.

"If you'd be okay with it," Gabby said, "maybe we could hang Hazel's ornament with the boys'—all together."

"Yeah?" He hesitated.

"Bonnie and Hazel are a part of my history, too," Gabby said softly. "So don't you ever think that you have to stop remembering in this house, Seth Straight. They belong on this tree."

Seth hung the pink ball on a bough in the center, just a little above the boys' ornaments, a little closer to heaven, and he blinked back his emotion.

"Thanks, Gabs…" He swallowed hard.

Gabby slid a hand around his arm and tipped her head against his shoulder. She felt good here—warm, secure, a reminder that there was still life to be lived. Going on after heartbreak was the hard part, but with Gabby beside him, maybe he could face it. He pressed his lips against the top of her head.

"What about the party?" she murmured. "Do you want to go?"

"My aunt would never forgive me if we didn't," he admitted.

For one evening, he could act the part of a proper husband. She was right—it was best to get this out of the way early, and then they could get back to just being themselves.

CHAPTER TEN

GABBY HADN'T DRESSED up since before she got pregnant, other than her wedding dress, and that didn't seem like an appropriate choice for a Christmas party. But she did have a black dress with a high waistline and a fuller skirt that fit again. Her body had changed after having the babies; her waist was thicker and she'd grown rounder in all the other places, too. It was like getting to know herself all over again as she looked in the mirror. She used to be slim, but now she'd become downright curvy. Not only did her figure look different, but a sparkle of gold shone on her left ring finger as well, and as she looked in the full-length mirror on the back of Seth's bedroom door, that was where her gaze was drawn.

"I look married…" she murmured.

The door creaked open and Seth poked his head in. "You ready?" His gaze landed on her and he froze for a moment. "Wow. You look great, Gabs."

"I look...different," she qualified, and she pulled her lipstick out of a pocket in the skirt and put some on.

"You look beautiful," he said, and when she looked over at him, his expression was completely serious.

It felt good to hear it coming from him. Funny how childbirth could both give her new amazement in her body's ability to bring life into the world, and at the same time leave her feeling like a visitor in her own skin. She didn't know how to dress her figure to her best advantage anymore, and she felt like she hardly recognized herself.

"You ready to leave?" he asked.

"Do we have any last diapers to change?"

"I hope not." Seth smiled wanly. "I've got the boys all downstairs."

He was getting more comfortable with the babies, and she'd been surprised to see how quickly he'd adjusted to diapers and packing the babies around the last couple days.

"You're getting good at this," she said.

"I'm trying real hard." He grinned and stepped back to let her through the door.

"I guess we're ready, then." She felt a little tickle of nerves as she said it. "Let me just grab the diaper bag."

She was meeting the Straight family tonight in a totally new way. She knew a lot of them already from her years of friendship with Seth, but tonight she'd be introduced as his new wife. This was the kind of thing she'd wanted for years...a husband of her own.

But Seth's family knew him better than anyone... Would they see through this sham, or would they buy it? Because if they didn't, the rumors would fly around Eagle's Rest and her boys wouldn't have that protection from the gossip she'd been so desperate to provide. And when rumors started, they didn't stop. But it wasn't only about the personal impact of rumors; it could affect her husband's employment, as well. Suspicion of insurance fraud was nothing to toy with.

GABBY TUGGED HER coat a little closer as Seth parked the truck along the street outside a bungalow. The night was already dark, and the lights from inside shone welcomingly over the snowy yard. The house was lined with multicolored Christmas lights, and a stunted apple tree out front was wreathed in lights, too. The driveway was already full of cars, the back end of one of them hanging out into the street.

"Are we late?" Gabby asked.

"Maybe a little," Seth said.

She looked over her shoulder into the back seat, where the babies were all sleeping after that nice forty-minute drive into Eagle's Rest. "Let's go before I lose my nerve."

"You know some of these people," he said. "You'll fit in with the rest, too. Trust me on that. My family is already primed to like you."

"How do you know?"

"You won over Selena. The rest is easy." He shot her a smile. "Let's go."

It was her chance to see his family—and somehow that felt more intimidating than introducing him to hers. Hers was smaller, for one, and more willing to accept a few oddities. Seth's family was filled with long-time married couples, kids, grandkids, cousins, siblings... And Gabby was willing to bet they'd be able to detect a fraud. Or maybe she was just afraid they would.

Seth got out of the truck and came around to open her door. It was a sweet gesture, one she appreciated, since she had to get the babies' car seats out of the back seat. When they were out, Gabby carried Aiden's, and Seth carried Beau's and Andy's. By the time they got halfway up the walk, the front door opened, Nat King Cole Christmas carols filtering out into the winter air, and an older man with iron gray hair and dark eyebrows waved with a smile.

"You've met Uncle Doug, right?" Seth asked, glancing toward her.

"Yeah, once or twice," she said, forcing a smile.

At a family picnic, maybe, or a barbecue? And Seth and Bonnie's wedding, of course. She'd met most of his family, but back then she'd just been a buddy and decidedly out of the spotlight.

"You're here! Come on in. Gabby, it's great to see you—and welcome to the family." Doug bent down and bussed her cheek as she came inside. The house smelled of cinnamon and baking, and as Seth came in behind her, Doug took Beau's car seat and looked down into the baby's sleeping face.

"Oh, my goodness, it's been a while since I've been around a baby this small," Doug said with a grin. "Do you think I could hold this little guy?"

"Doug loves babies," Seth said, giving Gabby a smile.

"And babies love Doug," Selena said, coming up to give them each a hug. She was wearing a red turtleneck and a holly-patterned apron. As Gabby took off her boots and coat, Selena and Doug each got a baby out of his car seat and snuggled them close. Gabby watched as Doug shut his eyes for a moment, a goofy smile on his face.

"We won't go far, Gabby," Selena said. "We'll stay right here in the living room."

Gabby appreciated Selena's thoughtfulness. She obviously understood a new mom's anxieties. Seth's hand settled onto the small of Gabby's back, warm and strong. He took her coat and hung up both his and hers in the closet. She looked out into the living room, which was full of people—most sitting, some standing by an upright piano, wineglasses in their hands. Most had stopped talking, looking toward her with half smiles and curious expressions. She picked up Aiden's car seat and held it in front of her, somehow feeling safer with a baby to redirect their attention toward.

"They're staring," Gabby whispered.

Seth emerged from the closet and met her gaze with a mischievous smile of his own. "Then let's give them a show."

But Gabby wasn't in the mood for a show. Yes, she didn't want to be embarrassed by the truth about their union, or risk any suspicion, but did she really want to act the part of a doting couple? It was a little late to change her mind, though, because Seth caught her free hand in his, tugging her with him. She felt herself smiling in response to that eager pull.

"Let me introduce everyone," Seth said, his voice low and warm in her ear. He gave her hand a soft squeeze. Then he raised his voice. "Everyone, this is Gabby. I'm sure you've heard the news... As for the triplets— let me see... Doug's got Beau, Selena's got Andy. This little fellow here with his mom is Aiden."

So this was what it was like to have an attentive husband...warm and safe—a little too good for her to comfortably enjoy. Gabby smiled hesitantly as all eyes turned toward her. Aiden started to squirm, so she put the car seat down and unbuckled him, then picked him up. Aiden nuzzled into her arms, giving her a brief escape from having to look back at everyone. This had been a silly idea. They hadn't been married long enough to even sort out a united front, much less polish up their image in public. Family was the final test, not the practice grounds!

"I can't believe you're married!" A young man came up and shook Seth's hand. "Congratulations, Seth."

"Thank you," Seth said, then he put his

arm around Gabby's waist. "Gabs, this is my cousin Len."

Seth's arm was strong, but his touch was gentle as he nudged her into his side. He was muscular, solid—something she'd been noticing about him lately. She'd always appreciated his good looks, but she'd never been the one nestled against his side before. She felt her cheeks heat, since the touch of his fingers on her waist was more intimate than she was used to from him. For a moment, she felt so warm and protected that it almost brought tears to her eyes.

But this was an act. This whole tender, gentle husband performance was just that—something meant to convince the family that their marriage was a legitimate one based on love and passion. And damn, was Seth a good actor!

"I don't think we've met," Len said, giving Gabby a smile. "We're all glad you're taking this idiot on, though."

Gabby forced out a breathy chuckle. "What can I say? I'm nice that way."

Seth laughed, his own voice sounding casual and easy. "Are you hungry, babe? I could get you some food while your hands are full."

Babe. She looked up at him in mild surprise. His cheeks pinked slightly, and he shrugged just the tiniest amount. At least she could see through his role, which was a strange relief. Her buddy was under there somewhere—and she preferred regular old Seth to this polished, romantic guy…because her buddy wouldn't be touching her in a way that made her heart speed up. He wouldn't be meeting her gaze with a flirtatious glitter in his eye that spoke of some pent-up longing.

"I'll be back," Seth murmured, and headed toward the kitchen, leaving her alone with Len. The food did smell great, and when she looked around she noticed a young woman standing nearby, watching her hopefully.

"Hi," Gabby said.

"Hi, I'm Natalie. Seth's cousin. There are a lot of us."

"Nice to meet you," Gabby said.

"This little one is really precious," Natalie said, cocking her head to one side to look at Aiden. "How old?"

"He's six weeks now," Gabby said. "But he's only two weeks past his due date, so he's still pretty small."

"Do you think I could hold him?" Natalie asked.

"Sure." Gabby eased Aiden into her arms,

and Natalie shot her a grin. "He's just beautiful. We've all been waiting to meet you and to get our hands on these little guys. I'm taking early childhood education in college, by the way, so if you ever want a qualified babysitter, I'd be happy to lend a hand."

"Really?"

"Of course. What's family for?"

"Thanks," Gabby said. "I appreciate it."

She'd started out with very few people able to pitch in, and in a matter of days, she had more offers to babysit than she'd ever need.

"So how is it with three babies at once?" Natalie asked, looking down at Aiden with a gentle smile.

"Busy. And it requires a lot of strict scheduling," Gabby replied.

"I'll bet!"

Across the room, Seth had a plate loaded with finger foods, and she watched him pause to chat with a few people, smiling, nodding, occasionally glancing over to where she stood. His gaze met hers and his lips turned up in a slow smile. He'd never smiled at her quite like that before. It was tender, warm…promising. Her heart skipped a beat, and she looked away.

"So how did you two decide to get married?" Natalie asked.

There it was—the question she'd been preparing for.

"It just…happened," Gabby said. "I came home to Eagle's Rest with the babies, and we hadn't seen each other in a long while. We got together to catch up, and just ended up talking for hours. We realized then."

"That's so romantic." Natalie smiled, but then it fell. "My boyfriend and I have been together for three years, and still no ring."

But she'd had three years of a legitimate, romantic relationship, and Gabby felt a little tweak of envy. This young, beautiful Natalie had a man who obviously cared for her—probably even loved her. And right now, that felt like it counted a whole lot more than a wedding ring and a fake story.

"Don't rush it," Gabby said quietly.

"You sure?" Natalie asked with a low laugh. "I don't think three years is exactly speeding."

"Is he good to you?" Gabby asked. "Is he open, kind? Have you met his family?"

"Yes to all of that," Natalie said. "He's wonderful, and trustworthy, and…not ready for a ring."

But at least that relationship was real.

"Enjoy it," Gabby said, lowering her voice. "I'm serious. Just enjoy it. Let it happen naturally. It's part of the experience."

"What choice do I have?" Natalie asked, just as Aiden started to squirm and whimper. "I think this little guy is done with me."

"Here, I'll take him," Gabby said, and she eased Aiden into her arms, where he immediately settled. Her boy... At least her babies' preference for her wasn't for show. She looked over at Seth, who was talking to an older man. Seth leaned in, said something, and the man looked toward her with a smile. Then Seth headed toward her with that plate of food.

"Dinner," he said, when he arrived at her side.

"I'm going to get myself something to eat before it's gone," Natalie said. "Congratulations, Seth. So nice chatting with you, Gabby."

Gabby smiled, and Seth held the plate in front of her temptingly. She picked up a cheese cube with her free hand and popped it into her mouth.

"Thanks," she said.

"Getting to know people a bit?" he asked.

From across the room the tinkle of silverware tapping glass started, and then the sound grew as more people joined in. Gabby's heart sank, and Seth gave her a look of mild panic.

"You know what they want…" he murmured.

"Yep." She swallowed.

"Come on, Seth!" someone called. "Kiss your bride!"

There was some cheering and encouragement, and Gabby could see there was no getting out of it.

"You ready for this?" he murmured, and he slipped that warm hand around her waist once more. Her heart sped up and she opened her mouth to say something, but nothing came out. He leaned down toward her, his lips brushing hers ever so lightly.

A couple of his cousins groaned.

"Oh, come on, Seth!" Natalie laughed. "Kiss her properly. Like you mean it!"

"We'd better do it," Gabby said with a reluctant laugh. "Let's just give them what they want, and they'll leave us alone."

"You sure?" A smile tickled the corners of his lips.

"I don't see a way out," she said.

Seth tugged her closer and put a protective hand over Aiden's back, covering her fingers with his. His mouth came down over hers once more, and this time, his kiss wasn't hesitant or polite. It started out firm, then softened as he held her, his lips moving over hers in a thorough exploration. He smelled good and his kiss tasted ever so faintly of punch. He pulled back, dark smoldering eyes meeting her gaze as she blinked hers open again, and then he kissed her again, a peck, and then another softer peck, before he pulled back.

The family laughed and cheered, and Gabby's heart pattered in her chest.

Now *that* had been a kiss.

"Better!" Uncle Doug laughed. "Much better!"

Someone started playing a Christmas carol on the piano, and the Nat King Cole music was shut off as they turned their attention to the live music.

Seth looked down at Gabby, but this time, there was something else in his eyes—an intensity, maybe, that hadn't been there before. If she didn't know better, she'd think he was considering doing it again.

"Can we go home?" she asked breathily.

Seth blinked. "Yeah. Sure." He paused. "Look, Gabs—"

"It's fine." She looked over to where the other babies were being cuddled by two other women, but she couldn't keep the tremor out of her voice. "Duty done."

She wanted out of here. She needed to get back to their house, where their relationship made sense. Because his kissing her like that hadn't been fair.

They didn't love each other, and yet they were married. The way that kiss reminded her of the romance she'd written off was cruel. They'd agreed to this marriage for very good reasons, but teasing her with the kind of intimacy that they'd never share...

"Gabs." He caught her arm. "I'm sorry, but you did say to kiss you."

"I know," she said, swallowing hard. "But you didn't have to do it quite so well!"

THE NIGHT WAS COLD, but there was no wind, thankfully. These were the things Seth had started to think about more seriously now that there were tiny babies to consider. Gabby was silent in the passenger seat, her expression granite. He'd ticked her off tonight—that much was clear.

In the back, the babies were all sleeping, soothers bobbing in their mouths. And through the open curtains in the house, Seth could see the party still in full swing—one of his cousins standing with his back to the living room window, an aunt shading her eyes to look outside.

They'd left early, though he wished they could have stayed a bit longer. Family—his own family, who had known him since he was tiny—mattered more than it ever had before. He had been avoiding his extended family ever since Bonnie's death. They kept trying to cheer him up, and he hadn't wanted to feel better. He'd wanted to mourn. But with Gabby here, he had a good reason to be opening up to them again, and he felt more alive than he had in a long time. With Gabby and the babies in his home now, he was reminded just how much he needed a supportive family, and he'd been looking forward to an evening out with his family and his wife.

His wife… He still stumbled over that, even mentally.

"Gabs, I don't think I've done anything wrong here," he said.

"You've been married before, Seth," she said. "You should know better than to start like that!"

Right. And he did. But Gabby wasn't Bonnie.

"You know what?" he retorted. "If our relationship were…different…maybe I'd tiptoe more. But it isn't. You and I were friends first—and we're friends still. We tell each other the truth. At least, I thought we did. So I'm being honest here. I don't think I was wrong. If you didn't want me to kiss you, you shouldn't have told me to do it!"

He put the truck into Drive and pulled away from the curb. A few flakes of snow were spinning down from the sky, visible in the streetlamp's glow.

"It wasn't the kiss," she said after a moment. "And you weren't wrong. I told you to kiss me, and you did. It's fine."

"It doesn't seem fine to me," he said.

"It's all of it," she said. "This act—the doting husband. Don't get me wrong, it's wonderful. You're sweet, attentive, affectionate... You can pat yourself on the back for being very good at that stuff, but it's too much."

Seth signaled a turn at a four-way stop. Too much? He'd been nice. Sure, he'd put his arm around her, but they were newlyweds, after all, and there were a few expectations. But they'd talked about this! She'd said she wanted him to act the part of a loving husband, but now that he was doing it, she was upset.

"We had an agreement," he said. "We were going to act the doting couple, I thought.

Getting mad at me for doing exactly what we agreed to do is ridiculous! Besides, it worked. Everyone is convinced that we got married for the most romantic of reasons, and the stories will be in your favor."

"In my favor?" she snapped back. "This is about convincing our community we aren't committing insurance fraud!"

"It's also about how people see us—how much they respect us as a couple," he countered. "This is personal, too."

"Fine."

She fell silent, and he navigated the familiar streets, heading for the highway.

"I'm not mad at you," she said at last. "I'm just… It's not your fault, okay?"

"So if it wasn't the kiss, what's upsetting you?" he asked.

"It's…hard for me to see you like this— and know it isn't real."

"Real? Our marriage *is* real. Our vows to take care of each other are real. We're both in this for the long haul. The only thing that wasn't real is a romantic connection…but then, a lot of couples act happier or more affectionate in public than they are in private. So, what's real, anyway?"

"You've had the real thing," she said with a sigh. "I haven't. So experiencing a fake version of it stung more than I thought it would."

"I'm sorry."

"You don't need to be," she said. "I'm just looking forward to the stage where people no longer expect us to be honeymooning. I think it'll be easier then."

He smiled ruefully. "We can be a more distanced couple. I thought you wanted that—the attentiveness, the food fetching."

"I thought I did, too," she admitted quietly. "Turns out I don't."

Fair enough. But not all of it was an act. He'd liked having her with him, looking across the room and knowing she was there. And he'd honestly thought she could use a little bit of doting—hanging out with a family she didn't know too well, being out with the triplets...

And she'd been beautiful—the sparkly, holiday kind of beautiful with her black lace dress that made her skin look so creamy and her eyes so bright. He'd been caught up in the moment. Apparently, she hadn't been.

"Okay," he said. "But I think we need to be really clear and honest with each other when it comes to our expectations and all that. Our feelings aren't going to get hurt over the same things as other couples', at least. So let's agree to be completely honest."

She was silent for a moment, and he thought maybe she wouldn't answer him. Then she said, "If you ever want an amicable divorce so that you can move on in a more real way, I'll give it to you."

Any rebuttal he'd been thinking up evaporated. He looked over at her, and found her gaze fixed on her hands in her lap.

"We talked about this…" he said.

"One of these days, you'll heal, Seth," she said quietly. "And you'll feel ready to face romance again. I'm just saying, you aren't stuck with me."

"We have an agreement," he said. "I'm not going back on that."

"I'm just saying."

"Are you okay?" he asked hesitantly.

"I'm fine."

But was she? The snow started to fall a little thicker and faster as he pulled onto the highway. A semitruck thundered toward them and whipped by, pushing the pickup with a gust of wind. These mountain passes could be dangerous this time of year. He glanced over at her.

"It seems to me that you're the one who's regretting this marriage a little bit," he said.

"You don't want to be reminded about the romance, the love…"

"I don't want the reminder right now," she agreed. "But that doesn't mean I want to go find a boyfriend, either. I know what I want—to raise my boys. I want to be a good mom. And I want our oddball relationship to work out, too."

"Good. So where is this coming from?" he asked. "Why are you worried about me wanting out?"

"Your aunt and I were talking when she came to visit," Gabby said. "And she was telling me about Bonnie, and how when she wanted to move to town you two butted heads over it a lot, and—"

He clenched the steering wheel in a tighter grip. "She told you that?"

"Yes."

"That was private."

"I thought we told each other private things," she said.

"Gabs…"

"I told you everything. I wasn't holding back. I told you about boyfriends and family, and—and…" She tapered off, and he remembered countless conversations where she'd opened up. Sitting in his truck, hanging out on a summer night, watching movies together in the winter—she'd talked. Constantly. Openly. He was more of a listener. It was what made their friendship work.

"I just don't talk as much," he said feebly.

"Well, maybe you'd better start," she replied. "And I'm on your side, Seth! We have to understand each other. I need to know what's going on with you so I can be your support. We aren't romantic, but we're definitely a team."

"So what else did she say behind my back?" he asked. His aunt wouldn't be keeping those little nuggets just between her and Gabby. He knew how family gossip worked.

"She said that you blame yourself for Bonnie's death because of that friction between the two of you."

He heaved a sigh. The highway's downhill slope was growing shallower as he steered past a rest stop with a view of the towering peaks behind them. How much had his family discussed behind his back? And how much were they going to unload on Gabby?

"That's not true," he said after a moment.

"You sure?" she asked.

Seth sighed. "Maybe a little bit. I wasn't there when she needed me. That tends to haunt a guy."

"I'm just saying," she said. "You can tell

me stuff like that. We need to know where each other is coming from. We need to be open with each other."

"And how is my marriage your business?" he demanded. "I'm struggling to see how it's even Selena's!"

"Because if you decide you want out of *this* marriage, I don't want it to come out of left field!" Gabby said, her voice shaking. "I don't want to be sideswiped! I'm your best friend, Seth, and if you're able to heal and you meet someone who interests you, I want us to be able to end this honorably! I don't want to lose my best friend!"

What was she imagining happening, exactly?

"You're afraid I'll cheat?" he asked, struggling to get his mind around her worries here. "Because I'm not like that."

"I don't know," she said. "Could I blame you for finding romance with someone else? Does it even count as cheating if we're married for other reasons?"

He thought he could see what was happening here. She wasn't secure in their relationship because it wasn't based on the normal things—passion, desire, love. But that didn't mean she couldn't count on him.

"Okay..." he said quietly. "You need me

to be transparent and open with you so you can trust me. Is that it?"

"I guess that sums it up."

"Gabs, you matter to me," he said. "I mean, you *really* matter to me. Just because we don't share a bed doesn't mean I want to risk losing you. I'm not going to lie to you or do anything behind your back. You can count on me."

She didn't answer, and when he looked over, he saw tears shining in her eyes. It suddenly struck him what was worrying her—and it probably wasn't how much he told her. She'd been lied to a lot. The father of her children had cheated on both her and his wife. Seth reached over and took her hand. She squeezed his hand back.

"I'm not like Craig," he said earnestly. "Okay? I need you to know that. I'm not following a feeling, and I'm not going to lie to you. I made a promise, and you can count on it. I'm coming home to you and the boys. I meant those vows."

But he did have to be more open with her. This marriage wasn't an easy way out of anything. They'd have to trust each other, open up with each other, talk stuff through, just like any other married couple.

They fell into silence as Seth navigated

the winding highway down toward the foot-hills. He didn't pull his hand back, though. It felt good to hold her hand. He was glad they'd gotten married for more logical reasons. He'd fallen in love once already—and he'd experienced the gut-wrenching loss of a woman he'd relied on for everything. He didn't want to go through that again, but he didn't want to be alone, either.

"Gabby, I'll open up more," he said quietly. He glanced over at her.

"Yeah?" she said, meeting his gaze.

He looked back to the road, at the trees growing high and black on either side. He thought he saw the green flash of a deer's wide eyes in the foliage, reflecting the truck's headlights, but then they zoomed past. "You're right. We have to trust each other. And I do blame myself for Bonnie's death. But it wasn't because she wanted to move to town."

"Then why was it?" Gabby asked.

He'd never said this aloud before, never admitted it to anyone. Those closest to him obviously saw that he blamed himself, but it wasn't for the reasons they thought.

"We fought," he said, his voice low. "It was stupid. She was upset about some email you'd sent me. It was just our regular way of chatting, but Bonnie didn't like it. I showed her the reply I sent, and she thought I'd been a bit flirtatious. I hadn't meant to be. I was just trying to be polite, and I'd been excited about the baby coming, and having that news to share, and maybe I'd come off wrong. Not to you—you understood me. But to Bonnie. Anyway, it was just a stupid couple fight. Everyone has them. But I was tired and stressed out, and so was she. I just wanted air. So I left for a while."

"And you missed her call," Gabby breathed.

"I hadn't turned my phone off." He needed her to understand that part. "But the service dropped, and..." He licked his lips. "She needed me, and I'd left because I wanted some space. And she and our daughter died because of it."

"I never thought you were flirting," Gabby said.

"I know."

"You couldn't have known what would happen, either," Gabby said.

"I'm just explaining."

"I'm sorry, Seth. I didn't know it was me—" Her voice caught.

"It wasn't you," he said curtly. "It was me and Bonnie. You and I were never romantic.

Ever. She just couldn't believe you weren't in love with me, I guess. Because she was."

"I'm glad you told me," Gabby said.

"If I'm going to open up more, I have to trust you to keep this stuff between us," he said.

"Of course, Seth."

He felt better, a bit lighter. He smiled faintly in the low light of the cab. This was a partnership. And of all the women he could have chosen, he felt safest with Gabby Rogers. They'd always been a good team. And he was glad he had her in his life. But what made them best was that they didn't have those silly romantic squabbles, the kind that tipped him off balance and brought out his worst. He'd watched his father be a jerk to his mom during that acrid divorce, and he never wanted to be that guy.

He'd be more open with Gabby, and he'd do his best to keep their balance. Their strength, as always, was in their friendship.

CHAPTER ELEVEN

THE NEXT DAY, Seth went to work. It was a relief to have a regular schedule back—at least Seth seemed more relaxed, more cheerful. He left just as Gabby was getting up, and he waved as he grabbed his thermos from the counter.

"See you for dinner," he said.

"See you."

She'd been standing there in her bathrobe, her hair all mussed from sleep, and she'd realized belatedly that this would be the image of her he carried with him all day. Bleary, mussed-up Gabby.

The rest of the morning she spent with the babies, and she went online a little bit, looking at her father's employee profile. It was him; she could feel it. And he hadn't written back. He probably wouldn't. Part of her was tempted to send a second email, just asking for confirmation, but that was silly. If it was her father, it was clear he didn't want to hear from her.

Grace called her just before noon, and they chatted on the phone for a little while. Poppy was home from school, sick with a stomach bug.

"So how are you doing?" Grace asked. "How's married life treating you?"

"It's…" Gabby felt a lump rise in her throat. "It's not quite what I expected."

"Oh…" Grace's tone softened. "You know, no one warns you about this, but the first year of marriage is tough. It isn't that you don't love each other, because you really do, but you're adjusting to living together, and when you love someone that much, your feelings get hurt when they let you down. It's normal to fight, so make sure you make up just as passionately…if you know what I mean."

Gabby forced a laugh. "Right. Of course."

"You sound upset," Grace said.

"I'm not. I'm just…tired, I guess. Three babies do that to you."

"I can only imagine," Grace replied. "Billy and I are trying for a baby right now, and I'm a little bit daunted, I have to admit!"

"Are you really? Oh, that's great, Grace! You're already a great mom," Gabby said. "I'm really happy for you. You married your best friend, and you've got it all right now."

"So did you," Grace said, a smile in her voice.

"Yes, I did." But it wasn't the same. When Grace married her best friend, it had been because they'd fallen headlong in love with each other and couldn't face the thought of a life apart. They'd had to juggle all sorts of things to make it work, but it was worth it. Gabby's story was a whole lot more pragmatic, and while hiding the truth had seemed like a viable option last week, it wasn't easy.

In the background, Gabby heard the sound of Poppy getting sick.

"Oh, shoot—" Grace said. "I've got to go, Gabby!" Then her voice softened. "Poppy? You okay, sweetie? Come here…" The phone hung up.

Gabby envied her friend just a little bit, even with a sick kindergartner on her hands. She really had hit the jackpot with Billy, because it was *real*. But Grace had always had a good head on her shoulders, and she'd chosen good guys, even the boyfriends who hadn't worked out. Gabby's heart led her in the wrong direction—every time.

That afternoon, Gabby packed up her sons and drove the forty minutes into Eagle's Rest to see Aunt Bea. She was tired of keeping up appearances. What she really needed today was her aunt's practical wisdom. Life could get tangled, and Bea could shake it all straight again. You might look like a fool once she had, but at least things made sense.

Less than an hour later, Gabby sat at Bea's kitchen table, and Bea slid a plate in front of her. It held a thick slice of pie with apples and a syrup spilling out onto the plate, and its aroma was sweet and comforting.

"This looks good," Gabby said with a grin. "I needed this."

"I made it yesterday," Bea said. "Pie is always best after a night in the fridge."

Afternoon sunlight spilled through Aunt Bea's kitchen window. The babies were asleep in their car seats, and Gabby picked up a fork and pushed it into the flaky crust.

"So how are you enjoying married life?" Bea asked.

"Everyone's asking me that these days. And it's more complicated than I thought," Gabby admitted past a bite of pie.

"It would be," Bea said. "How's Seth doing with a houseful of babies?"

"He's doing great, actually," Gabby replied. "He's been changing diapers, doing bottles... He can tell them apart now, too." She paused. "It's easier, Bea. Having a husband. I mean, he isn't around all the time, but if the boys are awake he always has one of them in his arms. It's another person to love them, and feed them, and…it's nice. I feel less stressed out."

Bea nodded thoughtfully. "I'm glad. Did the health insurance kick in?"

"We sent in some receipts," Gabby said. "Fingers crossed. The formula is prescribed by the doctor, so unless we hear otherwise, we should get reimbursed."

"Your mom is really happy for you," Bea said. "She was telling me that you look content, and she figures Seth will be good to you."

Gabby nodded. "Mom is really supportive."

"Are you going to tell her the whole story?"

Gabby shook her head. "Nope. She's happy. Let it go." She sighed. "She is rather annoyed that I want to contact my dad, though."

Bea frowned. "And why would you contact him?"

"Well…" Gabby stopped, eyeing her aunt. "Did Mom tell you about this?"

"She mentioned it," Bea admitted. "And I agree with her on this one, Gabby. Contacting him is a bad idea."

"Seriously?" Gabby sighed. "Auntie, I really thought you'd have a different perspective. I understand why my mom is bitter about him, but you, too? What's the story here that you two aren't telling me?"

"There isn't a story," Bea said. "I just don't think he's the wonderful father figure you're looking for."

"I'm not looking for a wonderful father figure," Gabby countered. "I just want to meet my dad. And I want him to meet my babies. People can change, and it's been thirty years. You knew him. What was he like?"

"He was a jerk," Bea said. "He made your mother miserable and broke her heart."

"Okay, but personality-wise. She loved him once. There must have been some good," Gabby pressed.

"He was a guy's guy," Bea said. "He... he didn't care enough about either of you to come back. He isn't worth your heart, Gabby. This is what I'm worried about— you getting hurt when he lets you down."

"I'm thirty," Gabby reminded her. "I'm not a child anymore."

"But your boys? He's not a nice man, dear."

That felt like a low blow. Of course, she

thought about her sons constantly, and she stared at her aunt, not answering.

Bea took a bite of pie. "I can't stop you, but I'd advise against contacting him."

"I already did," Gabby said quietly.

Bea stopped chewing, her gaze locked on Gabby. "And?"

"I haven't heard back," she said. "At least I think I've contacted the right man. He has the right name, and he's working in California for a marketing firm. The details seem like they'd add up to the right guy."

Bea swallowed. "And he hasn't messaged you back?"

"It's been a few days," Gabby said. "And you might be right. This might be my father, and he might not care enough to even reply. I don't know… Being a mom now, I just see things differently, I guess. I know my sons will need a father in their life. It makes me realize I might need one, too."

"You took care of a father for your boys," Bea said shortly. "And your mother took care of you by giving you a good godfather."

"No matter how wonderful Seth is, my boys will want to meet Craig," Gabby said. "And he will very likely let them down, but it'll be their right to meet the man who fathered them."

Bea reached for her mug of tea and took a swig. "You might feel differently about this when they're older, dear girl. They're infants now, and all of this is so far away that it's cushioned in noble wishes for their future. But when you're facing the complicated emotions of your precious boys meeting an older, possibly more bitter Craig, your instincts might be exactly like your mother's."

"I don't blame her," Gabby said. "I know why Mom didn't want him back in our lives, and I'm not upset. I had a wonderful childhood. I was loved and cared for, and I didn't lack for anything. But knowing that my dad didn't want me…that messed me up a bit."

"Not all men are worth being messed up over," Bea said.

Gabby didn't answer that. Her aunt was very likely right. And if she had found her father, he hadn't answered, and she'd promised herself that she wouldn't email him again. She wouldn't beg. She'd given him the opportunity to connect with her, and if he refused it, then he was the one who'd have to live with that.

Except she'd live with it, too—with his rejection.

"Why didn't he want to know me?" Gabby asked quietly.

Bea shook her head. "He just never came back, dear. He never checked up on your mom, either. Focus on what you do have— your mom, your godfather, your boys, your... husband."

Gabby noticed her aunt's hesitation there.

"What?" Gabby asked.

"Was your choice to marry a friend instead of a lover...was that because of your father?" Bea asked quietly.

"Maybe," Gabby said. "I don't know. How much can you blame an absentee father for? I was always attracted to losers, and I've often wondered if that was because of some DNA quirk that drew me to them, or if it was just my subconscious way of chasing after men just like my father... So the other men I wasted my time on are probably my father's fault. But choosing Seth was a conscious effort to get out of that rut. He's different. He's *better.*"

"He's a good man," Bea agreed. "Even if you did get married for all the wrong reasons."

"Just different reasons," Gabby said with a low laugh. "It seems to be working for us, so…"

And there she was—still keeping up those appearances. She didn't want to admit that this might have been a mistake. She had hoped they'd be able to sort it all out.

When her visit was through, Gabby packed the babies back into the car and waved goodbye to her aunt. It felt good to come into town. Maybe she'd married Seth for pragmatic reasons, but without him, she'd be slipping deeply into debt just to feed them, and these boys wouldn't be seeing a doctor. This morning, she'd called and made an appointment for their first checkup here in Eagle's Rest in the week before Christmas.

Sometimes marriage was practical. Sometimes it was for the children. Was that so wrong?

Gabby's phone pinged as started the car. That would be an incoming email. As her car warmed up, she fished the phone out of her purse for a quick look.

She pulled up the email, and she stopped short when she saw the name: Hank A. Rogers. Her father. He'd replied. She sucked in a ragged breath and touched the email alert, pulling up the full message.

Dear Gabby,
I was on vacation last week, and I only got your email today, so I'm sorry about the delay in replying. I'm the man you're looking for—I was married to Carol for three years about thirty years ago. Maybe it was four years by the time the divorce was finalized. But I think there has been a big misunderstanding. Maybe it's better we talk on the phone. This is my number. Feel free to call me.

Gabby's heart hammered in her chest. A misunderstanding? If he was the man she was looking for…it sounded like there was more to this than her mother or Bea were telling her. She'd tried getting answers from them, to no avail. If she wanted his side of it, her dad was willing to talk.

She dropped her phone into her purse and backed out of her parking spot. She'd wait until she got home, give herself a chance to feel ready for this conversation. She'd waited thirty years for this chance, and she needed to be able to remember his words once she hung up.

Because for the first time in her life, she was going to speak to her father, and the only question that she wanted answered right now was: *Why didn't you love me?*

CHAPTER TWELVE

SETH HAD BEEN thinking about that kiss from the Christmas party all damned day. It had been a little more than he'd expected. He'd figured it would feel as staged as it was... except it hadn't felt that way at all. Her lips had been soft and yielding, and while he'd intended to give her something a smidgen longer than a peck, he hadn't pulled back... and neither had she.

Seth put the truck into gear and pulled away from the barn. He was tired and hungry, and it was time to go home. But he wasn't going to be able to reheat some leftovers and sit in the silent living room, beating himself up. He was going home to *her*.

What had happened last night? Because after some time to think today, he knew the kiss had gotten away from him. Was he that lonely? Was that what it was—kissing a woman again after so long? Feeling connected in the physical way that he'd been missing so much? Because having Gabby and the baby in his arms had felt so right. He'd been protective of her, but he'd felt something deeper, too, something he wasn't comfortable with. It was probably best to keep that emotional door tightly shut.

The gravel road was slick with snow. They did plow the roads when there was a good snowfall, but a lot of the accumulation got packed down into something close to ice after a while. He slowed as he came around a corner, then sped up again.

So maybe he'd been a *little* bit wrong in that kiss; he should have kept it short and sweet and chaste instead of giving in like that. He should apologize properly for that. Because all day long, he'd been remembering the feeling of her in his arms, her lips against his, the smell of her faint perfume, the glimmer in her eyes when he looked down at her...

He was doing it again. He shoved the memory back. The problem was, while he could accept that he had crossed a line, he couldn't quite regret it, either.

What they needed was a chance to get out together without the babies. Most married couples had date nights and that sort of thing, because it refreshed the friendship. No matter the kind of marriage, that foundation of friendship mattered! So if he wanted to solidify things with Gabby again, maybe getting out together would be the answer. Not a date, just…an outing.

It had been probably ten years since they'd gone riding together. The last time had been before he'd met Bonnie, and he and Gabby had gotten caught in a rainstorm. They were drenched when they got back, and they'd wrapped up in towels and heated up a can of mushroom soup to share between them. He could still remember the way her wet hair had looked smoothed away from her face, a fluffy white towel over her shoulders. She'd hogged the crackers for her soup, but he hadn't minded. It had just been something to tease her about.

Maybe Gabby would be game to go riding again. It might get them back into their comfort zone, away from the pressure of their new legal status of husband and wife.

His house came into view. The curtains were open and the inside glowed golden. He could see the Christmas tree in the front window, lights twinkling. He'd gotten used to coming back to a dark house, and he was almost scared to get used to domestic comfort again…a woman waiting for him.

He parked the truck in his regular place

in the carport. He was looking forward to seeing her. And the babies, too. It felt good to pack around the little tykes, look down into earnest little faces… He liked it.

Seth headed around to the side door and kicked the snow off his boots before letting himself in. The house smelled good—was that beef stew?

Gabby was standing by the counter as he peeled off his outerwear, her cell phone to her ear, and she looked over as he came in, but she didn't return his smile.

"…you said there'd been some sort of mis-understanding," Gabby was saying into the phone. She paused, listening.

"Wait…" She rubbed a hand over her fore-head. "But my mom was pregnant when you left—" She nodded, listening for a lit-tle longer. "Oh…" She shut her eyes. "Yeah, that's…understandable."

Her father? Seth's heart sped up, and he tried to catch her eye, but she turned away from him. Right—she might want some pri-vacy for this. Seth watched her for a mo-ment, then headed to the living room, where the babies were in their bouncy chairs facing the Christmas tree. Beau and Aiden were asleep, their faces turned toward each other, but Andy was wide-awake, those round brown eyes blinking up at the tree.

"Hey, buddy," Seth said softly, squatting down next to him. "How're you doing?"

Andy waved a little fist, and Seth scooped him up and settled him against his chest. Andy smelled of baby powder and milk. Seth smiled down at the little guy.

"That tree is something, huh? Well, I've got news for you, kid. Santa's coming, and that's going to be really exciting. Just wait until you get old enough to wrap your mind around that."

He looked back in the kitchen again, where Gabby stood with her back to him.

"Yeah, thanks," she was saying. "I appreciate you telling me this… No, no…it's better to know the truth, right…? Yeah… You, too. Merry Christmas."

Gabby hung up the call, but didn't turn. She stood frozen in the center of the kitchen.

"Gabs?" he said softly.

She turned then. He hadn't known what he'd expected to see on her face, but she looked calm. Too calm. He came into the kitchen.

"That sounded like it was your dad," he said.

"It was… I mean…" She swallowed. "It

was the man I was looking for, but he's not my father."

"What?" Seth couldn't help the incredulity in his tone. "It sounded like—"

"Oh, he's the right guy," she said, the calm starting to crack. "He's just not my biological father."

"How does he figure?" Seth asked.

"Hank and Mom were having a lot of marriage problems, and they hadn't been… intimate…in about six months. He said maybe longer. So when Mom told him she was three months pregnant with me, Hank was absolutely positive he wasn't my father. That's why he left."

Andy wriggled in Seth's arms, and he readjusted the baby, his mind spinning. Someone was lying, Carol or Hank. And he'd never heard a good thing about Hank, so he knew who *he* suspected.

"Do you believe that?" he asked after a moment. "Because I've known of guys who claimed kids weren't theirs in order to avoid the child support. It's cowardly and cheap, but it happens."

"I think he's telling the truth," she said.

"Why?"

"Because he felt awful. He has a wife and three kids now. He said he had no idea

I was raised believing he was my dad. He said it felt cruel to him, and that was why he wanted to talk to me over the phone, to make sure I was okay."

"And you think your mother lied to you for the last thirty years?" he asked. "Did he say who your father was?"

She shook her head. "Hank said he knows, but it wasn't fair to my mom to tell me that. He said she should be able to tell me about that in her own words."

That did seem rather noble of the guy, Seth had to agree—grudgingly.

"To top it off, he told me that my mom is a good person," Gabby went on. "He said that he wasn't a good husband back then, and that their divorce gave him the kick in the pants he needed to pull his life together and revaluate a lot of things, namely, how he treated the women in his life."

"So he's grown and changed?" Seth muttered.

"Apparently." Gabby heaved a sigh. "I did believe him while he was saying it, but Seth, I find it really hard to wrap my mind around my mother cheating on someone. She's not the type."

"Was there anything that didn't quite add up when you were growing up?" Seth asked.

"Um…" She shrugged weakly. "I don't know. Isn't that just life? Lots of things don't add up."

"Like what?" he asked.

"I mean, lots of things don't make a lot of sense on the surface," she said. "You need more details to understand."

Seth frowned. "Not really. The truth normally sounds like the truth. It's pretty rare when something sounds like a lie and it turns out to be true. In my experience, at least."

Andy started to whimper, so Seth eased him into his mother's arms. Gabby smoothed a hand over Andy's downy hair, then looked up at Seth.

"Mom always said I shouldn't look for my father because he didn't care about us," Gabby said. "And she stood by that. I used to wonder why she wouldn't let me at least see the jerk he was, but she said it wasn't worth it."

Seth met her gaze. "But you believed your mom, obviously. It's understandable."

"When you love someone, you believe their version of things. That's loyalty," she said, then shook her head. "Maybe I wanted to believe Mom's version. I don't know. It was easier to resent him than to believe my own mother might be lying to me."

"*If* she was…" Seth scrubbed a hand through his hair. "He could be the liar. Some people are awfully good at it."

"Don't I know it," Gabby said with a sigh. "Most of my boyfriends have been accomplished liars."

Seth didn't know how to answer that. She always had been attracted to the wrong kind of guy, and he'd hated that. She deserved so much better than she'd been willing to accept.

"What am I supposed to do, demand a DNA test?" she asked bitterly. "Mom was the one who loved me and raised me. She was the one who was there for me. She's my family, not the man who might be my biological dad, but was never in my life."

"I agree," he said. "Maybe she'll have some insights. I know you're being facetious about the DNA test, but maybe you should get one, just to put your own mind at ease."

"He isn't supposed to matter!" Gabby said, tears welling in her eyes. "I told myself he didn't—everyone told me he didn't! He wasn't a part of our family. He dumped us. Whether he acknowledges me or not isn't supposed to affect my balance! But he does matter, after all. Maybe he did all along."

"What do you need right now?" Seth asked quietly.

"I guess I need to go talk to my mom," she said.

"Is she home?"

"She should be soon." Gabby pressed a kiss on the top of Andy's head, but her chin trembled.

"You want to leave the triplets with me and go talk to her?" Seth asked.

"You'd be okay?" she asked hesitantly.

"Gabs, I'll be fine," he said. "I can do diapers, I can do bottles and I can hold them. I might not be able to do anything else while I'm at it, but I can cover the necessities."

"That would be nice, Seth. You're very sweet."

"I'm your husband," he said, lowering his voice. "This is part of the job description."

Gabby smiled wanly. "You really did get yourself the short end of the stick on this, didn't you?"

"Nah," he said. "Here, give me Andy. You go ahead and see your mom. I'm sure you'll get the answers you're looking for."

Gabby slid Andy back into Seth's arms, her warmth emanating against his biceps for a moment while she kissed her son's head once more. She smelled like the savory stew she'd been cooking. He wished he could hug her, but he wasn't the one who'd make her feel better.

"We'll be right here when you get back," Seth said. This was what he could offer—stability for both her and these boys. They were safe with him.

GABBY HAD FORTY minutes of driving to revisit Hank's words. She didn't feel entirely comfortable referring to him as her father, even mentally. Either he was not her biological dad or he was—and such an accomplished liar that it was staggering. Either way, he wouldn't be the man she'd been mentally creating in her mind all these years. She wanted the whole story, once and for all.

When she got to her mother's building, she turned off the car and sat there for a moment. This conversation was going to change everything. Funny—she'd always assumed that it would be a conversation with her father that would do that. Or maybe the conversation she'd just had with him had already started the transformation.

Gabby got out of the car. The sun had sunk behind the western peaks, and the streetlights glowed golden. Her breath hung in the air in front of her in a cloud. When she got to the front door of her mother's apartment building, she punched in the buzzer code and waited.

"Hello?" Carol's voice crackled over the fuzzy line.

"Hi, Mom, it's me," Gabby said.

"Gabby? Do you need help with the babies?"

"No, I'm alone."

"Okay. Come on up, sweetie."

There was a buzz and the door unlocked. Gabby went inside, peeling off her gloves as she made her way to the elevator. By the time she got to her mother's door, it was already ajar, and Gabby let herself in.

"Hi, Mom!" she called.

"Hi, sweetie," Carol said. She came out, wearing a bathrobe and a towel on her head. She cast Gabby a smile. "Where are the babies?"

"At home with Seth," Gabby said. She shut the door and took off her boots. "I wanted to come alone."

"That's nice," Carol said. "Just the two of us. How's married life?"

Gabby sighed. "Fine."

"So not fine." Carol's face fell. "Gabrielle, it's going to be hard. It just is! But you've got to stick with it. Seth's a good one. He's nothing like your dad, and—"

"Mom, I meant it. It's fine," Gabby said, interrupting. "Seth is the ideal husband— sweet, accommodating, great with the boys…" She swallowed. "I came for something else, actually."

"Oh…" Carol eyed her uncertainly. "You okay? You aren't pregnant again, are you?"

"No!" Gabby looked down at herself. "Do I look pregnant?"

"Not a bit," Carol said. "Maybe I should stop guessing and you should just tell me what's wrong."

"I contacted Hank Rogers."

Carol's expression froze, and then fell. She licked her lips. "When?"

"A few days ago. I found a Hank A. Rogers working at a marketing firm in California. I took the chance and emailed him…"

"Was it him?" Carol asked breathlessly.

Gabby nodded. "Yeah, it was."

Silence stretched between them for a couple beats. Gabby wondered what her mother was thinking, because she stood there with her hands clutched in front of her, sucking in measured breaths as if she were doing a calming exercise or something.

"I see…" Carol said at last, and nodded toward the couch. "Maybe we should sit down, then."

Gabby shook her head. "I don't feel like sitting down, Mom."

"Gabby, just sit!" Carol's voice rose, then she sighed. "I'm sorry. Just sit."

Gabby went over to the couch and perched on the edge of it. She didn't want to relax. Something had changed at the mention of her father. This wasn't the same old tension about him.

"I know you didn't want me to contact him," Gabby said. "But I've spent years wondering about him, and I kind of needed to see what kind of man he was. Even the worst of him. I just needed to know. He's half of me, you know—"

"Is that what he said?"

"No," she admitted. "He said he wasn't my father."

"He isn't," her mother said woodenly.

"So he wasn't lying?" Gabby asked hesitantly.

Carol sank onto the couch next to Gabby and pulled the towel off her damp hair. "What did he tell you, exactly?"

"He said that he was certain he wasn't my dad," Gabby said. "He, um…he said that you and he hadn't been close in about six months, so when you found out you were pregnant with me, there was no question there. He knew that he wasn't the father."

Carol nodded thoughtfully. "Anything else?"

"I asked who my father was," Gabby said. "And he said I needed to talk to you about that."

"Did he…" Carol swallowed.

"So, Hank isn't my dad," Gabby said.

"No, he isn't." Carol sucked in a shaky breath. "Ted is."

Gabby stared at her mother in shock, the information skimming the surface of her heart and refusing to sink in. Ted was her father?

"I should probably start at the beginning," Carol said.

"Why did you let me believe that Hank was my father all this time, when—"

"Because it was better for you to think that your father was a cad than it was for you to know what I'd done!" Carol blinked back tears. "It was complicated—all of it. From start to finish."

"So Ted—my godfather—is my actual dad," Gabby said. The words felt foreign on her lips.

"Yes."

"If that's true, why all this stupid godfather business? Why didn't he just acknowledge me?" Gabby demanded, her mind finally seeming to catch up with the shock.

"Because he was married at the time. And so was I, obviously," Carol said. "Hank was hard to be married to. He was mean. He drank. He was awful in a lot of ways, and I was *so* unhappy. But I saw a lot of Ted because he and Hank were best friends. Ted kept telling Hank to treat me better, and I was so grateful to anyone who would stand up for me that our emotions got involved. Neither of us were proud of it.

"Before I found out I was pregnant, we'd already stopped the affair. Ted loved Ramona, and he wanted to focus on his life with her. And I didn't want to be the kind of woman who cheated on her husband—no matter what kind of a jerk he was to live with. But Hank was right—there was no question about him being the father."

"He said he left you when he found out," Gabby said.

"That's true." Carol smoothed her hand over her lap. "I mean, it took a little longer than that. We fought for a couple of weeks. He had it out with Ted and punched him in the face. And I called the cops on him for that, and he said I was choosing Ted over him, and…" She shrugged. "Then he left. He never came back."

"But Ted—" Gabby swallowed. "He obviously stuck around."

"He was your father," Carol said softly. "But Ramona was heartbroken. She hated me. She hated Ted. But those two did love each other, and after a while she calmed down a bit and she told him that it was all just so humiliating to live in the same town with me…and you. She knew that she couldn't demand that Ted give up his child. So we agreed to tell a story that made us all look a little better."

They'd covered up the truth, smoothed over the embarrassing mistakes, and told the town a version that was more palatable. And suddenly, it all made sense—Ted's dedication to all Gabby's school concerts, how he was like a dad in her life all these years, while Ramona was more distant. Seth had been right—it *was* weird. That wasn't a regular godfather relationship, was it?

"Did anyone else know the truth?" Gabby asked hesitantly.

"Ramona," Carol replied. "She knew, but it was better for her if no one else did. And Ted, of course."

"And Aunt Bea, I'm assuming," Gabby breathed.

"Yes. Ted needed to focus on his wife and marriage, and I needed someone else I could talk to about my feelings. So I let Bea in on the secret."

And they'd all kept it… They'd all let her believe that her father had walked away and never looked back. The realization was only slowly sinking in, and as it did, anger rose up to meet it.

"Do you have any idea what that did to me?" Gabby demanded. "Do you have any idea how it broke me to believe that my own father hadn't cared about my existence?"

"You had *me*!" Carol's voice shook.

"I also had a *father*!" she said, her voice rising in spite of herself. "I had a dad who, it turns out, was in my life this entire time!"

"And we made sure he'd be there for you," Carol said. "You had a father figure—"

"I had a *god*father," she retorted. "With some weird boundary issues, might I add! My God, do you know how many times I've heard people say that Ted was in a little too close for comfort? And every time they said something like that, I'd tell them that was the role of a good godfather. But they were right! That whole setup was weird!"

"That setup was your family!" Tears sparkled in her mother's eyes. "I did my best! Would it have been better to grow up knowing that you were the product of an affair? To have the whole town know it? Would you have preferred that?"

"You mean like my boys?" Gabby demanded. "Because the word is out on their parentage."

"No..." her mother breathed.

"Oh, yes. I saw Terry Schwartz in town, and she filled me in on all the stuff she'd heard. So my kids are going to grow up with everyone knowing how they came to be. I think they'll survive it."

"Well, I didn't think that *I* would," her mother said. "I made sure that Ted was in your life, that you had him there for a good role model. I let you believe that you were conceived inside a marriage. And there are a lot of kids who didn't know their fathers. I didn't think it would make that big of a difference. But if you'd thought I was some home-wrecking floozy—"

"You think my boys will think that?" she asked icily.

"You didn't know Craig was married, Gabby!" her mother shot back. "You were in the dark. You can fully and truthfully blame Craig. I couldn't do that. I chose to cheat on my husband with a married man. It was completely different."

"Maybe…"

"So now you know the truth, maybe you do think that of me." Carol straightened her spine as if she was bracing herself.

"No!" Gabby felt her eyes mist. "You made a mistake. I think that's forgivable, actually."

Carol looked over at her, a tear escaping down her cheek. "Do you *really*?"

"Oh, Mom…"

Gabby leaned over and wrapped her arms around her mother's neck. She clung to her, her face against Carol's damp hair. Her mom squeezed her back as she cried softly into Gabby's shoulder.

"I'm sorry," Carol whispered. "I'm sorry I lied. I was just so ashamed of myself."

"Hey, at least you had me." Gabby pulled back. "Right?"

"Yes." Carol gave a wobbly smile. "And I don't regret *you* for a second. But do you see how that might have been a tough one to explain to an inquisitive six-year-old? How I wished I'd never made the mistake that brought you into the world? I didn't want you to be messed up by my stupid choices or think I hadn't wanted you…"

If Gabby had grown up with that story, she'd likely have a whole new set of issues to untangle right about now. And her mother had had to make a choice on the story that would shape her daughter… Much like Gabby was trying to give her sons. A different story.

"Mom, you loved me," Gabby said.

"Heart and soul," Carol said, putting a hand on Gabby's cheek. "Down to the bone. You're a piece of me, Gabrielle. And I've only ever done my best."

Gabby had questions—oh, so many questions. But at least she no longer wondered why she wasn't loved. Because she had been, by both her parents. And she still was.

"I don't think I can call Ted 'Dad,'" Gabby said after a moment.

Carol shrugged. "I don't think Ramona would like it, even now. So it's not much of a problem, sweetie."

Gabby wiped tears from her cheeks. "So, I think it's time you told me the real story… like about my birth. And about my…father."

It was time for the whole truth.

CHAPTER THIRTEEN

SETH DID UP the last of the snaps on Beau's sleeper, then laid him in the crib next to his brothers. He'd fed them all, changed them all, cuddled them all, and this time he'd tackled dressing them, too, because there was no way he was going to put them to bed without their warm sleepers on. And he was wiped. Three babies at once was a huge job, and he had a whole new respect for Gabby's days with her sons.

Seth glanced at his watch. It was almost nine, and outside the sky was black. The moon shone fuzzily from behind some thin cloud cover, and Seth looked at it for a moment before he pulled the curtains shut. He flicked off the light, leaving just a soft night-light glowing, and Beau's cry started up. Seth felt a wave of wonder. Just a few days ago, he'd had trouble telling them apart just looking at them, and now he could tell by their cries.

"Hey, buddy…" Seth went back to the crib

and picked up the baby. Beau settled again once he was in Seth's arms, and he smiled down at the little guy. "You scared of the dark?"

Beau stared up at Seth with round, serious eyes. Yeah, Seth had things on his mind, too. He'd gotten a call from a cousin earlier this evening congratulating him on his marriage. And he'd stood there in the kitchen, the babies dozing in front of the Christmas tree and a bowl of savory beef stew in one hand, telling his cousin that married life was good, and he'd felt a sudden surge of guilt.

It was one thing to be in the house with Gabby. Her presence did something to the very walls, changing the space for the better. But with her gone, even with the changes she'd made around here—the Christmas tree, the fruit bowl on a different counter, a plate of Christmas cookies that always got refilled, no matter how many he swiped—it was like the old days crept back. And he looked around at the kitchen that he used to share with Bonnie.

This had been Bonnie's home—albeit one she hadn't necessarily wanted. Gabby was happy here, though. There were no arguments with her about where she'd rather live, and he felt guilt at enjoying these new comforts. Because if he'd been more attentive, if he'd stopped to look at things from Bonnie's point of view instead of just reacting and marching out on her, Bonnie might still be here. Heck, maybe he would have moved her to town and made her happy, or maybe they'd still be butting heads over rural life.

Instead of Gabby's sons in that crib, it might have been his little girl. She'd be a toddler… And life could have just carried on. He'd deserved the loneliness of his empty house. Going on to love three more babies, to enjoy the feminine presence of another woman in this home who really did enjoy being here wasn't fair to the family he'd lost.

Bonnie had deserved so much better. And Hazel hadn't even had a chance to sleep in this crib her daddy had assembled for her. Doing this for Gabby was one thing—she needed support, too. So did the triplets. But enjoying it this much…

A lump rose in his throat.

"You gotta sleep, big guy," Seth said huskily.

Beau's eyes drifted shut, and Seth felt a wave of protectiveness for this little boy. Maybe it was even love. It was hard not to feel something pretty profound for three little boys who needed so much. The thing with babies was they never asked to be brought into this world, but once they got here, they just begged to be loved. And who could resist?

He heard the growl of a car's engine outside, and he moved the curtain to see Gabby getting out of her vehicle. She was home, and Beau here had just drifted off. He brought Beau back to the crib and laid him down next to his brothers. Seth paused to look at them, all lined up together.

They were trusting him to be the man they needed him to be. It was all a baby could do.

He headed down the stairs and met Gabby. She shivered and stamped the snow off her boots before she bent down to take them off.

"They're all asleep," Seth said, and he glanced around the messy kitchen. "I'll clean this up. Sorry, I was maxed out with the babies."

She smiled tiredly. "I know the feeling."

"So, how did it go with your mom?" he asked.

"I learned a lot." Gabby took off her coat and hung it up, then came into the kitchen. She picked up a gingersnap from the plate on the table.

"Yeah?" Seth went and filled the kettle, then pulled open the dishwasher. He might as well get some of this cleaned up while she talked.

"First of all, Hank isn't my father," she said. "He wasn't lying about that."

Seth eyed her in surprise. "Really?"

"Ted is my dad," she said with a sigh, and she sank into a kitchen chair. "I had a father in my life the whole time... I had no idea. I thought my dad didn't want me."

"Ted..." Seth shook his head, trying to sort out these new details. "Why not just tell you?"

"Because he loved Ramona and it was incredibly embarrassing. So they all hid it. You were right, though. Ted's relationship to me was a bit weird for a godfather."

"Yeah..." He'd thought it was a little strange for Ted to be *that* close to Gabby. But this was a shock. "So what about Ramona, then? I mean, she was okay with Ted spending an awful lot of time with you, but not telling you the truth?"

"My mom said that when I was born, Aunt Bea was in the hospital room with her. And when I'd arrived, she called Ted and told him. Ted arrived to see me, but he had Ramona with him, and while Ted and Bea held me and counted my fingers and toes, Ramona had a heart-to-heart with my mom."

Seth frowned. "That sounds ominous. While she lay there in the hospital bed?"

"That's what she says," Gabby went on. "Ramona told my mother that she loved Ted, and she wasn't giving him up. She also wasn't going to hurt him by refusing to let him be in his daughter's life. But there would be no visits alone. Ramona would be there for it all."

"Was she?" Seth asked. "There for all of it, I mean."

"No," Gabby replied. "She must have realized that she could trust Ted, or else seeing me was just too painful for her. Whatever the reason, Ted ended up spending time with me alone most often, but he did stay devoted to his wife, so...it worked out for them."

Ted and Ramona had managed to get through the worst disaster that could befall a marriage, all because they loved each other too much to let their union fall apart. They'd soldiered on...

"Ted really loved her..." Seth said, and turned away, not sure he wanted to share the emotions coursing through him. He grabbed some dishes from the counter and started to load the dishwasher instead.

"Yeah. And I'm glad. At least my mom hadn't broken them up."

The dishwasher loaded, Seth turned back to Gabby and found her gaze locked on him. Her eyes were filled with conflicting emotion, and she looked pale and vulnerable. She stared at the half-eaten cookie in her hand, then put it on the table in front of her.

"Are you okay, Gabs?" Seth came back over to the table and pulled out a kitchen chair and sat down next to her. "This is shocking for me... I can't imagine how much it's shaken you."

"You know, it actually explains some things," she said quietly. "I put a lot of effort into explaining away our family oddities, but it turns out it was pretty simple, really."

He reached out and took her hand in his, running his thumb over her knuckles.

"But every single man in my life..." Her chin trembled. "Every one of them—they weren't what I thought. Boyfriends who lied to me, Craig who had an entire family hidden away from me... Ted who was supposed to be my godfather. Hank, who I spent the last twenty-odd years agonizing over because he hadn't loved me... None of them were who I thought they were."

"Except for me," Seth said quietly.

"That's true." She pulled her hand from his. "You were always a straight shooter. That's probably why you weren't my type."

Right. She'd never been attracted to him in that way. That shouldn't sting, but it did. Because he was finding himself feeling all sorts of things he didn't want to feel toward her these days, and it would be nice if he wasn't alone.

"How are you now?" he asked.

"I feel betrayed." She shook her head slowly. "I was lied to...a lot. I feel like I don't even know who I am anymore. I'm a mom now, and that changes everything. But even the stuff that messed me up has turned on its head. I can't even count on that stuff to stay constant."

Gabby laughed bitterly, and Seth smiled.

"I get it," he said.

"You know what I need?" she asked.

"What?"

"A day off. I need to just...think."

"How about riding?" he asked. "I have the afternoon off tomorrow, and I wanted to get out on horseback in those snowy fields and just...go. I was going to suggest you come with me, anyway. I was thinking it might do us both some good to go out, just the two of us, away from everyone else. Get our friendship back to where it was...before."

Gabby met his gaze, her expression brightening. "We have more babysitting offers than we know what to do with. We could make use of one."

"Is that a yes?" he asked hopefully.

"That would be perfect," she said. "I just need to process a bit, you know?"

"Yeah, I know."

He had to process his own stuff, and he realized wryly that this outing would be like a honeymoon, of sorts. Wasn't that what honeymoons were all about—a couple taking some time alone to get their balance again after a huge amount of change?

"I'm going to go to bed," Gabby said, standing up. "I'm so tired all of a sudden. And maybe I just need some time alone to think this all through."

"Okay," he said. "I get it."

Gabby cast him a smile and headed for the stairs. But Seth stayed where he was, sitting in that kitchen that was awash in memories all over again. This home didn't just belong to the past anymore. It was part of his future with Gabby, too, and he was feeling more excited about that lately. He had a family again. It brought a strange relief mingled with a burden of guilt.

Getting back to their easy friendship—that might help straighten out his emotions a little bit. He was the one man in Gabby's life who hadn't lied to her...and he wanted to keep it that way. He had to get these feelings under control.

"I'M NOT SURE I should be going," Gabby said, looking over at Seth, who stood by the door, ready to leave. His hat was on his head and he held a pair of leather gloves in one hand.

"Really?" Seth sighed.

The problem wasn't maternal guilt, although she could probably blame her change of heart on that. It was that keeping their friendship intact was incredibly important, and going out alone with him on horseback might not be the best way to make that happen. They'd gone riding together before and it had never been romantic—adventurous and fun, perhaps, but not romantic. He'd been the guy she could count on not to try for more, and she'd really valued that trait in Seth. He'd also been the man who knew her best.

Living together was changing things between them, though. And it wasn't just his kisses. It was her. If only Seth were a little less attractive... Last night she'd lain in bed trying to read another chapter of her book, but her thoughts had been filled with him. Not her confusion. Not all the lies she'd been told. *Him.*

Gabby was getting attached, falling for her oldest friend in ways that she had no right to. She'd meant it when she told him that she'd step back once he healed from his grief. And he *would* heal...and he'd fall in love again. She'd be better off with her heart intact so she could give her boys a loving and supportive godfather for the male influence they'd undoubtedly crave.

But going out riding with him? Her heart wasn't ready for this...

"It'll be fine, Gabby," Aunt Bea said with a smile. "I've really missed the boys since you left. I'll have a chance to snuggle them again. They'll be fed and dry when you get back. That's a promise."

"I know, but..." If only that were the problem.

"Dear." Bea's voice firmed and she angled her body away so that Seth couldn't hear her when she lowered her voice. "Time with your husband alone is a good thing. These boys will only be happier if their parents are happy and solid in their relationship, however you two define that. Now take a deep breath, and go out there and have a date with your husband."

"You know this isn't a regular marriage," Gabby whispered.

"I have no idea what your arrangement is after dark," Bea whispered back. "Nor is that my business. But you'd better be taking care of your friendship if you expect to raise these boys together harmoniously." Bea met Gabby's gaze for a moment. "Now go."

Gabby sighed. "I hate it when you're this right."

"You'll survive." Bea met her smile with one of her own. "Every couple has to learn this lesson. You've got to put your relationship first, or all of you will suffer. Go figure things out. You can't hide from him by doting on your sons."

"I'm not hiding!"

"I'm glad." Bea nodded. "Have a good time."

She was being kicked out of her own home, but Bea had a point. Whatever their arrangement, Gabby and Seth's friendship was required to maintain it. She couldn't just run away from uncomfortable feelings, not when she was living with the man. Gabby bent down to kiss her boys' downy heads once more, and then went to the door, where she stepped into her riding boots.

"It'll only be a few hours," Seth said. "Come on, this will be good for us."

She could only hope that it would be.

They got into a rusted red Chevy truck—one that was used for ranch work—and as they pulled away from the house and turned down the gravel road toward the barn, Gabby glanced over at him.

"How long since you've gone riding?" Seth asked.

"I went riding last year, before I got pregnant," she said. With Craig.

"So it's high time you got on a horse. There are some trails through the forest that are really beautiful this time of year." Seth grinned. "It's time for us to have some fun, Gabs."

And there was something about his smile—happy, relaxed—that started to undo a few of the knots inside her, too.

Seth parked outside the barn and led the way around to the corral, where two saddled horses waited. One was a black stallion, the other a golden-brown mare. The horses' breath hung in clouds in front of them, and the mare shook her head with a snort as they approached.

"Do you really think this is a good idea?" Gabby asked.

Seth held open the gate for her until they were both inside the corral, and then he locked it again.

"It's an excellent idea," he said.

"I mean, for us—for our balance," she clarified. Was he feeling what she was feeling? That was what she wanted to know.

"Out there with family, with an audience," he said slowly, "we have to keep up appearances. We have to pretend we're something we aren't. And I think that getting away from all of that, just being us again, will help."

She met his gaze, then licked her lips. "So...you're feeling like things are off between us, too?"

"Yeah." He shrugged. "And I think getting away from it all is the answer. I'd take you on a honeymoon if I could—"

"*That* wouldn't help," she said with a low laugh.

"No one else would know. They might just assume we were two good friends," he said. "We could even pocket the wedding rings until we got back."

Gabby looked down at her hand—at the golden band shining in the watery winter sunlight.

"You know what? Let's do that," he said. "Take your ring off."

The suggestion sent a thrill through her. "What...now?"

"For today it's just us. We're going riding." He worked his own wedding ring off his hand and pushed it into his jeans pocket. "There. I feel better already."

Gabby felt the smile tickle her lips, and she followed his lead and pulled off her ring. It felt strange to take it off, and she looked at it for a moment before she tucked it into her own pocket, out of sight. He was right—they needed a little vacation from this marriage of theirs.

"This is Misty," he said, handing her the mare's reins. "Now, let's ride!"

Seth, on the back of his black stallion, led the way out of the corral and down the gravel road toward the tree line. Gabby's mount was a gentle animal, and she reached forward to pat the mare's neck. As she did, she caught sight of her left hand, now bare, and she felt a surprising surge of discomfort.

She pulled her fingers into a fist and straightened. If she didn't like the missing wedding ring, then it was probably a good exercise to be without it for a little while. Because that wedding ring was for health insurance, and that was all. She pulled her gloves out of her coat pocket and put them on.

"I got our Christmas tree down here," Seth said over his shoulder. "Mr. Ross doesn't mind. He chops his down from the same area. We plant a few saplings in the summer in the hope of getting the perfect sized Christmas tree in a few years."

"Speaking of Christmas, what should I get you?" she asked.

"Keep it cheap," he replied with a grin.

She chuckled. "That might be easier said than done. I don't know what to get you. I wrapped up some baby clothes to put under the tree for the boys. And that package of new soothers. It's just nice to get a few packages under there, you know?"

"What do *you* want for Christmas?" Seth asked. He slowed down a little as she caught up, and their horses continued side by side.

"Formula," she said with a rueful smile.

"Yeah, we covered that," he said.

"I have everything I need, Seth," she said.

"People will ask," he said quietly.

"Then we'll tell them we got each other

something private, and they'll assume all sorts of intimate things without us having to be too specific. My name on your insurance is all I could ever want. I'm serious."

Seth reined his horse left, through the deep snow toward the trees. He ducked his head when a shower of flakes fell from the branches of an evergreen as he passed beneath it. Gabby tucked her chin down, too, as she followed him, the spray of snow misting her face.

"I'm getting you a gift," Seth said, glancing back. His voice was low and gruff. "When people ask what I got my wife, I'm not lying."

Maybe she was tired of lies and half-truths, too. "Do you know what I'd really like for Christmas?"

Seth reined his horse in, and she came up beside him again. Her horse stamped her hooves against the snowy ground and snorted.

"What do you want?" Seth asked, and those dark eyes met hers with a strange directness.

"A book of poetry," she admitted.

"Yeah?"

She sort of expected him to laugh, but he didn't. He just looked at her.

"In the hospital, when I was sitting in the NICU, I had all this time to kill, and someone had left behind a book of Robert Frost's poetry. I liked it."

"I could do that," he said softly.

"So…what do you want, then?" she asked. "I need something specific. I'm too tired to be creative."

She also didn't trust herself to get the tone of the gift right for their relationship, either. She'd get something either too flippant or too intimate. They weren't ready for gifting—at least she wasn't.

"I wanted a picture of you and the boys," he said, and looked away. "For, um, my wallet."

"Really?" she said softly.

He was serious. Silence stretched between them for a moment, and she reached out and put a hand on his sleeve.

"I mean…" He looked back. "Yeah. Really. You're mine…in a way, right? We belong to each other. And I'm their stepdad, and I…" Color crept up in his cheeks.

He wanted to put a photo of them in his wallet, and the realization was so sweet that she nearly crumbled. No man had ever put a photo of her in his wallet…or even had a picture of her on his desk.

"Maybe that's dumb," he said, when she hadn't answered.

"No," she said quickly. "It's not. It's... sweet."

"I don't know how to do this!" He swiveled in his saddle toward her with more energy than she expected. "I don't know how to be your husband, but not care too much. I don't know how to be a dad to your boys but not feel something for all four of you!"

"Feel what?" she breathed, and she closed her fingers over the material of his jacket.

"I don't know...protective, I guess. I want to keep you all safe, give you everything you need. I want to..." He stopped and didn't finish the thought.

She was about to pull her hand back, but something stopped her. Was it so terrible to have this big cowboy want to protect them? She swallowed, and he put his hand over hers on his arm, pinning her to him.

"Want to what?" she whispered.

"I want to kiss you."

Her breath caught, and she opened her mouth to say something, but she couldn't think of anything. He wanted to kiss her... Did he have any idea how often she'd played his kiss over in her mind? His touch, his lips, the way he'd dipped back down and pecked her lips afterward, as if he weren't quite willing to stop...

Gabby dropped her gaze. "No rings, remember? Let's forget that we're married. Let's just be us."

Because maybe then he wouldn't want to kiss her, and she could push back the memories of his warm lips, his arms pulling her closer...

"I am just being me," he said. "I don't know how to look at you and the boys and not feel like you're becoming the reason for every hour I work, the reason why I hurry a bit at the end of the day so I can get home a few minutes sooner..."

His voice was bare, raspy, honest...and she raised her gaze to meet his once more. Of all the men in her life, Seth was the one she could trust to tell her truth—even when it was hard for him, even when he didn't know how to put it into words. It was a very attractive quality, she realized in a rush.

Seth leaned toward her, the saddle creaking with his movement, and he stopped a few inches away from her. His gaze flickered down toward her lips, and before she could think better of it, she tugged at his sleeve and lifted herself up on her stirrups so that her lips met his.

Her eyes fluttered shut, and for a moment it was just the two of them, the cold rush of winter wind and the warmth of their breath mingling together. When she pulled back, Seth's gaze was locked on her.

"Sorry..." she breathed.

Seth smiled, a faint half smile that tugged up only one side of his mouth. "For what?"

She felt the heat rise in her face. "I shouldn't have..."

"Gabby, we're feeling something—" Seth sucked in a deep breath. "And it's not just due to the legalities of our relationship."

But whatever they were feeling wouldn't last. He was starting to get his balance back, and she wouldn't lock him down. He was giving her a selfless gift in this ability to feed her children, and she wouldn't take advantage of his generous, but wounded heart.

"Robert Frost wrote a poem about being in the woods on a snowy evening," she said, licking her lips. "And the last lines are 'But I have promises to keep, and miles to go before I sleep.' And I feel like that, right now. We're at the very start of whatever this is. We have miles to go, Seth, and if we mess it up now..."

"We're not messing it up," he said gruffly.

"You sure?" Her voice shook.

Seth didn't answer that, and she felt tears prick her eyes. He was trying to take care of her because she had the babies now and she needed a little protection. But she needed to take care of him, too, because he'd lost everything two years ago, and he was still putting himself back together. She could see things he might not just now. But his silence suggested that he might see more of those pitfalls, after all.

"Let's ride," he said after a few beats of silence. He urged his horse forward, and she followed, ducking her head again to miss a snowy bough.

She'd promised Seth that they'd keep to their agreement. She wasn't supposed to be complicating his emotional life. He'd given her enough, and she could not ask for his heart, too. She pulled off her gloves and straightened her spine so she could reach into her pocket, and she pulled out the golden band, slipping it back onto her finger.

She needed the reminder—not of marriage, but of vows.

CHAPTER FOURTEEN

THE REST OF the trail ride was a quiet one, with horses' hooves plodding softly along the snowy path. She could hear the cry of an eagle, but she couldn't see it through the snow-laden trees. And while she rode behind Seth's mount, Gabby chastised herself for that kiss.

She'd done it because it felt right… In the moment, at least. But she couldn't be toying with their already complicated emotions. He'd said he wanted to kiss her, but he was grieving his wife. She was still trying to figure out what had been true and what hadn't been in every single story she'd heard in her childhood. They both had wounds they were healing from, but his simple request of a picture for his wallet had tugged at her heart. He wanted to protect her, and oh, how she longed to be protected. But that was the same feeling that had drawn her toward the older, more experienced Craig. She couldn't trust her own longings to lead her straight.

Either she was drawn to the wrong man or she was drawn to messing things up.

They headed back toward the barn, and by the time they had unsaddled and brushed the horses down, the sun had fully set, leaving a smudge of red along the western horizon.

They drove the truck back to the house, and when Seth parked, the lights in the cab came on. Gabby glanced over at him. He looked tired. It had been good to get out together, but the result hadn't been quite as helpful as she'd hoped. She'd wanted to feel that camaraderie again with her buddy, not that strange, growing attraction that kept building between them.

"Don't forget your wedding ring," she said.

"Right." He straightened so he could pull it out of his pocket, and he looked down at the band for a moment before sliding it back onto his finger. "Let's get in there."

Seth pushed open the truck door, and Gabby could hear the cry of one of the babies. Her heart immediately clenched, and she hopped out of the truck, slammed the door and headed around the side of the house to the side door.

Bea stood in the kitchen with a cloth over one shoulder and a crying Beau in her arms. Aiden and Andy were in their bouncy chairs, and while they were fussing a little, they weren't howling like Beau was.

"You're back!" Bea smiled tiredly. "I think they missed you."

Gabby took off her coat and boots and accepted Beau from her aunt. He pushed his little face into her neck, but he still wailed. Apparently, he wouldn't forgive her quite so easily. Gabby tipped her cheek against his head and shushed him softly.

"Mommy's home..." she crooned, and then she smiled over at Bea. "Thank you for watching them."

"Not at all. And I'll gladly watch them again," Bea said.

Seth came into the kitchen and crouched down in front of the other two in their bouncy chairs. "Are they fed yet? Changed?"

"Yes," Bea said. "You're catching on, aren't you, Seth?"

"Sink or swim," he said, but a smile tugged at the corners of his lips.

Just then, Andy started to cry, and Seth unbuckled him from his chair and picked him up.

"Dear, before I leave," Bea said, turning to Gabby, "I wanted to invite you and Seth over tomorrow night."

Another family event. They'd barely gotten through the Christmas party at his aunt's place, and she wasn't sure her heart could handle another evening of Seth as the doting husband. Besides, she was tired tonight.

"Oh...you know, Bea, we've been so busy..." Gabby started, and then she saw Bea's expression turn sheepish.

"It's a baby shower," Bea admitted. "And a bit of a wedding shower, too. We're covering all our bases with one big party to make sure you're set up. I was supposed to ask you before, but we got a bit sidetracked with Hank and all that... Your mom wanted it to be a surprise, but this close to Christmas, maybe that was silly. Everyone's coming. We didn't want to wait until after the holidays because you'll need baby things now, and..." Bea's voice trailed off. "You'll come, won't you? Both of you."

It would be a wonderful help in getting ready for growth spurts and the like. She'd been so focused on formula, but she needed all the baby accoutrements times three.

"That's really kind," Gabby said with a smile. "Thank you. What do you think, Seth?"

She turned toward him, and saw he looked mildly panicked with the wailing baby in his arms. He looked at Gabby, then down at the infant.

"We'll be there," Seth said, raising his voice over Andy's wail. "Thank you, Bea."

"I'll let you two take over, then," Bea said, heading for the door. "The party starts at seven. I'll tell them I ruined the surprise, so no need to pretend."

Gabby laughed softly. "Okay...thanks! See you tomorrow, Auntie."

Bea left, and Gabby smoothed a hand over Beau's downy head. His cries weren't quite so insistent now, but he still hadn't settled.

"It's nice of them to throw us a baby shower," Gabby said. "With three boys, there's just so much I hadn't even thought of getting yet."

"What's family for?" Seth said.

Just then, Aiden's little lip quivered and he started to cry, too. That was three for three, and Gabby looked over at Seth.

"Thank you for being here," she said.

"In my kitchen?"

"*Here*. Holding babies. Changing diapers, being so supportive," she said. "You mean the world to me, you know that?"

The words came out before she could think better of them, but they were honest. His friendship meant more to her than her own longing for something deeper. Because here she was in the kitchen with her wailing babies, and he was right next to her. Like he'd promised to be. She felt the heat rise in her cheeks.

"Let's take them upstairs," she said. "They might be easier to get into bed once they settle if we're already up there."

"Sure." Seth nodded. "You're better at this than I am."

Gabby took Beau and Aiden upstairs, with Seth behind with Andy in his arms. The babies continued to cry, their plaintive wails resounding through the house. Gabby heaved a sigh as she walked into the bedroom.

"Let's do diapers once more," she suggested. "See if that helps."

For the next hour, they soothed, rocked and snuggled the babies. When one would settle, the others would take up crying again. But Seth was surprisingly patient through the whole ordeal. Maybe it was that he wasn't their mother; his heart didn't pull toward three sobbing babies at once. She was glad for his help.

Aiden and Beau finally fell asleep, and she and Seth put the babies into the crib. Andy fought sleep a little while longer, and

Gabby paced the room, back and forth, patting his diapered bottom gently. Seth sank onto the side of her bed with a sigh.

"You want me to try?" he asked.

"We're almost there…" she whispered, not wanting to ruin any progress she was making. Andy paused his crying to yawn, and this time he didn't start up again. He blinked a couple times before his eyes drifted shut. "There we go."

"Nice," Seth said with a tired smile. He dropped back, his arms spread over the mattress. "That was a marathon tonight."

Gabby rocked Andy for another minute to make sure he was sleeping, then settled him into the crib next to his brothers. Seth patted the bed next to him.

"We need two more cribs," he said quietly.

We. Funny how natural that sounded tonight. Gabby went over to the bed and sank into it next to Seth. She leaned her head against his solid shoulder, inhaling the scent of him—horses, hay, a bit of aftershave. He was comforting for more than the babies.

"We do…" she said. "Do we go to town to get them, or—"

"I ordered this crib online," Seth said. He closed his eyes. "Granted, it was a couple of years ago, but I could probably find them again. They were shipped here to the ranch. It was surprisingly simple."

"Simple sounds good," she admitted.

"I'll place an order tomorrow," he said, but his voice sounded thick, groggy.

Easy as that. She didn't need to look at her bank account, try to find some cheaper option… He'd order two more cribs.

"Thank you, Seth."

Seth sucked in a deep breath, his breathing coming more evenly. "What are husbands for?"

Husbands were for more than providing, that was for sure. But she was deeply grateful all the same, and she wouldn't be taking him for granted. She could feel the steady beat of his heart against her shoulder and she shifted a little to get more comfortable, pressing her cheek against that soft bit of muscle between his shoulder and his chest.

She let her eyes drift shut, listening to his regular breathing. It had been a long time since she'd lain in bed like this next to a man, and she considered nudging him, waking him up. But it was early still, and this was just a catnap. It was okay to be comfy for a little while…

Then sleep took her.

SETH DREAMED OF Christmas lights. He was wrapping them around a tree out in the forest. He had an ax with him, but somehow he didn't feel like he needed to chop the tree down. Instead, he was putting lights on it—lights that were inexplicably glowing out there in the middle of a forest with no electricity. In his dream, he wondered where they were plugged in, and his gaze followed that string of glowing lights, winding down a path, around trees, across a frozen stream, until the twinkling lights disappeared.

I need a Christmas tree for my little girl, he was thinking. *She'll want a tree.*

She was old enough to like lights and trees, Santa letters and gifts. And he felt that solemn obligation to bring her just that—the kind of Christmas childhoods were made of.

But Hazel wasn't with him in that forest. He was alone, and he kept winding the lights around the tree, nestling them into the spruce branches, into the icy layer of accumulated snow. For her, for his little girl.

It seemed to go on for some time, and as he slowly woke up, the light from those bulbs faded away, the boughs of the tree evaporated. As he gradually came up to the surface of slumber, he could hardly remember the dream anymore. Just a strange feeling that he needed to do something, and it was important.

Seth lay on his side, one arm caught beneath a warm weight. He absently reached out and wrapped his other arm around someone, pulling her closer. She smelled soft and floral, and a tangle of her silken hair brushed up against his face. She felt good there—warm and sweet—and he tugged her closer still, inhaling the scent of her hair.

Wait...

He woke up fully then, realizing in a rush where he was. His arm was still close around her, feeling the rise and fall of her rib cage as she slept. Gabby felt so warm in his arms. She fit perfectly against his chest, and she leaned toward him in unconscious response to his touch. He shut his eyes again for a moment, allowing himself the luxury of having this woman in his arms.

How did he end up like this? He racked his brain, searching for answers. They must have fallen asleep atop the covers, and in their sleep, they'd rolled into this position— spooning on the edge of the bed.

Shoot. What was he doing? He looked toward the window and the splash of moonlight that fell across the changing table. He pulled his arm out from under her—most of it at least—and pushed himself up onto his elbow.

Gabby's golden hair was in a tangle, and her face looked milky in the glow of the moonlight. Her long lashes touched her cheek, and her mouth was open slightly, her breath coming slow and deep. She was tired; he could feel it in how heavily she slept. But my God, she was beautiful...

She had faint freckles on the bridge of her nose—how had he never noticed those before? She was lovely... *His wife.*

In all the rules of social convention, lying here next to the woman he'd married was perfectly acceptable. Holding himself back with her was getting harder and harder. Lying here next to her, watching her chest rise and fall with each breath, he was so tempted to just relax and pull her close, to let her sleep against him, to stroke her hair and feel her breath against his neck.

That would feel good...but she was trusting him to abide by their agreement, even when she slept. Maybe even especially when she slept. And what felt right in the light of the moon felt very different in daylight.

Seth eased himself the rest of the way free. The room was silent, except for the creak of bedsprings as he pushed himself up and over her, his feet landing on the floor.

He didn't belong here, wrapping his arms around her, listening to the quiet sounds of sleep. This was her space, and he was intruding.

He tiptoed to the crib and looked down. The babies were all sleeping soundly—for how much longer before they got hungry was anyone's guess. He ran his hand over the wooden crib rail, remembering how excited he'd been when he'd put this crib together. He was a different man back then—so oblivious to how much life could hurt. He'd been fully expecting to lay his baby girl in this crib.

And now it was filled with growing little boys.

It should be used, and he was happy they could use it. But he did miss the little girl he'd been able to hold only once. He missed her so much sometimes that his whole chest ached, and at this time of night, he seemed to remember her most clearly. It wasn't how she'd looked in his arms that he recalled, it was the crushing love that he'd felt for her— the terrible weight that he'd carry with him for the rest of his life. Someone had said that grief wasn't a loss of love so much as the weight of love with nowhere to go.

Seth swallowed against a lump rising in his throat and continued on out of the room, shutting the door gently behind him. Before Gabby came here to live, he used to leave that door shut, as if by closing it, he could lock the memories behind it. Looking in and seeing the empty crib and the piles of folded baby blankets had hurt too much to bear. Now, he was closing the door on his new family—the woman he dared not fall in love with, and the babies he'd raise as his own.

And even with the room so full of life and possibility, his heart still yearned for a tiny girl named Hazel.

Seth stood in the dark hallway for a moment, tempted to go straight to bed and crash. But the babies would wake and Gabby would have to get up to feed them. The least he could do was prepare some bottles and leave them in the fridge for her.

And maybe while he was down there, he could turn on the Christmas lights and look at that little pink ornament for his baby girl's first Christmas.

This Christmas would a first for more than just the triplets. It would be the first Christmas that he celebrated after losing

Hazel Marie and Bonnie, the first Christmas of his new marriage, the first Christmas where he let himself enjoy the glow of festive lights, even when his heart was heavy with love that had nowhere to flow.

Maybe it was all right to celebrate some good in the world while a man's heart was still damaged and bruised. Celebrating the good didn't negate the pain, but it might make it easier to bear.

CHAPTER FIFTEEN

SETH WOKE UP the next morning feeling lonesome. Waking the night before with Gabby in his arms had sparked a longing inside him. He was lonely. He wanted a family, yes... But he was starting to feel like a husband and father with Gabby and her boys—and he couldn't shake the guilt of Bonnie's worries. Was he proving her right?

So he poured himself into his work that day, trying to sweat out whatever it was he was feeling for Gabby. This hadn't been the plan—and yet, now that they were here, what was wrong with it? They were married, weren't they? They could be more to each other, if they wanted to be. It hadn't started earlier, even if Bonnie wouldn't have believed that. But he was innocent there, no matter how damning this looked.

He'd been willing to be a husband to his best friend and keep it strictly on a friendship level, but why not deepen that a little bit? He hadn't wanted his desire to take over, so he'd held back from touching her or cuddling her. But if she wanted the same thing, couldn't their arrangement grow a little bit? Was desire such a terrible addition to their marriage? She'd kissed him, too, so he knew that she felt this.

He finished up his work an hour early, then headed back to the house. When he kicked the snow off his boots and went inside, he found the kitchen empty. The oven was on, and the smell of roasting chicken filled the house. He took off his coat and boots, then peeked into a couple pots on the stove, finding rice and vegetables.

"Gabs?" he called.

"Upstairs!"

He paused. Was that an invitation to go on up, or was she just letting him know where she was?

He headed up the stairs, but stopped short when he got to the top. The bathroom door was open, and the warm smell of shampoo filled the hallway. He was about to retreat when she emerged from the bathroom, her bathrobe on and a towel wrapped around her head. Her cheeks were flushed, and she shot him a smile. His breath caught. She was just so…womanly. And standing there in his own hallway, he was half afraid to step closer.

"Hi." She padded barefoot toward her bedroom. "You're back early."

"Yeah, I managed to finish everything up already. I skipped lunch, since we had this thing tonight."

"You're kind of looking forward to this, aren't you?" she asked.

"I'm, uh…" He smiled uncomfortably. "I guess I want to make it up to you after last time."

"That…" She winced. "I may have over-reacted there."

"Yeah?" he asked uncertainly.

"I was just…" She sighed. "I like things the way they are between us. I don't want to change it! And you know I don't want to find someone I fall for again, because I don't trust myself, and I don't trust the guys I'm attracted to. But it's a very elemental part of me that longs to feel all those heady, roman-tic feelings. I don't trust them a bit, but…" She shrugged. "I know my weakness."

"You keep telling me I'll fall in love again," he said quietly. "I dare say you will, too."

"No, I have good reason to stay clear of that," she said with a sad smile.

"No better than mine," he replied.

"It's just taking me some time to separate a life with a man from the romance," she said quietly. "But I'll get there."

"You know how ironic it is that we're trying to do this, right?" he asked. "Most couples are trying to find that romance, not run from it. I mean, that kiss when we were riding—that *was* us just being us…"

Gabby dropped her gaze. "No, that was me being silly. Seth, you don't want romance with me!"

"Our kisses are pretty nice, and falling asleep with you, having breakfast with you… I want more of it."

"But here's the thing," she said. "You want more of it until you reach your limit of what you can give, because your heart is already taken. And I'll want more than you can give, which will make me frustrated, and we'll start fighting. Or maybe it'll be the other way around—you'll want me to be a regular, loving wife, but I come with a whole heap of baggage! I've been lied to by every man in my life but you. Every single one! Romantic expectations take a strong friendship and turn it upside down, and I think if we start this, we'll look back and realize we were better as friends."

She was right, of course. And there were some relationships that couldn't be rewound to an earlier, more comfortable state. Their arrangement wasn't something to be played with.

"Okay," he said.

"Really okay?" she asked earnestly. Behind her in the bedroom, one of the babies let out a moan in his sleep, and they both looked toward the open door.

"I'll have to be." But he smiled to let her know there were no hard feelings. She was right—he wanted the comforts of a wife, but his heart didn't even feel like it was his to give. And it was hardly fair.

"So, how do you want to do this party, then? You weren't crazy about my good-husband behavior the other night, so—"

"Let's just try to act more natural," she said.

"You aren't worried about what people will say anymore?" he asked.

"If they want to gossip, they'll gossip. I can't control that," she said. "I think we have something good here—and they'll never know the details. So if they want to wonder, let them."

"Yeah, I agree," he said. "Whatever we make of this marriage, that's our business."

She smiled. "So let's just act like us, then. No playacting for appearances. You okay with that?"

He nodded. "That would be a lot easier."

But his feelings for her *were* deepening, and his "natural" still might not be in line with her expectations.

She nodded toward the bathroom. "The shower's free." Then she disappeared into her bedroom, her voice filtering out into the hallway. "I'm just going to get dressed."

Her door shut.

Gabby deserved more than he could offer right now, and it was selfish of him to suggest that she settle for what he could give. At least she could see that clearly, even if he couldn't always.

THE BABY-AND-WEDDING-COMBINED shower was held at Bea's place, and when Seth pulled to a stop in front of the house, he could count another four vehicles already there. The driveway and that path leading to Bea's front door had been shoveled, and he could see a wreath of blue balloons bobbing in the front window. His stomach tightened, and he forced himself to inhale a deep breath.

He looked over at Gabby. She tucked her hair behind her ear, exposing her pale neck.

"You ready?" he asked.

"Yeah." She nodded. "Ted will be there, though. And I'm not ready to talk to him yet."

"That's understandable," he replied.

"I have to eventually, though."

"You have the right to take your time," he replied.

She looked at him a little closer. "Are you okay?" Gabby asked.

"Yep."

"Are you sure? Because you don't look okay." She turned toward him. "It's the baby stuff, isn't it?"

"We didn't get ours," Seth said. "Bonnie's friends had planned one, and it ended up being on the day they were buried." There was so much he'd missed—so much Bonnie had missed—and he was getting another chance at family that Bonnie never had.

Tears sparkled in Gabby's eyes. "Oh… Seth…"

"It's fine." He swallowed hard. "Like you said, we're going to need those gifts for the boys. And these are your friends and family…"

"Do you want to just drop me off?" she

asked hesitantly. "You don't have to do this, you know. I'll make up some excuse for you. These parties don't normally have the guy there, anyway."

He considered it for a moment, then shook his head. "No, I think I do have to do this. I'm their stepdad. I can't just duck out when it's hard."

"For the record, Seth?" She smiled sadly. "You're one great guy."

"Yeah, yeah." But he smiled back. "We're still just being ourselves tonight, right?"

She nodded. He wasn't sure what was natural between them anymore, but he'd try to relax a bit.

"Then let's get in there," he said, and he pushed open the truck door.

GABBY RANG THE DOORBELL. She could hear people chatting and some excited voices saying, "They're here! It's them!" But the door didn't open. The wind picked up, cold and prying, and Gabby looked back at Seth.

"Maybe just go in?" Seth said. "They're definitely expecting us."

"Hello!" she called, as she pushed the door open, and Bea came toward her with a grin on her face and her arms spread in welcome. Gabby's mother wasn't far behind.

"Come in, come in!" Bea said, and when Gabby and Seth came inside, there was a spattering of people calling out "Surprise!" and a few others saying, "They know already..." Gabby lifted the car seat and Bea took it from her hands so she could take off her coat and boots.

"They're here!" Poppy Austin came bouncing toward Bea, then skidded to a stop, her eyes wide. "Is that a baby?"

Bea lowered the car seat so the little girl could look inside. "It sure is. This is..." Bea looked up at Gabby questioningly.

"That's Andy," Carol said, and she leaned over to kiss her daughter's cheek. "You look wonderful, Gabby."

"Thanks, Mom."

Poppy sidled closer, and Carol took the other two car seats from Seth's hands, bringing the babies into the warmth of the living room as Seth shut the door against the winter wind.

"Ooh... He's so cute!" Poppy crooned. "He's so little..."

"Poppy, let's give them a bit of space," Grace said, coming forward to take her daughter's hand, and she cast Gabby a grin. "Don't worry about her being catchy or anything. Turns out that tummy bug was nothing more than a stash of jellybeans in her bedroom she'd been eating too many of."

"Are you serious?" Gabby chuckled.

"It's better than a full-blown flu," Grace said, then rolled her eyes. "Welcome to parenthood."

Carol got Beau unbuckled and out of his car seat, Bea picked up Aiden, and another family friend scooped up Andy. Poppy scampered off to sit next to them so she could hold the baby's hand.

"Let me hang up your coat." Seth's voice was deep and close to Gabby's ear. She glanced up at him and allowed him to help her off with her jacket.

"Thanks," she said, and it was then that her gaze landed on Ramona, who stood across the living room with her spine straight and her eyes locked on Gabby with an expression that could only be described as dread. She had stylish gray hair cut in a bob, and her makeup was impeccable. Uncle Ted stood next to her, and he looked uncomfortable at best, shifting his weight from foot to foot. He reached out and took Ramona's hand, and they intertwined their fingers, but their grip was white-knuckled. Gabby was willing to bet that they'd heard about her conversation with Hank by the way they were acting.

She looked back at Seth, who seemed to have spotted Ted and Ramona at the same time she did.

"You don't have to talk to them," Seth reminded her softly.

"I don't think I can avoid it," she breathed.

"You want me there?" he asked.

"Um… No, I'll do it myself," she said. "But thanks."

"So this wasn't a surprise, huh?" Grace said, coming over and giving her a squeeze.

"Actually, Bea told us," Gabby said. "But it's okay. I'm running on very little sleep. Everyone jumping out at me might just have given me a heart attack."

Grace laughed, and Gabby's gaze slid back toward Uncle Ted… She couldn't bring herself to call him anything different. She'd have to get this over with. She couldn't ignore them all evening.

"Let me make the rounds, then I'll come back for a chat," Gabby said.

"Deal." Grace nodded toward the boys. "I'm going to see if I can get a turn holding a baby."

"With three, your odds aren't bad!" Gabby laughed.

Seth's warm hand settled on the small of her back, then he slipped past her and shook hands with Billy. Ted and Ramona hadn't moved from their spot by the kitchen doorway, and as Gabby approached them, Ted forced a smile onto his face.

"Hey…" he said quietly. "Congratulations. Again."

"Thank you." Gabby swallowed, and she looked over at Ramona. "It was nice of you to come."

"I wouldn't miss it." Ramona nodded. "Your mother said you needed baby clothes in larger sizes for when the boys grow, so I made sure to get you matching outfits in a few different sizes. I assumed you'd like the boys to match—"

"Yes!" Gabby forced a smile. "I do. I really like that. It's just hard to afford sometimes, so I really appreciate that."

Ramona and Ted exchanged a look, and Gabby glanced over her shoulder toward Seth. He was watching her, his warm eyes almost seeming to buoy her up.

"Uncle Ted," Gabby said. "I know we have a lot to talk about, but I don't think this is the right place to do it."

"No, not the right place at all…" Ted let out a breathy laugh, then he sobered. "But I do want to talk. I was thinking that I could come by your place tomorrow morning. If that's okay, I mean. If you'd be home. I'll answer all your questions."

"I have quite a few."

"I know." Ted shuffled his feet. "And you're probably upset."

"I honestly don't know what I'm feeling right now," she admitted. "Confused, mostly, and—"

One of Bea's granddaughters brought a platter of finger sandwiches over, and Gabby shook her head.

"No, thanks."

Ted and Ramona did the same, and when they were alone again, Gabby said, "Obviously, we can't do this here. So, for tonight, let's just pretend everything is normal for appearances, then."

Ramona's expression melted, and tears welled in her eyes. "Thank you, Gabby."

"No problem." Gabby's voice sounded tight in her own ears. "Why don't you come by around nine, Uncle Ted. Ramona, you could come, too."

"No," Ramona replied. "This is between you and Ted. I can give you some space for that."

It was a kind gesture, and Gabby appreciated it.

"Nine works." Ted nodded. "I'll be there."

His voice softened, and for a split second Ted met her gaze with a look of unrestrained tenderness, but then he cleared his throat.

Gabby didn't have it in her to comfort Ted and Ramona right now, but at least she'd avoided a confrontation—that was something.

"Can I have everyone's attention, please?" Bea called out. "Tonight, we're celebrating Gabby's triplets—Beau, Andy and Aiden. They're still pretty small, so we're asking everyone to please use hand sanitizer before holding the babies. But that's not the only good news we have to celebrate. For anyone who hasn't heard yet—and I'm pretty sure gossip has taken care of spreading the news—Gabby and Seth got married!"

There was some clapping and a few whoops.

"Now, they had a private ceremony, so they didn't get a proper wedding cake. But we wanted to take care of that tonight," Bea said. "Carol?"

Gabby's mom handed Beau over to Grace and disappeared into the kitchen. A moment later, she wheeled out a trolley with a two-tiered wedding cake. It wasn't the biggest cake ever, but it was beautifully decorated with pearls and swirls of white icing. A plastic bride and groom stood on the top, and Carol shot Gabby a misty smile.

Yeah, this would have been her mother's doing—and while she appreciated what her mom was trying to do, she felt a wave of misgiving. So this was the plan tonight—pretending that Ted was nothing more than a family friend, and that Gabby's marriage was a legitimate love match. Admittedly, her mother knew about only one lie in this room. She looked across the room to where Seth stood, and he met her gaze evenly.

They'd have to get through this…gracefully, if possible.

"Seth, Gabby?" Carol said, holding up a kitchen knife with a white ribbon tied around the handle. "Let's cut the cake!"

Seth ambled across the room toward her, and when he got to her side, Gabby slid her hand into his. He gave her fingers a squeeze. This wasn't for show—this was for support.

"Wait, wait, we need pictures," Carol said, pulling out her phone. "Seth, you stand behind Gabby…" She arranged them both so that Seth stood behind and they each held the handle of the knife. "There. Now smile!"

Gabby turned toward her mother and put a smile on her face. Carol nodded a couple times. "Got it. Okay, go ahead!"

Gabby swayed toward Seth, her back pressing against his warm chest.

"You're doing fine," Seth murmured in her ear. "Let's just cut the cake. That's all they want…"

Together, they pressed the knife into the soft cake, and everyone clapped. Seth released the handle, and Gabby set to cutting pieces and setting them onto waiting paper plates.

"Now, Gabby and Seth—you have to have the first bite!" Carol said.

Gabby picked up a plate and fork, then looked over at Seth. "There's no getting around this, Seth."

She lifted a forkful of cake to Seth's lips and he took the bite, his warm gaze meeting hers. He chewed a couple times.

"It's good," he said. Then he did the same, feeding her a bite of vanilla cake.

Why was it that with every traditional event they participated in, they felt a little more married?

There was a plastic tapping sound—in the absence of silverware and glasses, people were tapping plastic forks against plastic cups. Gabby looked up at Seth.

There was no getting around another kiss—but what about their promise to just be themselves?

Gabby met Seth's gaze, and she saw the same misgiving in his eyes. And just then, she heard the cry of one of the babies. She looked over. It was Aiden, and the teenager who was holding him was patting him and jiggling him to no effect.

"Oh, come to Mommy," Gabby said, hoping her relief didn't show.

"No kiss?" someone called.

Seth caught her around the waist, leaned down and kissed her cheek. His lips lingered against her skin, his breath warm on her face and the scruff on his chin tickling her. Then he pulled back.

And it was nice. They'd said they'd just be themselves, and that had felt right…for the moment, at least. She smiled, and eased Aiden into her arms. Aiden settled down, his cheek against her shoulder, happy to be in her arms.

"We get a little shy with all the public kissing," Seth said, raising his voice. "But we really appreciate what you've done for us tonight. This is wonderful, and we're grateful. So thank you for all of this! And if there are any offers for babysitting, we will take that in lieu of wedding gifts!"

Everyone laughed.

"Thank you!" Gabby added. "Let's enjoy the party!"

They'd managed to avoid a romantic kiss... The relief she'd felt a moment earlier evaporated, and in its place was a deep sadness. It wasn't that she didn't like kissing this man. The problem was, she did. But was avoiding displays of affection both publicly and privately what she wanted for the rest of her life? It was one thing to help her in the short term with health insurance, but to stay like this...

Her heart hammered hard in her chest, and she felt tears threaten to rise.

Gabby might choose the wrong men, her heart might steer her wrong every time, but this wasn't right, either. Because if she had gotten what she truly wanted, Seth would have swept her up in his arms and kissed her senseless.

And then she'd have regretted that, too, because whichever way she looked at it, this marriage wasn't till death parted them. It was only a temporary arrangement for the sake of the babies. Whatever tricks her heart was playing on her couldn't be counted on to make a forever solution.

CHAPTER SIXTEEN

SNOW STARTED TO fall as Seth pulled onto the highway. The babies were all asleep, and he looked over at Gabby. Her gaze was turned toward the front window, so all he could see was her profile.

Everyone had been incredibly generous, especially considering how tight things could get this time of year for a lot of families. Friends and family had given them boxes of diapers, piles of clothes, baby blankets, some gift cards to Walmart. He'd felt just as grateful as Gabby had—and that had surprised him just a bit...how much Gabby and the boys felt like his tonight.

The highway wound around some curves as it descended from the mountains, and he squinted against the falling slow. A few cars came toward them, and he slowed down as the glare of the oncoming headlights made it harder to see the road.

"So what happened with Ted and Ramona?" he asked, glancing toward Gabby.

"Ted will come by tomorrow morning and we'll talk," she said. "Ramona... She's the one who chose all those matching outfits all the way up to toddler sizes. Remember that big box that was filled with matching triplet outfits?"

"That was them?" It had been a generous gift—a thoughtful one, too. All those clothes wouldn't have been cheap.

"It was *her*," Gabby said, her voice low. "Ted didn't choose those clothes. She did. That's the thing... Ted's my father. And while Ramona seems to have stayed in the background all that time, he couldn't have been such a huge part of my life if she hadn't backed him up."

Seth turned on the windshield wipers to clear some wet snow off the glass, his mind chewing over these new dynamics. "She's gone through more than anyone knew."

"I think she deserves a lot of credit," Gabby agreed. "I always noticed some tension between her and my mom, though."

"I guess that's to be expected," he said.

"I never understood it before," Gabby said. "I made up all sorts of reasons in my own mind to explain all this stuff, and most of it wasn't very kind to Ramona, I have to admit. I thought she was some shrew of a wife and Ted was henpecked. I no longer think that was the case. But my childhood—my whole life!—has been spent concocting these excuses and explanations to make up for the stuff that didn't make sense."

"I figure we all do that," Seth replied quietly.

"Not to the same level that I had to," she said with a bitter laugh. "When you're trying to sew untruths together, and you feel like you must be the one with the problem if it isn't working—"

"You get used to doing it," he concluded.

Keeping up appearances, explaining away problems... He knew what that was like. He'd done it in his own marriage. A strong marriage didn't show cracks—that had been their motto. But he still wondered what had gone wrong with them. Was it him? Was he the one who'd been too stubborn to make for a peaceful home?

"At least there's no faking with us anymore," she said, and her voice shook with the strength of her emotion. "I don't think I could take one more minute of pretending we're something we're not."

Seth was silent for a moment, his heart swelling in his chest. She wanted honesty.

"I'm faking things, still," he said, his

voice low. Gabby didn't answer, and when he glanced over at her, he saw the hesitant look on her face.

"This is the truth," Seth said. "Tonight, they wanted us to kiss after cutting the cake—"

"We agreed not to," she said.

"Yeah, we agreed to just be us—our natural relationship—and let them gossip if they wanted to."

"What's wrong with that?" she asked.

He remembered the way her hair had fallen behind her shoulders. He remembered the way her blue eyes had softened when they met his, and how his heart had sunk when she'd turned away.

"I wanted to kiss you," he said quietly.

"You did. You kissed my cheek," she said.

"That wasn't what we are!" he said, irritated. "Was it? It might have been what we were, before we got married and started getting closer, but that kiss on the cheek wasn't what we *are* anymore."

"We'd agreed—" she started, but the words evaporated when there was a loud popping sound, and the truck started drifting to the side. Seth pulled hard on the steering wheel to keep it on the road, and took his foot off the gas. Great—just what he needed right now. His heart was still pounding from his confession, and when his gaze flickered toward Gabby, he found her staring at him, wide-eyed.

What had shocked her—the flat tire, or what he'd just said? Up ahead, there was a rest area, and he eased his way toward it. The snow was coming down heavier now, and as he pulled to a stop, he could make out the mountain peaks disappearing into cloud. A truck thundered past them on the highway, headlights slicing through darkness.

Seth had said enough, and he wanted to get out of the vehicle and get some space. Breathe. Fix this stupid tire and get his head in order again. He'd probably already said too much.

"Stay in the truck," he said. "I'll check it out."

Leaving the engine running to keep Gabby and the babies warm, Seth slammed the door behind him and headed around to the back of the truck. He took out the wheel lock and jack box and settled on his haunches to get the rod put together that would lower the spare tire from where it sat underneath the back end of the truck.

He'd changed tires on this vehicle before, and it didn't take him too long to get the tire down. He was just getting the jack in place when Gabby's door opened and her boots hit the snowy gravel.

Her eyes glittered in the low light. A fluffy snowflake clung to a wisp of hair in front of her eyes and she brushed it away, tugging her jacket closer around her.

"Hey." He turned back to the jack.

"I know this isn't easy," she said quietly. "We'll find our footing."

"I thought we found it," he retorted, and he started pushing down on the jack handle, slowly raising the chassis.

"What did you want—for us to kiss each other in front of everyone?" she demanded.

"What I wanted was to be able to hold my wife in my arms and celebrate *us* a little bit," he said. "Instead of holding myself back all the time."

"Holding yourself—" Her breath came out in a cloud. "Since when are you holding yourself back?"

"For the last while," he said, but he wouldn't look up. He put his frustration into the tire instead, reaching for the tire iron. He fitted it onto the first lug nut and gave it a firm push.

"Holding yourself back from what?" she demanded.

He lifted his gaze to meet hers. "From kissing you. From holding you close. From showing you exactly how I feel about you."

"You don't really feel like that about me!" she said with a shaky laugh.

"Sure I do." He turned back to the job at hand, putting the first lug nut aside and fitting the tire iron onto the next one. Whatever she thought of him, he wasn't that out of touch with his own feelings.

"We said we wouldn't play with this—" she started.

"I'm not playing." The second nut came loose, and he unscrewed the next three, pulling both the lug nuts and then the tire free. Then he rose to his feet and faced her. A brisk wind blew her hair away from her face, and she pulled her fur-lined hood up. "You know me better than that, Gabs. I've never lied to you. You can trust *me*."

"I know that."

"Do you?" he asked. Because this mattered to him. He was many things, but he'd never lied to her. It wasn't who he was—and he valued their friendship too much. "I need you to know that, Gabs."

"I do know it," she said, her voice softening. "You're the one I could always count on."

"I'm tired of trying not to feel this, and

of hiding what I do feel," he went on. "We have something, you and me. It goes beyond our friendship."

"It's gotten complicated…" she breathed.

Seth stepped closer and dipped his head down, catching her lips with his. This was the kiss he'd wanted earlier—the honest one that bared his heart. He slipped his hand into her hood and behind her neck, sinking into the depth of her warm hair and pulling her close against him. His lips moved over hers slowly, thoroughly. And when he leaned back, he pressed his lips together, then rested his forehead against hers.

"It's not so complicated," he murmured. "I love you."

Gabby broke out of his arms, and he stared at her dismally as she took a step back, the cold wind cutting between them once more. As the words came out, he knew they were true. He loved his wife. She was going to have to remind him why they'd been running from this, because from where he was standing, he couldn't see a problem. They were married and raising three kids together—what was so wrong with a little bit of love?

GABBY STARED AT SETH, his words still settling into her heart. He loved her? Her fingers fluttered up to her lips, and she felt tears mist her eyes.

"Is this one-sided?" he asked huskily.

When she met his gaze she saw uncertainty swimming there, and her heart went out to him.

"We weren't supposed to do this!" she said, swallowing hard.

"Do what?" he demanded. "We're married, Gabby! We're raising your boys together. We're sharing a house and going to parties together... We're falling into each other's arms more often than not. I love you."

"You keep saying that!" She shook her head. "It's not helping."

"Are you saying that you don't feel it?" he asked miserably. "Because if you don't, I'll back off—"

"Yes, I feel it!" She hunched her shoulders against the wind. "But it doesn't matter if I've started falling in love with you—"

"It matters to me!" he interjected. Seth closed the distance between them again. "Gabby, we have something here."

"We have to keep things platonic," she breathed.

"Why?" he demanded. "I don't see a problem here!"

"I do!" She put her hands up on his chest and pushed him a step back. "Seth, I'm… I'm…" She looked around herself. "I'm a convenience! Like you said, I'm here. I'm in your house. I'm in the next bedroom. I'm a good friend, and you're slowly getting over your grief. I think it's good that you can imagine a life with someone again, but it's only a matter of time before you start feeling trapped in this marriage."

"I'm not feeling trapped," he said curtly.

"You will!" she insisted. "You'll feel like I tricked you. It's all fine and good when we both know what to expect, but when romance gets mixed in—"

"It's marriage!" he said. "Romance is supposed to be mixed in!"

"It's supposed to be the bedrock, not the garnish!" she snapped. "You didn't marry me because you loved me, Seth. You married me to get me onto your health insurance. Let's keep that in perspective!"

Seth opened his mouth to say something, then shut it. He scrubbed his hand through his hair.

"What do you even want from me?" she demanded.

"More…of this," he said. "We might as well explore our feelings a little bit, see where it leads—"

"We know here it leads!" she said. "To heartbreak! I can't share a bed with you just to see where it goes…"

"I'm not asking you to share my bed," he said. "I'm asking you to open your heart to a few possibilities!"

"I had no idea we had this chemistry," she said. "We didn't before. So how long will it even last? One day when your heart is ready to move on, you'll want a woman you actually fall for—not a friend you made an arrangement with. I'm not going to hold you down. I'm grateful for all you've done for me, but I won't be the one you make do with."

"I'm not making do," he said gruffly. "And what about your feelings for me?"

"They aren't enough," she said, and she blinked back a tear that threatened to fall. "Loving you, sharing a home with you, relying on you… It's making my feelings for you grow, but that isn't enough for me, either! Don't you get it? I don't want to be the woman who managed to snag you. I want something different—"

"A different story?" he said, shaking his head.

"I want a *true* story!" The tears she'd been

trying to hold back made it past her lashes and she dashed them from her cheek with her fingertips. "Mom, Ted and Ramona concocted a story for me—and they were wrong! I'm a little too damaged from all those lies, and I won't do that to my kids. I'm not giving them a story I think will sound believable. I'm giving them the truth. And if I'm not proud of the truth, then I have to change something."

"You aren't proud of us?" he said feebly.

"You aren't the problem, Seth. You're a very good man." She swallowed hard. "You'll see. This feels real…but I'm not sure that it is."

One of these days, he would thank her for this. She wouldn't take advantage of his kindness, or of his wounded heart.

"Every couple has a few secrets!" he said. "That doesn't have to be so shameful."

"It isn't about keeping private things private!" she said, her voice raising. "Seth, this is about what *I need*! I'm happy to have our marriage completely platonic. I can live very happily that way. But if romance is going to enter into this, I need the real thing! We're married—and I've told you before that I won't hold you to those vows. I'm grateful, deeply grateful that you married me. And when I can get myself onto my own two feet,

I'll let you go…" Gabby sucked in a wavering breath. "What if I was willing to see where these feelings took us? Really think about it."

He was silent for a moment. "I might have some guilt of my own to wrestle with."

"What if we hadn't gotten married for the health insurance?" she pressed. "What if I'd come home, managed to find a job with some good benefits, and we were just hanging out like we used to and these feelings started to spark…" She paused, swallowed. "What then? Would you want to date more casually, or would you want commitment and a wedding ring? Or would you be willing to move forward with any kind of relationship at all?"

"I'd still have fallen in love with you," he said quietly. "But you're right. It would be more complicated."

"The complication won't go away," she whispered. "Those issues will all come back, but instead of us being good friends who can work through them, we'd be lovers who felt let down. Giving in to this isn't just a risk, Seth. We'll lose everything—including our friendship!"

Gabby wouldn't be the woman who had cunningly trapped a great guy. And she'd end up losing him…

Gabby hadn't accepted his help in an effort to lock him down. This had been about her boys from the start.

"I'm not living a secret for the rest of my life," she said. "I'm not telling my boys a lie to make them feel better, because they'll end up just like me, trying to explain away their mother's marriage as normal. And I don't want them to marry their best friends! I want them to marry partners they're passionate about. I want them to have the real thing, too!"

"So what do we do?" Seth asked, his voice low.

"I don't know..." She shrugged weakly.

Could they go back to their previous arrangement and live together as friends? Or was that hopeless now? Sometimes, things changed too much to be repaired.

"Let me finish the tire," Seth said. "It's late. We need to get to the boys home."

Gabby heard the heartbreak in his voice, and wished she could take it back. For a little while, at least, it would be heaven. She could be held by him, loved by him, kissed by him... Until it wasn't enough for either of them and the resentment set in.

But it had always been about her triplets, and she felt her heart breaking open. If only she had a few less scruples, she could wind Seth closer in and set up the life she'd always wished she could have.

But that wouldn't be love. Real love wanted the best for the other person. And Gabby wasn't Seth's best.

Gabby watched him for a moment as he put on the new tire, then she got back inside the truck. She pulled the door shut just as the tears started to flow.

Love could make people do strange things, like accept relationships that weren't quite right. She'd spent her life accepting discrepancies in the name of love, and she wouldn't do that to Seth.

Integrity could be painful, but it would be worth it.

This had to be about her children. They needed formula and health care—and they needed to see a mom whose honesty they could count on, even when life got complicated.

Gabby might love Seth...but since when was love enough?

CHAPTER SEVENTEEN

GABBY SAT IN the kitchen, Beau in her arms as she fed him the last bottle. Aiden and Andy lay in their bouncy chairs, looking at a ray of sunlight that reflected off the cupboards. Aiden kicked his foot, making his chair bob up and down, much to his delight.

"You found something new, did you?" she asked him with a smile.

Seth had left for work early; he was gone by the time she woke up, but he'd left a hot pot of coffee. Just like him, sweet to the last. They hadn't talked much after last night, and her heart felt heavy. They weren't supposed to get their emotions involved—they'd planned to protect against this very thing! And yet here she was, exhausted from a night of restless sleep and crying.

The problem was, she *was* in love with Seth, and admitting it didn't make it any easier. He loved her, too, but how did that solve anything? He was still racked with guilt over Bonnie's death, his ability to be a good husband, his loss of his baby girl... He was still the same dear, sensitive, noble Seth who'd lost so much. And he'd never been hers.

Outside, the sunlight sparkled off the newly fallen snow, and Seth had shoveled a deep slice through it. The tree limbs were covered in a mantle of white. It was the perfect morning, the house smelling like pine from the Christmas tree, and yet her heart ached so deeply that the festive touches around the house only made it hurt more.

Maybe she could understand now why Seth had avoided it...

Beau finished his bottle, and she put a cloth on her shoulder, then lifted him up to burp him. He felt bigger in her arms this morning, as if he'd done some significant growing overnight. She'd find out exactly how much the boys had grown at their doctor's appointment tomorrow.

She heard an engine in the drive and looked out the window to see Ted's car. He had a bag in one hand and he looked hesitantly toward the house. Seeing her in the window, he waved.

So he was here.

Gabby opened the door as he came up, and she stood back to let him inside. Ted leaned over to kiss her cheek, but it was awkward and she felt his hesitation.

"Hi," Gabby said. "Come on in. The boys are all awake if you wanted to hold your... grandsons."

It felt strange to refer to him that way. Grandpa. Would they call him Grandpa Ted? She couldn't bring herself to call him Dad.

"Yeah, that would be nice." Ted chucked Beau's cheek just as the little boy burped, and he laughed softly. "Thanks for letting me come over, Gabby."

Ted put his bag on the table, and bent down to say hi to Aiden and Andy.

"Here, take Beau," Gabby said, and she handed the baby over to Ted.

"They're so handsome, Gabby," he said quietly.

"Thank you. I'm rather smitten," she said, and she sighed. "How long are we going to do this polite banter, Uncle— I don't think I can call you Uncle Ted anymore."

"Yeah, I get that." Ted settled Beau into the crook of his arm. "I bet this whole thing has been a real shock."

"You could say that..."

"Your mom told me how you found out," he said. "I'm sorry it happened that way, Gabby. I truly am."

"Hank wasn't the monster you all made him out to be," Gabby said. And somehow, Hank still felt like more of a father to her than Ted did.

"He wasn't good to your mom," Ted said firmly. "He broke her heart."

"I think maybe you did, too," she countered.

Ted sighed, but he didn't answer that. So Hank was going to remain the bad guy in their version of things, was he?

"Why did you lie to me, especially as an adult?" Gabby asked.

"I…" Ted met her gaze. "I was selfish."

Gabby hadn't expected that answer. She blinked at him, then felt suddenly embarrassed and dropped her eyes.

"I know that's not much help, but it's all I've got," Ted went on. "I've been thinking this over for days—how I'd explain it to you. Your mom wasn't keen on letting everyone know the truth, and I understood why. But we have different reasons. I didn't tell you sooner because…it was easier for us—Ramona and me. You see, when I cheated on Ramona with your mom, I nearly lost my marriage. And I realized that I loved my wife with all my heart."

"Really romantic," Gabby said dryly. Craig

had had a similar realization when his wife caught him cheating. What was it about cheating men who decided their love for their wives suddenly ran true?

"I know how it sounds," he said. "This is why we wanted to give you a better story. Your mom and I—it was passionate and burned out fast. It was filled with high feeling and little else. Ramona and I had been going through a lull in our marriage, and—" He stopped. "That's personal. She wouldn't like me to talk about that. But suffice it to say, when faced with a choice, I chose my wife. I love her."

"I'm glad you do," Gabby said, shaking her head. "I'm not actually wishing that you'd gotten divorced. I'm just trying to piece it together. So it was easier on Ramona to lie to me, then."

"Partly, yes," he agreed. "It was embarrassing all around. You can imagine how heartbroken you'd be if you found out your husband had gotten another woman pregnant." He paused and color rose in his face. "And I understand that you were on the receiving end of something pretty similar, so I'm sorry. But from Ramona's perspective, to have everyone know about the affair, about your conception—it was a hard time for her. In fact, I wasn't sure she'd even take me back."

"So why did she?" Gabby asked.

"Honestly? She loved me. I didn't deserve it," Ted said. "I swore to her that I'd live every day giving her reason to keep on loving me, and I've done that. I don't take her for granted."

"Was keeping the secret part of the deal?" Gabby asked.

Ted was silent for a moment. "At first, yes. But she also said she'd never keep me from being in your life. She said that if she chose to take me back, then she was accepting that you were a part of things. You were one of my children, even if you weren't hers."

Gabby nodded. That wouldn't have been easy, especially not in a town the size of Eagle's Rest.

"Does she resent me?" Gabby asked at last.

"Resent you?" Ted laughed softly. "Oh, Gabby, you don't know her well enough. No, Ramona is the kind of woman who knows exactly who to blame—me!"

Gabby smiled at that. "If she and I knew each other under different circumstances, we might get along."

"I hope you will get to know each other

better now," Ted said. "If you want to, of course. I just—" Beau started to whimper, and Ted adjusted him, then he turned back to Gabby. "Are you disappointed—knowing the truth?"

"Hank still kind of feels like my dad," she admitted woodenly. "I've gotten used to believing that my father didn't love me—"

"Oh, Gabby…" Ted's arms were full with Beau, but his gaze locked on Gabby's with deep apology. "I loved you. I was at every single elementary school performance—did you know that?"

"Yeah… I thought it was a little weird," she admitted.

He laughed softly, blinking back tears. "I tried to be a dad to you, even when I couldn't tell you who I was. I really did try. I never missed a birthday, or Christmas, or Easter. Well, there was one Easter when I took my family to Hawaii, but I made sure you had a special Easter basket from—"

"From my uncle Ted," she finished for him.

"I wanted to acknowledge you."

"Your kids—do they know?"

"Ramona and I are going to tell them together—when they get home for Christmas. We wanted to do it in person." He frowned.

"I don't know how they'll react. They may need some time. But people need to know the truth. And we should have been telling them a long time ago."

"Is Ramona okay with that?" she asked.

"Yeah." He nodded. "And she wants to spend a bit more time getting to know you, if you'll let her."

"I don't know…" Andy was starting to squirm, and Gabby bent down to pick him up. She settled him on her shoulder and looked at those plump cheeks and bright eyes. "I'm still adjusting to motherhood, and marriage, and—"

The words caught in her throat. Marriage. It wasn't an actual marriage she was getting used to, but a sham. And she wasn't sure that either of them could continue it.

"I understand," Ted said quickly. "I brought something for you…"

He placed Beau back into a bouncy chair and reached for his bag, then pulled out a small, slightly yellowed photo album. Ted opened it and passed it over to her. There were pictures inside of Ted and her at different ages. The last photo was of him standing next to her at her high school graduation, Gabby wearing the blue gown.

"And there's something else." Ted reached

into the bag once more and pulled out a jewelry case.

"You don't need to—" she started.

"No, this is important," Ted said. He handed the box over, and she exchanged it for the album. She cracked it open to reveal a string of pearls.

"Why?" she asked.

"Our daughters all got pearls when they got married," he said. "This necklace was actually Ramona's."

"Ted, I can't take this!" Gabby said.

"She asked me to give it to you," Ted said earnestly. "She always said that every woman should have a good string of pearls. She never knows when she might need to dress something up."

Gabby felt a lump rise in her throat.

"We might not be a traditional family, Gabby," Ted went on, "but you're part of ours. And these pearls—they mean something to Ramona. So if you would accept them in the spirit that she's giving them..."

Pearls, the gift their daughters got when they married... But those young women would have married for better reasons than Gabby had. As far as she knew, Ted's daughters—her half sisters—were happily married and living in another state. Oh, goodness...

she had more family she'd need to adjust to, to navigate a relationship with. She doubted any of Ted's four adult children would be thrilled to find out about their relationship to her... Which made Ramona's gift an especially kind one.

Gabby nodded. "Thank her for me."

"I will." Ted smiled. "We're proud of you. Both of us. You've made a good life for yourself, and you've married a good guy—"

"Yeah, he's great," she said quickly.

Seth's boots sounded on the step outside and the door opened.

"Is there anything else you want to know?" Ted asked. "I'm sure you have more questions."

"I'm sure I do, too," she replied. "But I'm kind of overwhelmed right now."

They were silent for a few beats, awkwardness stretching between them. Ted seemed to be leaping into the role of father rather easily, but she wasn't ready to be his daughter just yet. Seth came inside, pulling his gloves and hat off.

"I should be going, anyway," Ted said, rising to his feet. "We don't have to do this all at once. I know this has been a shock, and you can call me whenever you want. We can take our time and talk it all out."

"I suppose so," she agreed. "Thanks for coming by, though."

She was eager for him to leave. She had enough to chew over right now.

"Merry Christmas, Gabby. I left some Christmas gifts with your mom, like usual."

Like usual. Gifts from Uncle Ted that were always rather expensive, and just a little bit left of her actual interests. He'd always tried too hard, especially for a godfather.

"Thanks, Ted."

"Care to walk me out, Seth?" Ted asked.

"Sure." Seth put his hat back on and waited as Ted put on his. The men disappeared outside, and Gabby was left with that jewelry in her hands.

Untraditional families could still wrap children in love and raise them well. Despite the mess, hers had managed just that.

Gabby would find a way with her boys, but she wouldn't lie to them in words or in actions. Her gaze moved toward the window where she could see Seth standing with his back to her, talking to Ted by the car. Seth was tall, broad, strong, sweet... Seth was ever so easy to love. A lump rose in her throat, and she blinked back tears.

She knew what she had to do, even if it broke her heart to do it.

It was a frigid morning, the wind brisk. The snow had developed a hard shell on top since Seth had shoveled that morning. They paused when they got to Ted's car and Seth squinted in the bright sunlight.

"I know this has been a tough time for your wife," Ted said quietly.

"Yeah," Seth agreed.

"And I don't know what you must think of me," Ted said. "But I want you to know that even when she didn't know I was her dad, I knew it. I did everything I could to take care of her and develop a relationship with her, too. I didn't abandon her."

Seth nodded. "That distinction matters to you."

"Wouldn't it matter to you?" Ted asked. "Look, I wasn't perfect, but I did my best by her. I didn't leave her then, and I'm not leaving her now."

"It's just a lot to come at her at once," Seth said. "She has to erase all these stories she's been told and replace them with a brand-new version. Those stories form you as you grow up, and to find out they were lies…"

Ted nodded. "Yeah, I have four other children. I do understand that, and I feel terrible for my part in it."

"So, maybe just give her some time," Seth

said. He wasn't sure what Ted was wanting from him—an explanation, some reassurance that she'd forgive him?

"You're the father my grandsons are going to grow up with," Ted said. "You're a good man to step up to that kind of responsibility."

"I'm trying, too," Seth said hesitantly.

Ted smiled weakly. "I want to open my family to her, but I have a feeling she's going to be resistant to that for a long while. Don't get me wrong—I get it. But she needs someone looking out for her. She's not as tough as she seems…" Ted looked toward the house. "And this Christmas will be a hard one—for her and my other kids. I know I'm the one to blame for all of it, but… Christmas shouldn't be about this kind of thing, you know?"

"Christmas doesn't seem to be any respecter of good timing," Seth conceded. "Let's just get through the holidays."

Ted was assuming Seth had access to her heart. Gabby loved Seth, sure, but she didn't trust him to keep on loving her back. She'd been lied to one too many times by men like her father.

"And if you need anything at all," Ted said, "I'm here."

"Thanks."

Seth watched as Ted pulled out, the car

disappearing down the drive. Then he looked back toward the house. He'd ducked out early this morning before Gabby had even woken up, and he was feeling guilty for that now. It felt like they'd said it all last night, but they hadn't figured out how they were going to go forward yet. How would they maintain a platonic marriage when they were attracted to each other?

And Ted was right—Gabby was going through a lot right now, and she needed his support. Whether or not they could be more than friends, he'd vowed to be by her side.

He walked back to the house, kicked the snow off his boots on the step, then went inside.

"How did it go talking to Ted?" Seth asked.

Gabby was holding a white jewelry box. She put it down on the counter next to her. "He means well."

Aiden started to cry in his little chair, and Gabby squatted down in front of the boys, unbuckled him and picked him up. As soon as Aiden was in his mother's arms, he immediately quieted, his eyes drifting shut. She looked down at the baby and tears welled in her own eyes.

"I won't lie to them…" she said, her voice shaking.

"Me, neither," he said earnestly. "We'll raise them right."

"No—" She raised her gaze to meet Seth's. "I mean, I'm not going to live a lie, either. They'll only end up doing what I did—ignoring their own sense of what's believable and what isn't in order to believe me. This marriage—Seth, I am so deeply grateful that you've made it possible for me to get formula for my boys, but it can't go beyond that."

"I think we are beyond that," he said.

"And we went through this last night," she said. "It isn't enough. Not for me, and eventually, it won't be enough for you. It's some halfway marriage where we respect each other a great deal, and our hearts never quite get their fill."

Seth swallowed. "I'm doing my best here, Gabs."

"I know. Me, too." She smoothed a hand over Aiden's head. "I think I should go back to Bea's place."

"For how long?" Seth asked.

"Until I can get a job and my own place." She met his gaze pleadingly. "We can't go on like this."

She wanted to leave. She wanted out. All those times she'd reassured him that he could leave if he wanted, it hadn't been his escape route she'd been thinking of—it was her own. He felt like he'd been kicked in the gut, and he cast about inside himself, looking for where they'd gone so wrong. They'd agreed that this was going to be a lifetime together. But then they'd gone and fallen in love with each other.

"Then stay here until you get that job," he said softly. "You don't have to leave."

"I do." Her chin trembled. "If I stay, I'll cave in. I'll accept this…halfway marriage…and it won't be a strict understanding between good friends anymore. I know myself. I want to be loved just as much as anyone else, and I'll end up in your arms, and it won't make me happy. I'm still the same woman who is drawn to all the wrong situations. And you can't give your whole heart. We'll make each other miserable."

"Will we stay friends?" he asked.

"I think this is the only way we can stay friends!" she said. "We'll take some time, get our emotions in order again, and…"

"And hang out?" he asked miserably. "Go to a movie? Joke around about that Christmas we accidentally fell in love with each other?"

"It might take some time..." she conceded. "But I want you in my boys' lives. Just because we couldn't make a marriage work doesn't mean they should miss out on you!"

Seth felt tears sting his eyes. "I'll be the godfather."

"If you'd be willing..."

He'd be the one who looked longingly at their mother. He'd be the guy who did all the dad stuff with them, and they'd grow up wondering why their godfather had been so close—a whole lot like their mother had grown up. Except this time around, it would be because he was in love with her, but he was too broken to give her enough.

"Yeah, sure." He couldn't quite bring himself to turn his back on these boys, either. Maybe she'd marry someone else and they'd get a good stepdad, but in the meantime, they'd have him to care, to love them, to help steer them in the right direction.

Gabby pulled the wedding band off her finger and pushed it into his hand. "I'm going to go pack."

He looked down at that delicate circle of gold in his palm. He wanted to reach out and hold her, to kiss her, to promise that they could make this work, but it wasn't true. He'd gotten a taste of a real, honest life with Gabby, and it was sweeter than he'd imagined it could be. He wanted more of this beautiful, hectic life…but it couldn't work for either of them.

If he really loved her, he had to let her go.

CHAPTER EIGHTEEN

BEA HELPED GABBY carry in the last of the baby things. The babies were all sleeping in their car seats, so they let them stay there, all lined up against one wall, for the time being.

"What happened?" Bea asked.

"You aren't going to say you told me so?" Gabby asked, tears misting her eyes.

"Nope." Bea shook her head, then looked at Gabby a little closer. "You fell in love with him, didn't you?"

Gabby sighed, wiping a tear from her cheek. "It was getting a little too close to the real thing."

"And what's wrong with that?" Bea asked.

"He's still mourning Bonnie, and he blames himself for her death. I'm still reeling from all these revelations about my father, and I'm having a huge problem with trust at the moment. We're both—"

"Human," Bea said. "You're both flawed. Welcome to life."

"I can't do it," Gabby said. "This would

only have worked if we kept things platonic! Add romantic expectations into it, we'll only break each other's hearts!"

"It seems you have already," Bea said.

"Neither of us meant to." Gabby looked around her aunt's kitchen. There were some holly-printed cookie jars on the counter, a loop of garland over the window above the sink. "It's almost Christmas…"

"You're welcome to stay as long as you need," Bea said. "But give this situation some thought. Sometimes these things can work out. You never know."

If only it were a matter of both of them cooling off after a fight. Instead, this was something thought through and discussed quite calmly. Her heart wasn't being quite so logical, though. She *had* fallen in love with him…and it was the stupidest thing she'd ever done!

"What's next?" Bea asked, after a moment of silence.

"Most immediately, the boys' have a doctor checkup this afternoon," Gabby said. "And then I need to find a job with benefits."

"Maybe after Christmas," Bea said. "Everyone's focused on the holidays right now, and—"

"No, I'm going to the ski resort," Gabby

said. "Ted and Ramona might not have been planning to hire right now, but if he wants to help me, he can squeeze in another full-time position for me."

"You think he will?" Bea asked. "Didn't you ask him before?"

"I didn't know he was my father before." Gabby sucked in a breath. "I'm going to try, at least. Could you watch the boys after their doctor appointment?"

Because she needed a way to support her children, and she was willing to try just about anything right now to make that happen. And she couldn't ask any more of Seth.

THE DOCTOR'S APPOINTMENT went well. The boys were all growing well, and the doctor assured her that the formula they were on was doing its job. In a few months, she might be able to switch them to a less expensive formula, but for the time being the doctor didn't want to disrupt them. It only confirmed what she already knew—she needed a job with benefits. She wouldn't take advantage of Seth's generosity more than she already had.

When she brought the triplets back to Bea, they were sleeping soundly once more, so she headed back out to the twisting road that led up the mountain to Eagle's Rest Ski Lodge. When she arrived at the turnoff for the resort, her stomach fluttered in nervousness.

Gabby would be asking a favor, and it would be based on her biological connection to Ted. Because she'd asked before, and he'd said no. Would he bend now? Maybe not.

She found a parking spot near the front doors, and when she got out of her car, she looked up at the log lodge—three stories, all decorated for the holidays. Massive wreaths hung on the front doors, lights were strung along the roof, and more light-festooned wreathes hung on the outside walls. It was beautiful, but the Christmas cheer only made her miss that blue spruce back in Seth's living room all the more. Why was it that the house with Seth felt like home?

Gabby pulled open the front doors. Inside, instrumental Christmas music played softly, and two mammoth trees, decorated with color-coordinated ornaments, filled the lobby. A young woman sat at the reception desk, her attention focused on a computer screen, and Gabby took a moment to look around.

There was a door to the left with a brass name plaque that read Manager. That was

Ted's office—she'd been here a handful of times. But then the door opened and Ramona stepped out, a sheaf of papers in one hand, her glasses perched on the end of her nose. Her silver hair was tucked behind her ears, revealing dangling red earrings. She looked up, and it took her a moment to register Gabby, but when she did, Ramona froze.

"Hi," Gabby said. "I was hoping to talk to…Ted."

"He's not here right now," Ramona said, and she crossed the lobby toward her. "Did you need something?"

Gabby almost laughed at that question. Did she need something? She needed to feed her children! She needed the truth. She needed some sort of healing for this new gaping wound in her heart.

But Ramona had reached out, hadn't she? She'd given her a string of pearls, a gesture that showed she was willing to bridge this chasm between them, and if Ramona didn't agree to giving Gabby a job, Ted couldn't make it happen, anyway. Maybe this was a conversation between women, after all.

"I, um—" Gabby swallowed. "Could we talk?"

"In my office," Ramona said, and Gabby didn't miss the way Ramona's gaze flick-

ered around the lobby to see who had notice her arrive.

The manager's office was neat. The or-
nate decorating seemed to have missed this
little room, which was a strange relief given
Gabby's current emotional state. She sat
down in a visitor's chair and put her purse
on her lap.

"So…" Ramona said as she shut the door.
"You came to see Ted."

"Thank you for the pearls, first of all,"
Gabby said. "It was really kind of you to
give them to me."

"Oh…" Ramona's cheeks pinked slightly,
and she sat down on the other side of her
desk—a protected position, Gabby noted.
"You're welcome. I thought—well, there's a
lot to make up for. But we haven't talked to
our children yet. Vivienne arrives tonight,
and the others will come tomorrow, and…"
Ramona's voice trailed off. "I haven't told
them."

"I'm not here to make a scene," Gabby
said. "And I'm in no rush. So take your time.
But Ted said that if I ever needed anything,
I should ask."

"You need money?" Ramona frowned.

"I need a job," Gabby said, and as the
words came out, she felt her eyes blur with

tears. "Yes, I need money, but I need a way to earn it. I need a full-time job with benefits. You see, my boys require a special formula for the next few months, and it's very expensive, but health insurance would help cover some of that cost."

"Your husband's job doesn't have benefits?" Ramona asked.

Gabby dropped her gaze. Dare she tell Ramona the truth? She'd been trying so hard to appear as a happy newlywed, but her heart was broken, and people would discover that she and Seth had separated sooner or later...

"Since we share a few secrets already, could I tell you one more?" Gabby asked, her voice low.

"What's happening?" Ramona asked softly.

"I married him for the health insurance," she said, her mouth dry. "And yes, he knew that. I had asked Ted for a job when I came back, and he said he just couldn't do it. Looking back on it, having me around for forty hours a week might not have been nice for you—the constant reminder, and all that. But I didn't know what else to do, and Seth had the idea that if we got married, I could use his health insurance."

"And...you can't use it anymore?" Ramona ventured.

"It turns out that marriage is a whole lot more complicated than I thought." She forced a smile. "And I can't take advantage of Seth's generosity. I need to find a job of my own to provide for my boys. I'll work hard. I'll do anything—housekeeping, reception, shoveling snow. I mean it—anything."

Ramona was chewing the side of her cheek. "We have a staff of experienced employees who have been with us for years. We don't have any openings right now, and the wait list is long."

That sounded like a no. "Okay."

It had been a long shot, and she'd guessed that Ramona wouldn't want her around, anyway.

"But all the same, I'm going to give you a job," Ramona continued thoughtfully, and Gabby looked up in surprise.

"Really?"

"It will be a bit of a made-up position. I'd need you do some of everything—front desk from five in the morning to seven, then pitch in with housekeeping. Around noon they could use some extra help in the kitchen, and after that you could spell off some people on breaks—"

"I can do that!" Gabby said eagerly. "And I'll…" She felt her cheeks heat. "I'll try to stay out of your way."

Ramona smiled weakly. "That won't be necessary, Gabby. We're going to find a way to be a family. It just might take a bit of time."

"Thank you!" Gabby hugged her purse against her stomach. "I appreciate this. I'll work hard."

"Child care won't be a problem?" Ramona asked.

"I'll sort something out," Gabby said quickly.

"So now that your employment problem is taken care of," Ramona said, "maybe we could talk a little bit. I can tell that I've come off as the evil wife in this whole thing, but… I'm not. I was hoping I could tell you my side of things."

"Okay," Gabby said with a nod. "I'd like that."

"We'd been married for five years when all this happened. I discovered that my husband had had a brief but passionate affair with your mother." Ramona dropped her gaze. "I was crushed. Things hadn't been easy for me and Ted. Marriage was tougher than either of us had anticipated. Maybe you know that I was the one with the money when Ted and I got married. My parents thought I'd married down, so there wasn't a lot of support from them. And I refused to let them know what had happened with Ted and your mom because they'd only tell me they'd told me so..."

"Yeah, I know that feeling..." Gabby murmured.

"But I loved him," Ramona went on. "And he loved me. He swore he'd do anything to keep me and the kids—it was only Robert and Ryan then, and they were both under three. Even so, I was going to divorce him. That level of betrayal—it's a lot to bear."

"So why didn't you?" Gabby asked.

"It was my grandmother," Ramona said. "She was the grand old matriarch of the family, and she terrorized my father something fierce. But she found me alone one day, and she saw my face, and she must have guessed how miserable I was. She sat me down and told me something that made a whole lot of sense."

"What's that?"

Ramona lifted her gaze. "She said, 'So,

what, you're going to let some other woman try to love him better than you?'"

Gabby laughed. "I didn't expect that."

"Neither did I," Ramona said. "Grandma was fiercely opinionated and often rude, but she also tended to be right. Ted deserved to be punished for what he did to me, but I realized that if he was willing to earn back my trust, I wasn't letting another woman love him better. I loved him. I wanted a life with him—and I realized then that life isn't a perfect fairy tale. We experience bumps and bruises along the way. We—especially women—pretend it's perfect. It isn't perfect, far from it, but it's worth it."

"So that's why you stayed..." Gabby breathed.

"That's why I stayed," Ramona said. "And my secret wound is about to be made public, but I think I'm ready."

"We don't have to tell people," Gabby said.

"Yes, we do," Ramona said with a kind smile. "There is healing in facing the truth. And I still love Ted enough to face it with him."

"Ted is a good man," Gabby said. "He was a good dad to me, even though I didn't know he was my father."

"He's one of the best," Ramona agreed. "Just give me this Christmas to get my kids up to speed. You can start work on the second of January, if that's all right with you. I'll make sure your benefits start right way. Do you have enough formula until then?"

"I do," Gabby said quickly. "Ramona, thank you. Really. From the bottom of my heart."

Ramona smiled, and for the first time that smile lit up her face. She was beautiful, Gabby realized, when she was free of that tension and pressure.

"I'm glad Ted chose you," Gabby said, rising to her feet. "Things worked out the best way possible."

"Oh, Gabby," Ramona said with a smile. "I chose *him*!"

Then Ramona stood up and put out a hand to shake Gabby's. "We'll have lots of time to figure this out. But trust that there is room for you and the boys in the family...and Seth, too. If you decide."

"Thank you. I'll be here bright and early on the second."

But as Gabby walked back out into the biting cold, an image of Seth rose in her mind—his dark hair, those piercing eyes, the way his lips started curving at one side when he started to smile...and her heart sped up at the very thought of him.

Are you going to let another woman try to love him better?

Ramona was right. There was definitely healing in facing the truth, and maybe she and Seth could do some of that healing together. Life would never be perfect, but no one could love Seth better than she could... So maybe it was time she stopped hedging and chose her man.

SETH STOOD IN the living room in front of the Christmas tree, a mug of coffee in one hand. The house felt echoingly empty now, with no babies to cry, no bottles to make... no woman nestled next to him with her soft floral scent...

It was Christmas Eve, and he didn't have any plans for the holiday. He'd wanted to sit alone in this house and wait for the hours to pass. And he certainly hadn't planned to spend the time in front of a Christmas tree.

The lights on the tree blinked cheerily, but his heart was heavy. He missed Gabby more than he thought possible. Losing Bonnie was the worst pain he'd ever gone through, but this also hurt in a way he hadn't anticipated. It was a different kind of pain—like a whole new part of his heart got torn this time around.

He'd fallen in love with his best friend, and that had ruined everything. Gabby had always been a buddy up until the day he married her, and then he started seeing a different side to her…a tender side, the intimate woman behind the scenes. And he'd been able to share that space with her and her babies for a little while. Was she right that it was only because of their marriage of convenience he'd even seen this side of her? Maybe…but he *had* seen it. And he *had* fallen for her, which only made him feel more guilty…because he still didn't feel like he deserved a real family, with Gabby of all women, after tiny Hazel and his beloved Bonnie had slipped away from him.

His daughter's Christmas ornament hung next to those three blue teddy bears, and he heaved a sigh. He hadn't deserved Hazel and Bonnie, yet he'd loved them with all his heart. Maybe he should make his peace with being a godfather to those boys and accept his lot in life.

There was a knock on the back door, and Seth roused himself from his thoughts. Had Gabby returned? He headed back into the kitchen, depositing his mug on the counter on his way by, and he pulled open the door.

"Oh, hi," Seth said, stepping back.

"Don't sound so happy to see me," Billy joked. "You got a delivery. They left it up at the main house, and I volunteered to drive it down to you."

Billy hoisted a box and handed it over, then grunted as he reached for a second, identical box. The cribs—he'd forgotten that he'd ordered them.

"Right…" Seth cleared his throat.

"Is this your gift for Gabby?" Billy asked as he carried the box inside and leaned it against the counter.

"No, it's…" Seth sighed. "We just needed them."

"Where is she?" Billy asked, glancing around. "Grace wanted me to tell her that she's got some baby books for her, and…" Billy paused. "What happened?"

Was it so obvious? Seth pushed the door shut and nodded toward the coffee maker. "You want a cup?"

"Sure." Billy pulled off his gloves and tossed his hat on the counter. "What's going on?"

"She left," Seth said.

"Left…" Billy frowned. "Why? Did you fight?"

"Not exactly."

"Women don't leave you for nothing," Billy said bluntly.

"We didn't exactly fall in love and get married," Seth said quietly. "It was a little more arranged than that…" When he'd finished explaining, Billy heaved a sigh.

"So…you weren't ready for another marriage, even an arranged one," Billy said simply.

"I guess not," Seth agreed. "I wasn't the stellar husband everyone thought, you know."

"Ha!" Billy barked out a laugh.

"That's funny?" Seth wasn't in the mood right now.

"Seth, no one's the stellar husband they look like to everyone else. Whatever. Our women love us enough to make us look good to their friends. Take it for the compliment that's intended." Then Billy sobered. "Look, I wasn't ready to be a dad when Poppy landed on my doorstep, but you grow into it."

And Seth had been growing into the role with the boys; it wasn't being a stepdad that had held him back. That hadn't been faked.

What he felt for the babies had been pure and natural, and he missed them like crazy.

"I was doing pretty well with the babies," he admitted. "It's being a husband again I'm not so sure I'm ready for."

"Is it sharing the house, reporting back to someone…?" Billy asked quietly.

"I was fighting with Bonnie when she died," he said. "We were fighting about Gabby."

"Was there something between you?" Billy frowned.

"No! That's the thing. Gabby and I were buddies and nothing more. There was nothing for Bonnie to be jealous of. But maybe she sensed it—this possibility between us—"

"There are a thousand possibilities," Billy said. "And then there are choices. Marriage is a pretty big, legal, official choice. Could you have married someone else? Sure. But you chose Bonnie."

Seth was silent.

"The thing I learned with Grace," Billy went on, "is that we're both better people when we're together. I'm a better dad. She's even a better teacher. We're different together, and we're better this way. The Austins are stronger than we ever were when we were single. It isn't about who we are apart, it's about who we are together... She's the smartest choice I ever made. For what it's worth."

Maybe there was some wisdom there. Seth had been blaming himself for falling for the woman his wife had never trusted, but maybe it wasn't about that. Maybe it was trusting his heart and standing by his choices. He'd been faithful to Bonnie in every way, and now he was faced with another choice...

"Do you think a woman would be crazy to sign on to a life with me?" Seth asked.

"I don't know," Billy said. "You'd have to ask her."

Seth smiled.

"You want me to bring these cribs back to the main house?" Billy asked. "I've got to get back home. Grace and Poppy are waiting, and it's Christmas Eve, so..."

Did he want those cribs going back to Bea's house to help get Gabby set up there, or did he want those cribs upstairs where it felt like they belonged?

"I'm going to think about it," Seth said. "Leave them here. Go on home. Sorry to have kept you."

"That's what friends are for," Billy said.

"You want to join us tonight? You know, if you need the company—"

"No, no," Seth said with a shake of his head. "I'll be fine. Merry Christmas."

He closed the door behind his friend, then picked up the first box, hoisted it over his shoulder and headed for the stairs.

Seth knew that he and Gabby were good together, but they couldn't have a future if he wasn't able to forgive himself for his failings in his first marriage. Gabby had been right about that, and maybe she'd been right about pulling away, too.

She thought that their marriage was a sham. It might have started out that way, but he'd gotten to see what he and Gabby could be as a couple. And Billy was right— he was a better man with Gabby by his side.

Seth started up the stairs, the heavy box awkwardly balanced on his shoulder. He had a lot to think about, and he thought best when his hands were busy.

CHAPTER NINETEEN

GABBY SAT IN the rocking chair, Beau and Aiden in her arms as she rocked gently. Andy was already asleep in the bassinet by the Christmas tree, but the other two had been fussier tonight.

As soon as she'd gotten home from the lodge, she'd been busy with diapers, Aiden's upset tummy and Andy's general upset about missing her while she was gone. Bea was in the kitchen doing some dishes, and that had left Gabby alone with the boys.

She'd almost called Seth several times over the last few hours, but she stopped herself. Just because she could love him didn't mean that Seth was willing to open himself up again after she'd turned him down. She wasn't sure she could handle any more rejection this Christmas, but Seth had filled her heart all evening as she held the boys, fed them, rocked them, changed them...

Gabby picked up her phone for the hundredth time and looked down at the empty screen. Grace had texted her a cute picture of Poppy in her Christmas pajamas. Her mom had called from her late shift to say Merry Christmas, and they'd all get together in the morning. The tourists still wanted to eat, even on the holidays.

Ted had texted to say he was glad she'd be working with them in the New Year.

Gabby wasn't alone… So why did she feel so lonesome? She leaned her cheek against Beau's head and started typing one-handed into the phone: Merry Christmas, Seth.

She pressed Send. The other things that filled her heart couldn't be texted. They were too deep to be communicated that way, but she longed to hear from him, at least.

Her phone pinged, and she picked it up. Seth had replied: I'm here.

She straightened. A truck had stopped outside the house, and she could just see the headlights through the open curtains.

"Is someone outside?" Bea asked, coming into the living room. She shaded her eyes and looked through the window. "I think it's Seth."

"He just texted," Gabby said, looking down at the sleeping babies in her arms.

"I'll go let him in," Bea said, leaving the room again.

Gabby didn't have much choice but to wait, and after what felt like an eternity, she heard Seth's boots on the steps, the murmur of their voices, and he finally came inside.

"Hey…" he said quietly.

"Hi." She smiled. "I'd get up, but—"

"Yeah." Seth came over to where she sat and sank down on his haunches next to her. He reached up and touched Beau's cheek with the back of his finger. "I miss you."

"Yeah?" Gabby smiled mistily. "Me, too. So much."

He leaned closer and caught her lips in a brief kiss. "I've been thinking, Gabs."

"Me, too," she admitted. "But you go first."

"Well, the thing is, I've been blaming myself for falling for you. It felt like Bonnie was right—that she'd sensed some unfaithfulness in my heart, or something…" Seth said. "But I was faithful. I know that. And Billy had a pretty solid point about the choices we make. Could I have fallen in love with you first if things had happened differently? Maybe! But I chose Bonnie, and I stayed true to her. I've got to forgive myself for not having been enough. I'm not going to be perfect at being a husband or a dad, but—"

"Seth, who asked for perfect?" she whispered.

"Gabs, I love you," he breathed. "And I love the boys, too. I don't have much to offer—just my best. And that might not always be enough… I guess what I'm getting at is…" He swallowed. "Billy was pretty chatty, and he pointed out that marriage is about who you are together. And Gabby, with you, I'm better than I am alone. I don't know if you feel the same way about me, if I bring out the best in you, but…"

"We are a good team," she admitted softly.

"Yeah." He nodded. "You were right, I was holding back. I was guilty. But I was putting together the cribs upstairs after talking to Billy, and… I realized I'm just going to have to forgive myself. And I know you think I would never have married you if it weren't for the health insurance, but I want to prove you wrong. It's about who you choose, Gabby, and I'm choosing you."

Beau started to slip sideways in Gabby's grasp, and holding both babies, she couldn't easily change their position. Seth reached out and eased Beau into his arms, freeing her to cuddle Aiden a little closer. He looked down at the sleeping child he held.

"I want to be their dad, Gabs," he murmured. "And I want to be your husband. I want us to be a real family, not just a convenient one."

Gabby adjusted Aiden in her arms.

"I've been afraid to trust us," she said. "But I went to see Ramona today, and I asked for a job—with benefits."

"A job?" Seth's face fell.

"She gave it to me," Gabby said.

"So you won't need my health insurance," he concluded.

"Not anymore." Gabby's heart tore a little at the sadness that filled his eyes. "But Seth, I don't want to let another woman love you better than I can. I love you! And I know you're healing, and so am I, but I love you too much to step back and let someone else try to do better by you."

"Here's the thing," Seth said. "I can see two options here."

"Okay…"

"The first one is that we annul this marriage, and I prove to you that I'd still marry you if we dated like normal people. And I will. I'll take you out for dinner, cook for you, watch Netflix with you while the babies sleep… And then one day, I'll get you a proper engagement ring and ask you marry me…again."

Gabby felt tears fill her eyes. "It sounds wonderful, but…lengthy."

"That's what I thought, too," he said with a low laugh. "The other option is that you take back this ring—" he pulled her wedding ring out of his pocket with his free hand "—and you come home with me, and we just stay married. I don't want Christmas without you. I don't want another day without you. I love you, Gabs, and I want our family. This isn't convenient at all—but it's all I want. I want you to be my wife, in every way possible."

"Do you mean it?" she whispered.

"Yeah." He put a protective hand over Beau's head and back, then leaned over Aiden and kissed her lips tenderly. "I love you—for who you are, and forever. Can you trust that?"

Gabby nodded. "Yes."

"Then which option do you like better?" he asked. "Will you come home with me tonight, or will you make me work for it?"

"Oh, I'll make you work for it, Seth," she said with a chuckle. "But I want to come home… It's our first Christmas, after all."

"You don't have to take that job," he said.

"I want to," she said. "Plus, it'll give me a chance to get to know my dad's family a bit. Bea already said she'd help out with some child care. And my mom will pitch in where she can…"

Seth leaned over and kissed her once more, his lips lingering on hers. There was movement in the doorway, and he pulled back. They both looked over to see Bea standing there with her arms crossed.

"So it's all sorted out now?" she asked with a smile.

"We're going to go home," Gabby said. "I'm sorry to be such a bother, Bea. Thank you for putting up with me."

"It's no bother," Bea said with a shake of her head. "But I'll tell you this. In my day, we weren't such idiots as to play with marriages of convenience. We knew what stupid was!"

Gabby laughed softly. "I know, I know. I can't say you didn't warn me."

"We might have gotten the order wrong, but we got the vows right," Seth said, and he looked around the living room. "So where are the car seats?"

Seth seemed eager to get them home, and her heart flooded with love.

Gabby loved him—for better or for worse, for richer or for poorer—and she was looking forward to getting home to their Christmas tree, their kitchen, and to her husband's arms.

This Christmas, she and her boys would be exactly where they belonged.

EPILOGUE

SETH SHIFTED AS he woke up, and reached out, pulling Gabby closer against him. Her hair was strewn across the pillow, and it smelled like her shampoo—a scent that had sunk into his heart when he hadn't noticed. There were two quilts on top of them, cocooning the warmth around them. This felt right—his wife in his arms and waking up with her in the morning for the very first time.

"Merry Christmas," Gabby murmured, sounding groggy still.

"Merry Christmas," he said. Their bedroom door was open, and so was the door to the babies' room. He and Gabby had already gotten up three times last night to feed the boys, so they knew the arrangement worked.

Gabby rolled toward him, and he smiled down into her bleary face. She was beautiful like this, still mussed from sleep and blinking up at him.

"Our first Christmas," she said with a smile. "Are you hungry yet?"

"Are you?" he asked with a soft laugh.

"A little," she said, then stretched and pushed herself up onto her elbows.

"Hold on," he said, and he rolled over and reached for a little package he'd put beside his nightstand. He passed it over to her.

"Oh, Seth…" Her face dropped. "I didn't get you anything—"

He hadn't expected her to manage it with three babies to take care of and everything else she'd had on her plate. She was his wife for real, and that was gift enough.

"I wanted a picture," Seth said. "And I'm taking one this morning with you and the boys by the tree. I'm perfectly happy, I promise. Now, open it."

Gabby tore back the paper and pulled out the little volume of Robert Frost's poetry.

"You remembered," she said with a smile.

"You only asked for one thing," he said, and he reached up to brush her hair away from her eyes. "We have miles to go, Gabs. Together."

"Together…" She leaned over and her lips brushed his. He reached up to pull her closer into a proper kiss.

From the other bedroom, the sound of a baby's cry filtered toward them.

"The day is starting," Gabby said, then

tossed the blankets back and reached for her robe.

Seth lay there watching as she disappeared through the doorway. Her soft voice could be heard, and the baby's cry stopped.

His family... He smoothed his hand over Gabby's side of the bed, then tossed back the blankets and got up.

Today was Christmas, and his sons were going to have a proper one, complete with a breakfast he cooked for their mother, and that scattering of little gifts under the tree with baby items for the boys.

"Seth?" Gabby called.

"Yeah?" He pulled on his own bathrobe and ambled to the door.

"We have a bit of a diaper situation here..." she said, and he couldn't help but laugh to himself.

"I'll give you a hand," he said, and he headed into the nursery.

It wouldn't be all perfect Christmas moments. Their life together wouldn't be picture-perfect very often, he was sure. But it would be perfect for them. Diapers, bottles, bedtime stories, bicycles, back talk, homework...all of it—he was ready to be a dad.

But more than that, he was ready to be

Gabby's husband, heart and soul. They were in this together, and they weren't just making up a story—they were living it now. He couldn't wait to start the rest of his life.

* * * * *

*Don't miss Patricia Johns's
next book for Harlequin Heartwarming,
coming June 2020.*

*And check out the previous books
in her Home to Eagle's Rest miniseries:*

Her Lawman Protector
Falling for the Cowboy Dad
The Lawman's Baby

Get 4 FREE REWARDS!

We'll send you 2 FREE Books
<u>plus</u> 2 FREE Mystery Gifts.

Love Inspired® books feature contemporary inspirational romances with Christian characters facing the challenges of life and love.

FREE
Value Over
$20

YES! Please send me 2 FREE Love Inspired® Romance novels and my 2 FREE mystery gifts (gifts are worth about $10 retail). After receiving them, if I don't wish to receive any more books, I can return the shipping statement marked "cancel." If I don't cancel, I will receive 6 brand-new novels every month and be billed just $5.24 for the regular-print edition or $5.99 each for the larger-print edition in the U.S., or $5.74 each for the regular-print edition or $6.24 each for the larger-print edition in Canada. That's a savings of at least 13% off the cover price. It's quite a bargain! Shipping and handling is just 50¢ per book in the U.S. and $1.25 per book in Canada.* I understand that accepting the 2 free books and gifts places me under no obligation to buy anything. I can always return a shipment and cancel at any time. The free books and gifts are mine to keep no matter what I decide.

Choose one:
☐ **Love Inspired® Romance**
Regular-Print
(105/305 IDN GNWC)

☐ **Love Inspired® Romance**
Larger-Print
(122/322 IDN GNWC)

Name (please print)

Address   Apt. #

City   State/Province   Zip/Postal Code

Mail to the **Reader Service:**
IN U.S.A.: P.O. Box 1341, Buffalo, NY 14240-8531
IN CANADA: P.O. Box 603, Fort Erie, Ontario L2A 5X3

Want to try 2 free books from another series? Call 1-800-873-8635 or visit www.ReaderService.com.

---

*Terms and prices subject to change without notice. Prices do not include sales taxes, which will be charged (if applicable) based on your state or country of residence. Canadian residents will be charged applicable taxes. Offer not valid in Quebec. This offer is limited to one order per household. Books received may not be as shown. Not valid for current subscribers to Love Inspired Romance books. All orders subject to approval. Credit or debit balances in a customer's account(s) may be offset by any other outstanding balance owed by or to the customer. Please allow 4 to 6 weeks for delivery. Offer available while quantities last.

Your Privacy—The Reader Service is committed to protecting your privacy. Our Privacy Policy is available online at www.ReaderService.com or upon request from the Reader Service. We make a portion of our mailing list available to reputable third parties that offer products we believe may interest you. If you prefer that we not exchange your name with third parties, or if you wish to clarify or modify your communication preferences, please visit us at www.ReaderService.com/consumerschoice or write to us at Reader Service Preference Service, P.O. Box 9062, Buffalo, NY 14240-9062. Include your complete name and address.

LI20

Get 4 FREE REWARDS!

We'll send you 2 FREE Books
<u>plus</u> 2 FREE Mystery Gifts.

Love Inspired® Suspense
books feature Christian
characters facing
challenges to their faith...
and lives.

FREE
Value Over
$20

YES! Please send me 2 FREE Love Inspired® Suspense novels and my 2 FREE mystery gifts (gifts are worth about $10 retail). After receiving them, if I don't wish to receive any more books, I can return the shipping statement marked "cancel." If I don't cancel, I will receive 6 brand-new novels every month and be billed just $5.24 each for the regular-print edition or $5.99 each for the larger-print edition in the U.S., or $5.74 each for the regular-print edition or $6.24 each for the larger-print edition in Canada. That's a savings of at least 13% off the cover price. It's quite a bargain! Shipping and handling is just 50¢ per book in the U.S. and $1.25 per book in Canada.* I understand that accepting the 2 free books and gifts places me under no obligation to buy anything. I can always return a shipment and cancel at any time. The free books and gifts are mine to keep no matter what I decide.

Choose one: ☐ **Love Inspired® Suspense**　　☐ **Love Inspired® Suspense**
　　　　　　　　Regular-Print　　　　　　　　　　　**Larger-Print**
　　　　　　　　(153/353 IDN GNWN)　　　　　　　(107/307 IDN GNWN)

Name (please print)

Address　　　　　　　　　　　　　　　　　　　　　　　　　　　　Apt. #

City　　　　　　　　　　　State/Province　　　　　　　　　　Zip/Postal Code

Mail to the **Reader Service:**
IN U.S.A.: P.O. Box 1341, Buffalo, NY 14240-8531
IN CANADA: P.O. Box 603, Fort Erie, Ontario L2A 5X3

Want to try 2 free books from another series? Call 1-800-873-8635 or visit www.ReaderService.com.

LIS20

THE CHRISTMAS ROMANCE COLLECTION!

THE FORTUNES OF TEXAS COLLECTION!

18 FREE BOOKS in all!

Treat yourself to the rich legacy of the Fortune and Mendoza clans in this remarkable 50-book collection. This collection is packed with cowboys, tycoons and Texas-sized romances!

YES! Please send me **The Fortunes of Texas Collection** in Larger Print. This collection begins with 3 FREE books and 2 FREE gifts in the first shipment. Along with my 3 free books, I'll also get the next 4 books from The Fortunes of Texas Collection, in LARGER PRINT, which I may either return and owe nothing, or keep for the low price of $5.24 U.S./$5.89 CDN each plus $2.99 for shipping and handling per shipment*. If I decide to continue, about once a month for 8 months I will get 6 or 7 more books but will only need to pay for 4. That means 2 or 3 books in every shipment will be FREE! If I decide to keep the entire collection, I'll have paid for only 32 books because 18 books are FREE! I understand that accepting the 3 free books and gifts places me under no obligation to buy anything. I can always return a shipment and cancel at any time. My free books and gifts are mine to keep no matter what I decide.

☐ 269 HCN 4622   ☐ 469 HCN 4622

Name (please print)

Address   Apt. #

City   State/Province   Zip/Postal Code

Mail to the **Reader Service:**
IN U.S.A.: P.O. Box 1341, Buffalo, N.Y. 14240-8531
IN CANADA: P.O. Box 603, Fort Erie, Ontario L2A 5X3

*Terms and prices subject to change without notice. Prices do not include sales taxes, which will be charged (if applicable) based on your state or country of residence. Canadian residents will be charged applicable taxes. Offer not valid in Quebec. All orders subject to approval. Credit or debit balances in a customer's account(s) may be offset by any other outstanding balance owed by or to the customer. Please allow three to four weeks for delivery. Offer available while quantities last. © 2018 Harlequin Enterprises Limited. ® and ™ are trademarks owned and used by the trademark owner and/or its licensee.

Your Privacy—The Reader Service is committed to protecting your privacy. Our Privacy Policy is available online at www.ReaderService.com or upon request from the Reader Service. We make a portion of our mailing list available to reputable third parties that offer products we believe may interest you. If you prefer that we not exchange your name with third parties, or if you wish to clarify or modify your communication preferences, please visit us at www.ReaderService.com/consumerchoice or write to us at Reader Service Preference Service, P.O. Box 9049, Buffalo, NY 14269-9049. Include your name and address.

50BFT19R

Get 4 FREE REWARDS!

We'll send you 2 FREE Books plus 2 FREE Mystery Gifts.

FREE
Value Over
$20

Both the **Romance** and **Suspense** collections feature compelling novels written by many of today's bestselling authors.